# NATURAL TWENTY

ROLL FOR LOVE BOOK ONE

CHARLIE NOVAK

*Charlotte,*
*May there always be love, dice & books!*

*Love,*
*Charlie*

Copyright © Charlie Novak 2020

Cover by Natasha Snow

Editing by Susie Selva

All rights reserved. Charlie Novak asserts the moral right to be identified as the author of this work.

This novel is entirely a work of fiction. Names, characters, places, and incidents are the products of the author's imagination or are used fictitiously. Any resemblance to actual events, locales, organizations or persons, living or dead, is entirely coincidental.

*For Rosie, my badass nerd best friend.
I think our twelve-year-old selves would be proud.*

## CHAPTER ONE

*Peony — Prosperity, Happy marriage, Bashfulness*

**Leo**

THE BITING cold of an early January morning seeped into my bones as my footsteps echoed on the empty pavement. I buried my face a little farther into my scarf and dug my hands deeper into my pockets, trying to push away the chill.

It was still dark. The sun wasn't due to rise for another couple of hours at least. The pavement was lit by the glow of streetlamps and what little moonlight still remained. The sky was clear, and despite the light from the city, I could still see a glittering blanket of stars above me. It helped that Lincoln was a small place, and at six in the morning, there were still relatively few people and cars about. Not everyone wanted to walk to work this early on a Saturday.

I carefully sidestepped a patch of ice because the last

thing I wanted was to fall flat on my arse. Even if there wasn't anybody around to see. My mind was already focused on what I had to do that morning before the shop opened and what orders needed to be collected and delivered.

There were the flowers for the Bond wedding that needed to go out that morning and an arrangement for the Webb family funeral this afternoon. Plus a dozen or so special-occasion bouquets that had been ordered and whatever walk-ins we got during the day.

I'd never really dreamt I'd end up a florist, but life was funny like that. Now I couldn't imagine doing anything else. It was a little different to the rock star ambitions of my teenaged years though. After four years of drifting around after university, trying to find something I wanted to do with my life, I'd ended up helping my gran with the church flowers to pass the time.

Who'd have thought a gruff bloke from North Yorkshire would end up having a way with sweet peas and sunflowers?

The chiming of the cathedral caught my attention, and I paused to gaze up at the softly lit towers. I walked past it every day when I travelled to and from the shop. I'm not a religious man by any stretch of the imagination, but to me, Lincoln cathedral was the most beautiful building in the world. There was something calming about its intricate architecture and towering presence. Sitting on top of the hill, it stood head and shoulders above the rest of the city. You could see it for miles.

Beside me, a snuffling noise drew me back to reality. I

looked down to see Angie, my slightly pudgy Staffordshire bull terrier, nosing at the door to a bakery, clearly hoping to find some sort of a scrap for second breakfast. "Come on, girl. Nothing for you there."

Angie sighed and looked up at me forlornly with her deep chocolate eyes. I'd had Angie for about four years now. She'd been a timid little rescue puppy when I'd first met her, but it hadn't taken long for her sunny Staffy personality to shine through. Her forlorn look was the reason she got far more treats than she needed in the first place.

These days she was a bundle of love and affection. She absolutely loved sitting behind the counter in the shop and pottering out to get endless scratches and ear rubs from our regular customers. One of them had even taken to bringing her a doggy doughnut from the local bakery every week when he came in to buy flowers for his wife.

"You had breakfast at home," I said, shaking my head and chuckling as Angie huffed, clearly unimpressed with me. It was like I'd never heard of second breakfast.

I started walking again, making my way across the crossroads at the top of Steep Hill. To my left was the cathedral and to my right the castle. Before me lay the cobbled street that descended the hill into the main part of the city. It wasn't called Steep Hill for nothing, but luckily, I wasn't going that far. Although maybe the extra exercise would do Angie and I both some good. Her coat had been a little tight this morning when I'd done it up, and my diet consisted mostly of biscuits and strong cups of tea.

The street curved around a bend, levelled out for a

moment, and then descended down again, steeper this time. The narrow road was surrounded by little shops, and I always liked looking at the window displays as I walked past. Nothing much had changed, except for one.

A previously empty window now held a display of colourful books, each different and each with a spaceship zooming across the cover. A hanging, chalkboard sign read *I don't remember the title, but it had a spaceship on it*. I snorted, and my laughter rang in the deserted street. The sign above the door was painted black with white lettering and declared the shop The Lost World.

I hadn't seen the sign before.

The unit had been empty for a while, but over the past month or so I'd seen signs of occupation. However, since it had been the run up to Christmas, I'd been so busy that I'd hardly had time to focus on anything but work. I moved a couple of steps down to read a poster in the second window on the other side of the door.

THE LOST WORLD BOOKSHOP
GRAND OPENING
SATURDAY 18<sup>TH</sup> JANUARY AT 10AM
THERE WILL BE CAKE!
(AND BOOKS…OBVIOUSLY)

I hummed to myself. That was today. I made a mental note to try and pop up later to have a look inside.

I loved bookshops and could easily get lost in them for hours. Having one near the flower shop would be a great way to spend my lunchtime. Then again, it could also be very dangerous for my wallet.

Still, at least I'd be limited by what I could carry home. That meant I could only buy one book at a time… maybe two if they were on the small side.

I shook my head and carried on down the street until I saw the little yellow-and-white sign of the flower shop glowing under the nearest streetlamp. I'd named the shop Wild Things because my gran had played the song endlessly when I was a kid, and it suited my style of flower arranging.

I dug my key out of my pocket, opened the locks, and flicked on the lights as I stepped inside, breathing in the soft, sweet scent of flowers and foliage that perpetually lingered before locking the door behind me.

Pulling off my coat and then Angie's, I set to work, humming to myself while Angie settled herself in the padded dog bed that was tucked in behind the counter. The pinboard in the back room was neatly covered in notes and held a little clip of order forms as well as a reminder from Emily that I had a consultation for a wedding booked in at eleven.

We didn't do many weddings, but I enjoyed meeting with the occasional couple. These days I didn't even advertise it as a service. Any wedding business we got was mostly just through word of mouth from other vendors and a couple of local venues. I didn't have the storage space for a million white roses, which ruled out the more extravagant weddings I'd seen, and my style tended to be a little more alternative than what most couples were looking for. That and the fact that I looked like I should be in some sort of Hollywood motorcycle gang instead of wrapping pastel tea roses in ribbon. Even if both my tattoo sleeves were entirely made up of plants and flowers.

I flicked on Spotify, singing softly to myself as I began double-checking everything on my list and working on the last few orders, losing myself in the gentle rhythm of work.

I didn't even know Emily had come in until she tapped me on the shoulder.

"Good morning, Leo!"

"Morning," I muttered, carefully wrapping a last bit of ribbon around the stems of a small winter bouquet and pinning it carefully.

"How're you today?"

"I'm fine."

"Seriously? Two words. That's all I get?"

"I can make it one tomorrow if you want. Or just a noise if you want the full Yorkshire experience."

"Or you could go all out and make it three."

"Hmm, I'll think about it." I carefully placed the bouquet in a bucket, making sure the label was neatly tucked into it, then I placed it in the small flower fridge we had at the back of the workroom. It naturally tended to stay very cold in the shop, but I'd invested in the fridge a couple of years ago for some of our more temperamental flowers and finished bouquets. When I looked up, Emily was hanging up her coat and unwinding the giant knitted scarf that was wrapped around her neck.

I'd hired Emily nearly five years ago, not long after I'd opened the shop. I'd always been a man of few words, which wasn't necessarily conducive to running a customer-facing business, and I'd needed some help. Enter Emily.

She was funny and chatty and my total opposite in a lot of ways, but we'd clicked instantly. I'd wanted someone to manage the front and help with the day-to-day running of the business, and Emily was the perfect fit. If I'd ever had any doubts about getting someone involved in my new business, they'd all disappeared on the first day when she'd arrived with a box of homemade cupcakes and a list of ideas for the front of the shop.

Emily wasn't a florist when I hired her, but she was naturally very creative, and when I'd asked if she was interested in learning the trade she'd said yes immediately. These days I made most of the arrangements, ordered stock, and did consultations, while Emily dealt with customers, made sure orders were processed and paid, and kept everything running like a well-oiled machine. She also took care of the occasional walk-in order and gave me an extra pair of hands when we needed it. During Christmas, Valentine's Day, and Mother's Day, we spent hours working on orders together, and I was always incredibly grateful for her help.

"Is that a new skirt?" I asked in an attempt to make conversation. I knew Emily made a lot of her own clothes and seemed to have more skill in her little finger than most people did in their entire bodies.

"It is! I saw the fabric and couldn't resist." She smiled at me and flicked on the kettle in the corner.

"It's nice."

While I generally stuck to t-shirts, jeans, and thick jumpers, Emily's style was all fifties pin-up. It suited her.

Today's skirt was dark blue with classic red and white rocket ships all over it. It made me think of the bookshop window, and I smiled to myself as I turned back to my workbench, selecting a couple of pieces of eucalyptus.

"Did you see there's a new bookshop opening? Just up the hill," I said.

"Oh? Where the hairdresser was?"

"Yes. They're opening today."

"Are you going to go up and say hi?" she asked, and I heard the clinking of mugs and teaspoons.

"I might."

"You could take them some flowers! You know, a nice little 'congratulations you did it' present. Opening a new business is difficult, especially in January."

"Maybe." Emily's suggestion was a good one; I couldn't deny that. And having some sort of flowers with me would make any sort of conversation easier.

"You never know, you might make friends with them." The kettle clicked, and I shook my head.

"I'm not five."

"No, but having friends who aren't Daniel and I would be good for you. I worry about you. You work too much."

"I'm fine." I looked over at her. Emily raised an eyebrow and pointed a teaspoon threateningly at me. "Okay. I'll take them some flowers." Emily wasn't going to drop it, and the more I thought about it, the more I liked the idea.

Plus it would give me a chance to have a good look inside the shop. I wasn't sure my bookshelves had much space left on them, but I could always get more shelves.

I looked around to see what I had nearby, my brain

turning ideas over. I had a few coral peonies leftover from the Bond wedding. I'd bought a few extras in case any got damaged while I was working. They weren't typically available this time of year, but one of the suppliers I used had some in, and I hadn't been able to resist. Right now, their brightness was just what I wanted.

Emily set a large mug of tea down beside me. "Peonies?"

"For prosperity. And some of the alstroemeria for wealth and good fortune," I said, carefully selecting some stems. All flowers had a meaning, good and bad. The Victorians had given flowers a language, and it was something I loved using in my work when I could. Even if I was the only one who understood what it meant.

"You're such a romantic at heart."

"Since when is wishing people good fortune romantic?" I raised an eyebrow.

"You know what I mean. You do sweet things for people all the time. You love making people happy. You've got a romantic soul, Leo."

"I'm still not seeing the connection."

"You just wait. One day you'll find someone, and you'll want to give them the moon," Emily said, collecting the order forms from next to me and beginning to pull things out for delivery so her husband, Daniel, could load them into the van. Daniel helped out with deliveries on busy weekends. It would mean he could drop me and the wedding flowers off at the venue and then make the rest of the bouquet deliveries before picking me up. A two birds, one stone approach.

"You are unusually happy today. What happened?"

"Can I not just be happy?"

"You're always happy, but you seem extra happy today." I reached for some deep purple alstroemeria stems. The colour would add a nice balance. Emily was quiet for a second, and when I turned to look, she was twisting her hands and looked about ready to burst.

"Daniel and I got approved to be foster parents."

"Holy shit, Em. That's amazing." I grinned and opened my arms, pulling Emily into a bear hug while trying to avoid her pompadour.

"Thanks." She let out a deep exhale. "I can't believe it's happening. It's only taken nine months."

"Well, let me know if you or Daniel need anything. I know it can be tough, so if you ever need to leave for anything just let me know before you go. I won't mind. And I won't have you making up time either." I released her, turning back to my workbench.

"You don't need to do that. Besides, Daniel will be home full-time since he can freelance around things like school and emergencies. And I don't work Mondays or Tuesdays. And we haven't even been matched with a child yet. That's going to be another couple of months."

"Yes, I do. Believe it or not, I can manage by myself when you're not here. I've done it before."

Emily hummed and then grinned. "You're a big ol' softie really."

"Oh no, the man who works with flowers all day and whose pampered dog has two seventy quid beds is actually a soft touch. Go figure."

"Sarcasm before nine? You spoil me."

"Don't you have work to do?"

"Don't you?"

"I am working." I pointed at the half-formed bouquet in front of me. "See? Work."

Emily chuckled. "Fine, fine. But I'm on to you. Leo the lion is a kitten at heart."

I snorted and pretended to ignore her. We both knew she was right, even if she and Daniel were the only ones who'd ever seen it.

## CHAPTER TWO

*Stock — Affection, Lasting beauty, You'll always be beautiful to me*

**Leo**

It was mid-afternoon before I managed to take the flowers up to The Lost World.

I'd managed to get the bouquet finished before I'd headed out on deliveries with Daniel, but it had taken longer than I'd wanted to set up the flowers for the Bond wedding, and by the time I'd gotten back, the shop had been rammed. I'd only had a chance to snatch half a sandwich before my wedding consultation.

The couple had been lovely, and we'd spent ages discussing potential ideas. I always loved it when clients came in with ideas and pictures, but these brides had arrived with a whole Pinterest board. They were getting married at a local barn venue in September but wanted something a little different from rustic mason jars filled with gypsophila. I'd spent far longer with them than I'd intended, but I didn't mind. We'd decided on big, bold, and colourful with trailing ribbons for both of their bouquets as well as conical flasks full of flowers to line the aisle and decorate the tables for the reception. They'd also given me free rein on the types of flowers, and my fingers were already itching to get to work. I kept having to bring my mind back to what I was doing instead of getting lost in ideas.

All I had to do now was remember to draw up the quote this evening and send it across. Maths had never been my strongest suit, but when I'd first started the business, my uncle had built me an enormous spreadsheet that would help calculate everything for me. All I had to do was input the details.

"I'm just going to take this up to the bookshop," I said as I grabbed my coat. "Do we have any vases left? I doubt they'll have anything to put it in."

"I think there are a couple," Emily replied, rummaging under the counter. I usually had a few spare vases lying around because we occasionally sold bouquets in them or offered them as an extra to customers, but I hadn't restocked them lately, and I couldn't remember seeing any in the back room. "Ah! One left."

Emily placed the simple glass vase on the counter.

"Cheers. Remind me to get some more."

"I'll put it on the order list. We need some more stem tape and floral foam too."

"Thanks." I grabbed the vase and carefully placed the

finished bouquet inside it. The peonies were just starting to bloom, and their bright coral looked beautiful next to the deep purples, greens, and pastel pinks of the rest of the arrangement. I hoped the new shop owner would like it.

Angie whined and looked up at me from her bed. "Sorry, girl, but you'll have to stay here. I don't think they'll allow dogs in the bookshop." She huffed at me, as if in disapproval, and then snuggled deeper into her bed, resting her head on one of the high padded sides. For a small dog, she could be incredibly dramatic.

The freezing January air nipped at my cheeks as I stepped into the street, and the sun was already starting to set. I knew in an hour or so it would be gone again. I was starting to miss the warmth of spring sunshine and the longer days that came with it.

There were still plenty of people around as I made my way up the hill, clutching my delivery to my chest. The bookshop looked warm and cosy, golden light glowing in the windows. I pushed the door open and stepped into the warmth as a little bell jingled above me.

The shop was divided into two rooms. To my left there was a little alcove with two sets of stairs. One of them had a little cordon across it which I assumed led upstairs to some sort of stock room. The space was packed with neatly arranged shelves, and in front of me was a counter dotted with little extras, including what looked like a bowl of badges. Hanging on the wall behind the counter was an enormous rainbow pride flag. I smiled. Just knowing this was a safe place for queer people made my chest flood with warmth. We needed more spaces like this.

There were people milling around, mostly in the large room to my right, which seemed to be floor to ceiling books, and I heard more voices floating up from downstairs.

"Can I help you?"

I turned to see a tall, slim man with sharp but pretty features and piercing blue eyes smiling at me. His waist-length platinum hair shimmered under the shop lights, and all I could think was that this man distinctly looked like he was related to Legolas or Thranduil from the *Lord of the Rings* and *Hobbit* films.

Since he was the one who'd spoken, I assumed he was the owner, and it almost seemed fitting.

"Oh, hi. I'm Leo," I said, giving an awkward half wave. "I run the flower shop, Wild Things, just down the road. I wanted to bring you a bouquet to say congratulations on your grand opening."

The man's smile widened until he was practically beaming. "Well, aren't you charming? Sadly, I'm not the owner of this fine establishment, but I'll get him for you."

He walked over to the stairs, leant over the cordon, and left me standing awkwardly in the middle of the shop.

"Darling, you have a visitor," he called. There was a moment of silence and then a crashing noise. The man chuckled and looked at me. "He'll be right down. Can I interest you in some cake? We have rather a lot left. I think I over ordered."

"Sure." I felt more awkward by the second. I was never very good in social situations at the best of times. "That'd be nice."

"Perfect. Chocolate or lemon?"

"Lemon, please."

The man nodded and then sighed as another crash came from upstairs. "I warned him to get the stock room in order," he muttered. "He's going to break something at this rate. Most likely himself."

"I heard that," came a second voice from the top of the stairs. There was a clattering of footsteps, and another man appeared, clutching a cardboard box in front of him. I couldn't see much of his face because it was hidden by both the box and a wall, but I caught a flash of dark skinny jeans and a red hoodie.

"I meant you to."

"You said there was a visitor?"

"Yes, this lovely gentleman here." The elven man pointed at me. The man in the hoodie turned, and I nearly swallowed my tongue.

Holy fuck. He was gorgeous.

His fluffy dark hair stuck out all over the place as if he'd run his hands through it, and he had large, dark eyes framed by thick-rimmed glasses. His full mouth curled into a smile, and I noticed a little lip ring on the side of his bottom lip. His ears were pierced too, and various rings and bars glittered in the light.

My mouth went dry, and my chest suddenly felt far too tight.

I'd always had a weakness for tattoos and piercings on people, and although I couldn't see any of the former, the latter were definitely present. My traitorous brain immediately began wondering what might be under the long sleeves of his hoodie.

"Hi," he said as he climbed over the cordon and down the last step, shifting his box into one hand and sticking out his other. "I'm Jay."

"Leo." I shook his hand while trying to force my tongue to work. I'd rather not look like a complete and utter twat in front of him. I actually wanted to be able to come in and browse, and if I couldn't even string two words together in front of the cute guy who owned the shop, then my future as a customer was going to be very painful. "I own Wild Things. We're the florist just down the hill a bit. I thought I'd bring you a little welcome gift. Or more of a congratulations gift, I guess." I held the flowers out and then realised that was probably stupid since Jay was still holding the box.

"Oh, that's so nice of you. Thank you." He smiled, and I was mesmerized by the way the damn lip ring curled around his lip and how full and plush said lip was. He put the box on the counter and took the vase, a long finger grazing over the petals of one of the peonies. He had nice fingers.

I squashed those thoughts because they wouldn't lead anywhere good. Maybe the six months I'd taken off from attempting to date had been a bad idea since the sight of one sexy man had me ready to malfunction.

"They're beautiful."

"I'm glad you like them," I said. "I brought you a vase too because I wasn't sure if you'd have one."

"That was a good call." Jay smiled and let out a little half laugh. "I mean, I don't think I do. Well, I might, but it's probably buried somewhere among the boxes upstairs. And I've tripped over the boxes enough times that any that I might have had are probably broken."

"Then I'm glad I brought one."

The was a pause, and it seemed neither of us knew what to say. This was why I let Emily deal with people. I could deal with plants, but humans were a whole different kettle of fish.

"Would you like some cake?" Jay asked. "We've got a ton of the stuff left. Edward ordered half a fucking bakery."

"I think he already went to get me some?"

"I did," said the blond man I assumed was Edward. He passed me a napkin that had a generous slice of lemon cake on top of it. He passed another napkin with a slab of chocolate cake to Jay. "I'm Edward, just in case Jay didn't mention it."

"It's nice to meet you."

"Edward is my business partner," Jay said, breaking off a piece of cake with his fingers. I glanced down at my own cake, trying not to watch as Jay slid the piece of cake past his lips. That would definitely count as weird, especially since we'd only just met. I broke off my own piece of cake instead.

"Silent partner, darling. This is your shop. And you also forgot to add fabulous best friend."

"You've done a cracking job," I said, looking around again as I ate more of the cake. I spotted a shelf with a little sign that said "New Releases" painted neatly on a panel at the top. There were at least a couple of books I wanted to look at. "I like your window display. With the spaceships."

"Oh, yeah. I saw a display about blue covers a library did on Twitter, and I thought it would be fun to do something similar. Plus, everyone needs to read more cool, new science fiction. I know loads of people who still think stuff from twenty years ago is new, but there are so many amazing books out right now."

"Maybe you could give me some recommendations?" I wasn't sure what prompted me to ask, but I was grateful something in my brain had decided to override my failing conversation functions. It was probably for the best. "I haven't read anything new in ages, and I don't really know what's come out recently."

"Of course!" Jay grinned as he put his cake on the counter, throwing words over his shoulder. "Edward, watch the till."

Jay steered me towards the second room where there were a few people perusing the shelves. "We've got sci-fi, fantasy, horror, and crime up here. Then downstairs we've got a YA and children's section, a little bit of romance, and a little less literary fiction. And there's a small games section too. Obviously I haven't got enough room to focus on everything, so I decided to focus on the things I like best. Oh, and I want to curate a really good selection of LGBTQ books across all genres because that's something that's really important to me." He paused, looking up at me. Now that he stood next to me, I realised he was quite a bit shorter than I was. My heart fluttered. I'd always liked dating people shorter than me. I loved being able to wrap my partner up in my arms and kiss the top of their head.

Jay looked almost nervous for a second as if he was expecting me to react negatively.

"I think that's amazing," I said, clearing my throat. "We need more bookshops like that."

"Thanks. I really want this to be a safe space, y'know? Somewhere queer people feel welcome. Especially young people. Like, I know it's so much better now, but not everyone has a good time. Sorry, I don't know why I'm telling you this. You wanted recs, and here I am rambling at you." His cheeks flushed and he looked away.

"It's fine. You can ramble."

"You might regret that," he said, flashing me another dazzling smile. "I'm a bit of a chatterbox. Edward says I could talk the hind leg off a donkey." He waved his hand. "Now, what sort of thing are you looking for? I can recommend everything from lesbian necromancers in space to epic political space operas. Or if you're looking for fantasy, I've got a gorgeous duology based on Mogul India with the most amazing characters and worldbuilding."

I left thirty minutes later clutching two new books and a little stack of postcards with the shop's details that I'd offered to hand out to my customers.

But it wasn't my purchases my mind kept wandering back to throughout the rest of the afternoon, and later that evening, while Angie and I were curled up on the sofa watching reruns of a cheesy eighties detective show on Netflix called *Last Call*. My thoughts were full of Jay's wild curls and wide smile and the way light glinted off his lip ring as he spoke.

## CHAPTER THREE

*Poppy (Yellow) — Wealth, Success*

## Jay

"Well, that went well." I clicked the lock closed, leant against the door, and breathed for what felt like the first time in hours.

I'd been so fucking nervous about the grand opening, convinced it was going to be an absolute shitshow and a complete disaster, but it had ended up being anything but. At least in my opinion. We'd had customers, and they'd bought things. That was more than I'd expected. Then again, my expectations had been really fucking low.

"It went more than well," Edward said from his seat behind the counter where he was drinking tea and eating the last of the lemon cake. "In fact, I'd go so far as to say it was a rousing success."

"Not sure I'd go that far, babe."

Edward raised one eyebrow, fixing me with a withering stare. "First of all, you sold lots of stock, people enjoyed themselves, and you made an excellent first impression on everyone. Secondly, we had cake. And thirdly, you were gifted flowers from the sexy mountain man who owns the local florist."

"Okay, first of all," I said as I began to straighten the shelves and make mental notes of what I needed to restock, "Leo was only being friendly. He just wanted to welcome me to the area and wish me luck. And I never ever said he was sexy."

"You didn't need to. I saw the way you looked at him. The way you couldn't stop looking at him, actually. You were practically drooling."

"Well... I..." I felt heat prickling my skin and running down my spine. Edward was right; I hadn't been able to stop looking. But what was I supposed to do when a fucking god of a man walked into my bookshop? Ignore him?

"Fuck you," I said childishly. Edward smiled sweetly and sipped his tea. I gestured at the nearest shelf. "You could help you know."

"I will. After I'm done with my tea. And my interrogation."

"Is that what this is?" I shook my head and moved onto another case, making sure everything was neatly displayed.

"I didn't think it was necessary to go full inquisition just yet."

"Will you need a silly hat and red robes?"

"Nobody expects the Spanish Inquisition!"

I snorted and shook my head. "You're an idiot."

"We all know that, darling, but you're still avoiding the topic. Admit you think our lovely local florist is sexy, and you'd like to climb him like a tree. Many, many times."

"You know I don't date." I called out as I slipped into the second room, heading for my next set of shelves. I was glad to see the science-fiction section had been thoroughly perused.

"I never said anything about dating." I sighed to myself and ignored Edward. I hadn't dated anyone since my last relationship had ended in disaster nearly a year ago, and it wasn't something I was looking to revisit anytime soon. Edward seemed to take my silence as permission for him to continue. "You could just go for a drink and then let him fuck your brains out."

"No, Edward."

"It would be good for you. When was the last time you went out and did something fun? Without me."

"I don't know."

"Then it's been far too long."

"Can you please just drop it?" I asked, a flash of irritation lacing my voice. "Even if I did want to go out with someone, which I don't, I wouldn't have time anyway. I'm far too busy getting this place going. And I know you're suggesting just a one-night thing, but you know that's not for me. It never has been."

I squatted down to tidy the bottom of the nearest shelf. My dedication to work was what had caused problems in my last relationship, and I wasn't going to make the same mistake again. If I wanted the shop to be a success, then any sort of dating would be on the backburner for the foreseeable future. I was fine with that.

I heard Edward moving, and a moment later his laced, heeled boots came into view. He dropped down beside me and put an arm around my shoulders.

"I'm sorry, darling. I didn't mean to upset you. I was only teasing, but still, that doesn't justify it."

"It's okay." I leant awkwardly into him. My thighs were burning from squatting, and I felt myself wobbling, but I didn't want to ruin the moment. "I know I'll have to get back out there one day, just… not yet."

"Not everyone is Kieran, my love," Edward said. "There are many men out there who manage not to be humongous douches."

I snorted and then wobbled, falling backwards to land on my ass and taking Edward with me. We lay sprawled out on the floor, giggling together.

"You know," I said as I stared up at the ceiling, "I really should have painted the ceiling before we put the bookcases up."

"You hate heights though. You'd have lasted five minutes on the ladder. Tops. And that's if I'd even have let you climb the ladder in the first place. The last thing we needed was you falling and breaking something."

"Okay. I should've gotten you to paint the ceiling before we put the bookcases up." I rolled onto my side and looked at Edward. His hair fanned out around him like he was some sort of sleeping fairy-tale prince. Even after six years of friendship I was still bowled over by how beautiful he was.

I'd met him on Tumblr back in my early twenties when I was deep into a vampire anime fandom. He'd posted a picture of himself in cosplay from the series, and I'd messaged him to tell him how awesome he looked. I hadn't expected him to reply because he'd been a big-name cosplayer even back then, but he had. We'd spent hours talking about the show and whatever other random shit popped into our minds. And that was it. Our friendship had gone from there. We'd finally met in person two years later when I'd managed to get a ticket to London Comic Con. He'd been cosplaying as Thranduil as played by Lee Pace in the *Hobbit* movies, and he'd looked every inch the haughty elven king... until he'd seen me, squealed loudly, and jumped on me, nearly crushing my ribs to the amusement of several thousand onlookers.

When everything had turned to shit in London, and my relationship with Kieran went sideways, he was the one who'd come to fetch me. He offered me his spare bedroom, even though it was over a hundred and forty miles away, and turned up in his tiny, battered old Mini to help me pack.

He'd never asked for anything from me except friendship and the occasional bit of help with a costume he was making. He was my best friend and one of my greatest loves, even if he could be an overdramatic bastard. There were times I didn't know what I'd have done without him.

I certainly wouldn't be here, lying on the floor of my dream bookshop and staring up at the stained, off-white ceiling.

"I would have done it if you'd asked," Edward said. "And I wouldn't have complained once."

"That's a downright lie and you know it."

"Probably." He sighed and glanced over at me. "You know, just because you don't want to date Leo, doesn't mean you can't be friends with him. You need more friends."

"I know. I just... Do you think it would be weird if I tried to be friends with him? I mean, I'm sure he's very busy. And what if we don't have things in common?" I rubbed my eyes, jostling my glasses, and then ran my fingers through my hair, tugging at the wild curls. I could never get my hair to behave, and these days I'd given up and given it free rein.

"Jacob." Edward fixed me with a glare. The fact he was using my proper name meant he was being serious. Or at least trying to be. "You two spent thirty minutes animatedly talking about books, and I can guarantee you would have spent longer if he hadn't had to go back to work. And even if he was just being polite, he still brought you flowers and bought books you recommended."

"Maybe I should return the favour?" I mused, twirling a piece of hair in my fingers.

"That's an excellent plan! Ooh, you should invite him to game night too. You said you wanted it to be a community thing. Invite him."

"Hold your horses. Let's start with something small." Edward huffed but didn't say anything, and I smiled to myself.

There were several other books Leo had expressed an

interest in earlier. Maybe I could take him one as a little thank you for the flowers and for supporting the shop. I knew I shouldn't really be giving away books, but one wouldn't hurt, and I could pay for it.

Besides, it would be nice to see him smile.

## CHAPTER FOUR

*Snowdrop — Hope*

**Jay**

I WAS BEGINNING to think this was a mistake. What if I was massively overstepping? What if he already owned this book? I mean, I know Leo had said he didn't, but that had been four days ago, and it only took two minutes to order something on Amazon.

Curse stupid Edward and his stupid plans.

I sighed, shaking my head, my curls falling in front of my face. Since I already stood outside Wild Things it would probably look weird if I didn't go in.

Why was making friends with people so hard when you were an adult?

Not that I'd found it much easier as a child.

I pushed the door open and heard a little electronic beep before I stepped inside. The shop was wide and low with a paved floor that was covered in flowers. There was a wooden counter at the side with a cheerful looking woman standing behind it. She was wearing a cardigan with flowers embroidered down one side, and her red hair was swept up into an elegant pompadour. There were a couple of enamel pins shaped like pokéballs attached to her cardigan. One was blue, pink, and purple and the other was pastel pink, white, and blue.

"Hello! How can I help?" she asked.

I approached her, trying to look more confident than I felt. Inside I felt like I was in primary school all over again, asking to see if one of the other kids wanted to come out and play. "Oh, hi. I'm Jay. I run The Lost World bookshop just up the road." I pointed in the vague direction of the shop, then realised how stupid I looked. "Is Leo around?"

"So you're Jay! I'm Emily. Leo mentioned you the other day. He said your shop is gorgeous, and you gave him the best book recs. I think he's just sorting some orders. Hang on. Lemme grab him."

I smiled and nodded, leaning on the counter while I tried to stop my heart from racing a million miles a minute. I'd never felt this nervous before. What was it about seeing Leo that had my stomach in knots?

A snuffling noise distracted me, and I looked over the counter to see an adorable pair of brown eyes gazing up at me.

"Hi there," I said, reaching my hand tentatively down to gently rub the dog's head. The brindle fur was soft under my fingers. They pushed into my hand, happily demanding more ear rubs. From the look of them, I thought they might be some form of Staffy, but my knowledge of dogs was iffy at best. "Aren't you cute?"

The dog huffed happily, and a pink tongue darted out to lick my hand. I chuckled.

"I see you've met Angie." Leo's gruff voice made me look up. He stood in the doorway behind the counter, tattooed forearms crossed and a little twinkle in his amber eyes.

"Shit. Sorry," I said, pulling my hand away.

"Don't apologise. She likes the attention. Don't you girl?" An uncontrollable grin slid across my lips as I watched Angie potter over to Leo, plopping down next to him and resting her head against his leg. He reached down to rub behind her ears and my heart melted.

I know I'd told Edward I wasn't interested in dating, but surely it was still okay to look. It wasn't my fault Leo was genuinely the most handsome man I'd seen in forever or that he unwittingly ticked all the boxes on Jay's checklist of attractiveness.

He was tall and muscular but not in a way that suggested he spent hours at the gym. He definitely looked strong enough to pick me up though, and I was not going to even consider how much that idea turned me on. His dark hair was pulled up into a messy topknot, and his neatly trimmed beard didn't hide his wide mouth. And then there were the tattoos.

Lord have fucking mercy.

I'd always found ink attractive, and I had enough of my own, but when I looked at Leo, my lizard brain wanted to strip off his clothes and lick his entire body. I'd seen his two full tattoo sleeves—each one a beautiful series of vines and flowers, intricately woven down his arms—and the simple black geometric pieces that decorated the backs of his hands. Looking at him now, I could also see hints of ink poking out of the collar of the thick knitted sweater he was wearing, the sleeves pushed up to his elbows. Even the idea that he had chest and neck tattoos made my insides squirm.

I wanted to pin him down and see what else he was hiding.

Jesus fucking Christ. I hadn't felt this horny in fucking forever.

Maybe Edward was right. Maybe one night would get this out of my system and I could go back to not wanting to drool on him.

Except I already knew I didn't want that. One night would probably mean we'd either never see each other again, or it would be really awkward whenever we did, and that would be so much worse. I hardly knew Leo, but the tug in my stomach and the way he'd spoken to me on Saturday made me want to get to know him better.

And I could really do with a friend who wasn't Edward.

"She's really cute," I said, watching as Angie snuggled farther into Leo's leg.

"Yeah, she is. And she knows it." The small smile on his face told me everything I needed to know. He absolutely adored her.

"How long have you had her?"

"Four years. Got her as a rescue puppy. She was so small I could cradle her in my arms like a baby. She still likes it now, but she's a lot heavier these days."

So the gruff, shy florist was also a total softie at heart. I could cope with that. It wasn't like my brain had ceased all operations or anything.

"So, what can I do for you?"

Oh shit. I'd forgotten I was actually here for another purpose other than to coo at him and his adorable dog. "Oh, yeah. Sorry. I just wanted to give you this." I pulled the book, which was wrapped in a brown paper bag, from my coat pocket and pushed it across the counter. "It's a thank you. For the flowers. I know you said it looked interesting, and you were looking for some fun reads, and I just… thought you might like it."

Leo stepped forward and scooped it off the counter, sliding the small novel from the bag. It was a pulpy, historical-fantasy adventure called *Fury from the Tomb* that featured a young archaeologist who had to face down mummies, grave-robbing ghouls, and evil monks while accompanied by a gunslinger, a young orphan, and the daughter of his patron, who was so incredibly badass I wanted a series of books about her. It was a fun adventure novel you could lose yourself in for an afternoon.

"If you like it," I continued, trying to fill the silence, "there's a sequel. It's a murder mystery set in the mountains. It's really good."

"Thanks." He smiled at me, turning the book over in his hands. "You didn't have to do this though."

"I know. It's just a little thank you. For the welcome. I'm still kinda new to this, and I'm really grateful."

"You're welcome."

I wasn't quite sure what to say next, but I knew I didn't

want our conversation to end just yet. "So, um, I'm looking at setting up some events at the store, like a book club, gaming nights, things like that. Y'know to get the local community involved. Maybe give some young queer people a place to hang out that isn't a bar. But I'm looking at starting the game night in the next few weeks. It'll most likely be role-playing games and board games, and it would be great if you wanted to join us." I held my breath, waiting for a response.

"That sounds fun. Does it matter that I haven't played any RPGs since university?"

"No, not at all. I mean it depends what you want to play, but I've got some spare rulebooks you can borrow. What did you play?"

"Dungeons and Dragons. Mostly third edition, since the fourth edition didn't come out until my third year."

"Awesome. The fifth edition is super easy to pick up, and I think it's mostly the same as older editions, just with some new mechanics that they introduced to streamline things a bit. And there're a ton of resources online these days that are great for character creation and they track loads of stuff for you. What was your character?"

"Barbarian," Leo said with a wry smile. "The party needed a tank, and it was something simple to get me started. I didn't have to figure out how to be charismatic."

I chuckled and felt myself start to relax. I could talk about Dungeons and Dragons for hours. I was an unashamed geek at heart. I always had been.

Kieran had once said it was cute how much I liked all this "weird, nerdy stuff", but I always got the impression the older we got, the less he liked it. He'd always encouraged me to grow up and try some different hobbies, but I'd never been into sports or going to the gym or anything he thought was suitable. I'd tried, but it had just made me miserable. Instead, I'd made friends online and stopped sharing things with him.

Now that I looked back on it, Kieran had really been an asshole. I'd just been too close to the situation to see it.

"What about you?" Leo asked.

"I've tried a few, but my favourite so far is a druid. It's my mission in life to try playing all the character classes at least once. Next on my list is a bard, which I'm kind of excited about, even though I can't sing to save my life."

Bard was also next on my list because Edward had offered to run some of the games, and I was really hoping I'd be able to spend half my time teasing him and driving him nuts. I was calling it revenge for the last campaign we'd played. I'd been the Dungeon Master and Edward had made it his character's mission to flirt his way through the game like some sort of louche layabout. The annoying thing was that he'd succeeded. His character had also been highly skilled with a rapier, so he'd skipped along happily, seducing my non-playable characters left, right, and centre and murdering those who disagreed with him.

"I don't know if being good at singing is a necessary requirement."

"You say that now, but I can guarantee you you'll feel differently once you've heard me." I grinned and Leo chuckled.

"Will you have sign ups beforehand or do I just need to come along?"

"Shit. Good question. I hadn't even thought of that. I'm still in the planning stages and seeing what interest there is." I'd asked Leo because I'd thought it would be a good idea, but I hadn't actually thought through much more than asking the initial question. I'd always been a leap before looking sort of person, and now it was going to bite me in the ass. Unless...

"Can I let you know? Maybe you could give me your number and I could message you? Maybe put together a WhatsApp group?"

"Sure." I pulled out my phone, and Leo rattled off his number. "Just give me a heads up and I'll come along."

"Oh, can I come too?" Emily stuck her head around the door frame. "Daniel and I love board games!"

"How long have you been lurking there?" Leo asked, the gruff note in his voice softened by the way his lip curved into a smile.

"Long enough," Emily said before turning to me. "Are you looking for other ideas for events?"

"Sure. Hit me."

"Pop-up pampering! Haircuts, manicures, make-up lessons, that sort of thing. It can be tricky to navigate when you're queer, and make-up is super fucking daunting if you're just starting out." Emily shrugged. "Like, YouTube is great and all, but if you have no idea where to start, a video on a cut crease isn't going to help."

"That actually sounds like a great idea," I said, my mind already turning over the possibilities. The only snag I could see was finding people to run it. Edward knew a bit about make-up, but his was all for cosplay, and that could be a little on the extreme end.

"I'm happy to run it," Emily said as if she could read my mind. "My sister's a hairdresser so I'll get her to come along and do the hair bit, and her wife's a beautician so she can do things like nails. And I can do make-up. I only started doing mine about eight years ago, so I totally get how hard it is at first. I think Dan's still got pictures of my first attempt somewhere."

"You've been planning this for a while," Leo said, chuckling as he looked at her. Emily shrugged.

"Everyone deserves to look fabulous. I was thinking about asking if we could do a class here, but if Jay's willing to host, that would be great. I think The Lost World would probably be warmer."

"Flowers don't like heat," Leo grumbled.

"And that's why I didn't ask." Emily smiled and stuck her tongue out at him while Leo rolled his eyes. They reminded me a little of Edward and me.

"It sounds great to me. Can I get your number too? Then we can talk dates when I get everything sorted. It might not be for a while though. Is that okay?"

"Sure. No worries at all."

We chatted for a few minutes more before I tore myself away, mostly because I didn't know what would happen if I left Edward in charge for longer than thirty minutes. Still, as I walked back to The Lost World, all I could think about was the way Leo had smiled at me. And the way my stomach had turned over on itself every time.

## CHAPTER FIVE

*Rose (Yellow) — Friendship, Joy, Gladness*

**Leo**

"Hey, you made it. Come on in." Jay waved from the top of the stairs leading to the lower level as the bookshop door closed behind me.

"Sorry I'm late. I got lost in orders."

It was the week before Valentine's Day, and I was already drowning in pre-orders and paperwork. I knew it was only going to get worse over the next seven days, and I'd be lucky if I managed to get any sleep next week. My shopping list for stock seemed to be getting longer and longer. I already knew I was going to have to request an additional delivery from one wholesaler next week as well as make at least two trips to the tiny, local wholesaler. That meant a five in the morning start so I could get there when it opened and then back in time to do my normal prep work. But a good Valentine's Day would make up for the normal quietness of January and February, so I wasn't going to complain.

I'd been debating whether or not to come tonight when Emily had shoved me out the door telling me it would be good for me to make friends. I'd wanted to argue that I was a thirty-two-year-old man and didn't need parenting, but the truth was I didn't have many friends. Not ones who lived locally anyway.

My family were all up in North Yorkshire, and the friends from uni I still kept in touch with were dotted all over the world. I knew a handful of people in Lincoln, mostly people Emily and Daniel had introduced me to, but that suited me fine.

That's what I told myself anyway.

After all, getting a business up and running was tough and time-consuming, and for the past five years I'd sunk all of my energy into making Wild Things a success. That hadn't left a lot of time for anything else. Now that I was in a place where I could look at spending more time on other things, I had no idea how to start. How did you even make friends when you weren't good with people?

But maybe things would be different with Jay.

"Don't worry about it," Jay said, running his fingers through his curls. "It's Valentine's next week, right? You must be slammed."

"Yeah, it's next Friday. This is the point in the year when I start to hate the sight of red roses." I sighed. There were so many other flowers people could use to show they loved someone, but they always stuck with roses. For once, I wished people would choose something else. Like tulips.

"I can imagine! Anyway, come on down. Is Emily coming too?"

"She'll be along in a bit. She's just doing a last bit of paperwork. I tried to get her to let me do it, but apparently I need to get out more… so here I am." I felt a bit stupid admitting that to Jay, but he just grinned and nodded as if he knew what I was talking about. I followed him down the stairs, careful to duck under the low ceiling. The last thing I needed was to brain myself before we'd even started. Luckily, when I got to the bottom of the stairs, it opened out into a long, high-ceilinged room. Similar to upstairs, there were plenty of packed bookshelves, but there were also some cosy looking armchairs and a selection of tables and chairs dotted about. There were quite a few people of all ages there already, and a couple of the tables had already started gaming. I saw the box for *Carcassonne* open on the one closest to me.

"I get that. Someone, who shall remain nameless, keeps telling me to do the same," Jay said as he flashed a pointed look at Edward, who was sitting at a table near the back of the room with a couple of other people I didn't know. "This is partly why I started this. To help people make friends, which is the hardest fucking thing to do as an adult!"

I nodded. "Especially when you're six four and look like you belong in some sort of fight club. Apparently, my tattoos are a little off putting."

"Seriously?" Jay stared at me as if I'd started speaking gibberish. "I think they're awesome."

"Thanks." I wanted to tell him that if he liked these, he should see the rest of them, but that felt really inappropriate, no matter what my libido said. This wasn't some badly written porno where Jay told me he liked my tattoos and I offered to show him more. We were here to play fantasy roleplay games for fuck's sake, not re-enact whatever fantasies my brain was trying to concoct. "Do you have any?"

"A few," Jay said with a wry smile, picking at the sleeves of his hoodie. I suddenly wished for the heat of summer so I could see him without it. That way I might be able to see what he was hiding underneath. Jay opened his mouth to say something when someone from one of the nearby tables called his name. "Sorry. I'll be back in a second."

He ducked away, leaving me standing awkwardly at the edge of the room. I really wished Emily had come with me. I wasn't really good with lots of people. I had a tendency to come off as surly even though I was usually just nervous as fuck.

"Leo!" A melodic voice from the back of the room caught my attention. Edward was waving at me and beckoning me towards him. I shuffled across the room, trying not to hit any of the tables. They were a lot closer together than I'd first thought. Edward smiled as I approached, leaning back in his chair and looking every inch like a king at court. His hair was elegantly braided, and he was wearing a long silver and blue frock coat with the most detailed embroidered flowers I'd ever seen. "It's good to see you. Jay mentioned you were coming."

"Yeah. I thought it would be fun."

"I'm so glad. He's been fretting so much over this." Edward's sentence was suspiciously open ended, and I assumed he'd said it that way deliberately. I wanted to ask whether he meant that Jay had been fretting about the whole evening or whether he'd been fretting about me. I guessed it was probably about the whole games evening, since it was the first one he'd run, but a tiny part of me hoped it was about me.

Edward looked up at me, a glint of mischief in his eyes. It was a look that made me nervous. I wondered what he was planning. "Do you know what group you're in?"

"No. Jay said he was going to wait and see how many people signed up." Had I missed something? Was there a message I hadn't gotten?

"Perfect," Edward said, pushing out the chair next to him and patting it. "You can join us."

"Are you sure?"

"Of course. I'm Dungeon Master-ing, and I promise it will be nothing but fun! Do you have a character in mind? If not, I have some suggestions. If you don't mind my assistance."

I had a few ideas, and soon Edward and I were deep in conversation with rulebooks and character sheets spread between us. Edward introduced me to the rest of the people at the table as well, drawing them into the conversation so we could start creating a party of characters. Daniel, Emily's husband, joined us not long after I'd sat down but not before giving me a giant bear hug. Something unclenched in my chest, and I felt slightly less nervous knowing there was at least one person here I knew.

Daniel was like Emily, easy-going and charismatic, with a carefully styled quiff and a colourful vintage-style shirt under an old bomber jacket. He was one of those people who could walk into a room and know everyone in five minutes. He had a way of making people feel like they'd known him their whole lives.

When Daniel was around, I always felt more relaxed because I knew I was never going to be the centre of attention. I was intrigued to see what type of character he was going to play.

Since I hadn't played in a long time, I wanted something simple so I wouldn't have to try and remember lots of spells and stats. I ended up creating a half-orc barbarian, who wasn't just strong but surprisingly smart. The only issue was he had more intelligence than wisdom, so I knew my character would struggle with anything involving common sense and perception. Still, he would be fun to play.

"We're just waiting for one more," Edward said, settling back in his chair and shuffling his notes behind the little screen he had. "Jacob? Where are you?"

"I'm here, I'm here! Sorry, I got side-tracked." Jay collapsed into the empty chair next to me, looking slightly stressed but still smiling. He glanced up at me, pushing his glasses up his nose, and I suddenly realised I was close enough to study all the beautiful details of his face. Like the way his thick eyelashes perfectly framed his dark eyes. "Hey. I see Edward adopted you."

"Yeah. He said your group had a spare space. I hope

you don't mind." Jay had mentioned he'd been developing a bard character, and during our sporadic messages he'd mentioned Edward running a campaign, but somehow I'd never put two and two together and realised that Jay would be playing too. I'd thought he'd be too busy.

Not that I didn't want him to play. I just didn't know how I was going to cope sitting next to him for several hours every other week without making a fool of myself. I'd always been a bit of a disaster around people I'd liked in the past. One of my previous girlfriends had commented on it and said it was adorable how flustered I got. My last boyfriend had said pretty much the same thing, although eventually he'd started to get frustrated with the idea that the Leo you saw wasn't quite the Leo you got.

"Of course not! I'm excited. Did you all build characters?"

"Yes, I'm your resident tank," I said, giving him a little smile. "Although I'm a little smarter than your average barbarian, just don't ask for common sense."

"Amazing! You can protect me when I inevitably irritate the DM and he decides to set a giant monster on me."

"Is that liable to happen?" I chuckled, and Jay flushed, his cheeks going an adorable shade of pink. It was the same shade as some of the little tea roses I'd been working with earlier.

"Probably."

"Jacob Morris, are you planning to be a pain in my ass?" Edward glared.

"No more than usual."

"Wait, hang on," said one of the other guys at the table.

He had shockingly blue hair, and I think he'd said his name was Sam. "Jacob and Edward?"

"Yes," said Edward, giving him a glare that would have turned most people to stone. "And I'll warn you now, any and all *Twilight* jokes risk incurring the wrath of the DM."

"Aw, man. Does that mean no vampire jokes either?"

"No. Those jokes went out of fashion ten years ago."

"Not even one?"

"Not even one." Edward glowered at him, then he turned to the rest of us and clapped his hands. "Are we ready to begin? We'll just take it steady tonight. A nice first session to get us going and let everyone introduce themselves. Okay, now for one reason or another you've all found yourselves in this bar called Shenanigans…"

## CHAPTER SIX

*Thornapple — I dreamed of thee*

**Jay**

I LET OUT an involuntary groan as I collapsed onto my bed, my body reminding me that I'd been up since six and it was now closer to midnight than eleven.

The game night had definitely been a success. I'd occasionally had to dash off to let people out of the shop or to help people find things, but everyone had been largely self-sufficient. We'd had more people turn up than I'd expected, but it hadn't been so rammed that it had been overly noisy or difficult to hear people speak.

One thing I did need to remember for next time was some refreshments. Even just a couple of packets of biscuits and some tea and coffee. Maybe I could even run it as a charity donation. It wouldn't be too expensive to fund out of pocket, and since I was charging people a little sit-down fee to cover the cost of being open later, it wouldn't hurt to get some cheap chocolate biscuits from Tesco.

I put my glasses on my bedside table and rubbed my eyes.

Now really wasn't the time to be thinking about it. I needed sleep. Any more ideas for improving game night could come tomorrow morning when I was awake and functional.

"Oh shit. Clothes," I mumbled to myself. I sleepily unzipped my hoodie and threw my t-shirt onto the floor, groaning again as I unbuttoned my jeans and slid them off along with my boxers. Wearing tight jeans for seventeen hours had not been a good idea.

Sure, they made me look good, but the lack of blood flow to my legs was a severe downside. Why had I even wanted to wear them anyway?

I crawled under the duvet and face-planted into my pillow. Luckily my flat was above the shop and therefore warm enough that I didn't need to worry about finding something resembling pyjamas. I wasn't sure I could find the energy to move again.

My brain rolled through the evening's memories. Dungeons and Dragons had been fun, and I had to admit that Edward had put together the perfect introductory session. It had been long enough to feel like a good adventure and solid enough that we'd all gotten to try out some of our character's abilities, but it hadn't been too dark and dangerous. It had been fun watching Leo emerge from his shell the longer the session progressed.

He'd obviously been nervous, so he hadn't said much at

first, but it had been fucking endearing when he'd started to get more involved. At least it had been to me. And the grin on his face when he'd left had me floating on a cloud all the way through clean up.

His smile was the last thing I saw in my mind's eye as I drifted off.

I groaned as two strong hands ran down my body, squeezing my ass and parting my cheeks, leaving me open and exposed.

"That's a beautiful hole." The voice was deep and rough, and it had me pushing back into the touch of his hands, desperately seeking more.

"P-please," I said, my voice sounding broken even to my own ears. I was so turned on, my cock was aching between my legs. I desperately thrust my hips forward, seeking relief. The sheets were cool and soft underneath me, giving me just enough friction to send me higher and higher, but then my lover smacked my ass sending shockwaves of pleasure through me.

"Stay still," he said on a low chuckle. "Push your hips up. Show me that perfect arse."

I did as I was told, pushing my ass up and back, preening a little as he moaned at the sight.

"Fuck. You're so fucking beautiful, Jay." I recognised his voice, but the knowledge of who it was remained just out of reach. My face was pressed into the sheets, and my glasses were gone, so even if I could turn my head, I wouldn't be able to tell who it was.

His hands were firm as they grasped my ass again. A desperate, needy moan slipped from my lips as I felt the roughness of his beard scraping against the sensitive skin. Then his tongue laved over my hole, hot and wet, teasing the sensitive muscle, and all my thoughts seemed to evaporate. I couldn't remember the last time anyone had done that to me. All I could focus on was the feel of his tongue, each flick sending waves of pleasure coursing through me. I clutched at the sheets as if they were some sort of life raft, the only thing keeping me anchored to reality.

"Oh God. Yes." My voice cracked as his tongue pushed inside me. "Yes! More. Please, I need more."

"Don't worry, I've got you." Somewhere nearby I heard the click of a lube bottle. I gasped as I felt cool wetness between my cheeks. My hips thrust abortively, desperately seeking some kind of touch as my cock dripped precum onto the sheets. Another whine slipped from my lips, the anguish at being left wanting clear as a bell. My lover gave a low hum, his hand running across my hip, soothing me instantly. "My poor, desperate boy."

"Touch me, please," I begged, the words dissolving into a moan as a thick finger pressed into me. "Fuck! Oh God."

His fingers were perfect, stretching me wide for him. When he fucked two into me, I heard myself begging for his cock, but he just chuckled and gently insisted on three, which was probably for the best. Somehow, I knew what my lover was packing, and I knew I needed more prep before he fucked me, but my patience was only going to last for so long.

"Please, give it to me. I need you."

"Roll over for me. I want to see your face as I fuck you."

I flipped myself over, collapsing onto the mattress before spreading my legs wide. My cock was hard and sticky against my hip, and I was so desperate I knew it wouldn't take much before I was painting both of us with cum.

My lover hovered over me, but I still couldn't see his face. I felt his hands on my legs, lifting me against his muscular thighs, and the press of his thick cock against my waiting hole. I moaned. I was tempted to reach up and push him over so he was flat on the bed, straddle his hips, and sink down on his cock. I wanted to ride him hard and fast and take my pleasure from him.

My muscles burned as he pushed inside me, and I was suddenly grateful for the three fingers. Holy hell. I hadn't expected this, but fuck, it felt so good.

"More. Fuck. More," I said, fisting the sheets beside me as I looked up into his face. His amber eyes twinkled, his thick, dark hair hung loose around his head like a wild mane, and ink spilled across his skin.

"Leo..."

The dream shattered around me, leaving me sweating and desperate in the middle of my bed.

I'd kicked the duvet off, and although the early morning air was cool against my skin, I felt like I was burning from the inside out. It was still dark outside, and I had no idea what time it was, but I didn't care. My mind was still fuzzy from sleep, but need had completely taken over.

My cock was rock-hard and dripping, and a groan ripped from my throat as I wrapped my fingers around my shaft, stroking the heated skin. I already knew it wasn't going to be enough. I needed to feel the delicious burn of something stretching me wide. I needed to be filled.

Fumbling around in the dark, I reached for my bedside table. There was a small bottle of lube in the little basket underneath it, along with my favourite dildo, "The Gorgon", aka George. It had been a self-indulgent purchase, and the first thing I'd bought after I'd left London. I'd ordered it online from a site that specialised in fantasy-themed sex toys. When it had finally arrived, I'd spent all afternoon in bed testing it out in as many positions as possible until I was exhausted, sore, sticky, and utterly sated.

The toy was cool in my hand. I dropped it onto the mattress next to me as I quickly poured lube onto my fingers, not caring if I made a mess. I could change the sheets later.

"Oh fuck!" I gasped out as I reached between my legs, pressing a slick finger to the furled skin of my hole. Sometimes I liked to draw things out, teasing myself before I finally gave in and slid my fingers inside me. This was not going to be one of those times.

I moaned as I pushed a finger in, fucking the digit in and out, barely giving myself time to adjust before I pressed a second in. It was awkward and rushed, but I didn't care. All I could think about was how fucking desperate I was. I flipped myself onto my stomach, reaching back between my legs to try and push my fingers in deeper as I added a third. I desperately wanted some friction on my cock, but that was going to have to wait.

My thoughts flooded with memories of my dream, and try as I might, I couldn't seem to push them away. So I embraced them. I imagined my fingers were Leo's, stretching me wide while he muttered soft praise and dirty words in my ear.

I wondered what he'd actually be like in bed. Would that soft, external façade melt away to reveal someone rough and controlling? Or would he be sweet and gentle, giving me everything I wanted? I wasn't even sure what I'd like best. I could be mouthy and pushy when I wanted, but I loved it when someone took care of me, letting me melt into their arms.

Oh God, would he let me top him? The idea of working my hands and tongue over his round, perfect ass was too much. Sure, I was half his size, but that just made the fantasy all the more delicious.

"Shit." The word tumbled out of me, laced with need. I pulled my fingers out and grabbed the toy off the bed, fumbling for the bottle of lube so I could pour more onto its thick, solid shaft.

Pushing myself onto my knees, I held the toy's base against the bed, pressing the bulbous head against my hole. I groaned as I slowly slid down onto it, my muscles burning at the delicious stretch. George didn't just have a thick head; he had a thick, ridged shaft that widened towards the base. It made me feel utterly and completely full, and I loved every fucking inch of it.

My breath came in deep pants as I held still, letting my body adjust to the toy's girth. Each moment seemed to last forever, and eventually my limited patience dissolved. I imagined Leo holding my hips and murmuring how good I looked on his cock and how much he wanted to watch me ride him. I lifted up on my knees, letting the toy slide a little way out before I dropped back down, gasping as it filled me again.

I began to ride the toy, bouncing and rocking on its thick shaft as its perfect ridges hit all my sweet spots. My hands came up to pinch my nipples, rolling my fingers over the barbells. I'd had them pierced years ago, and I loved the sensitivity that had come with it.

I slid one hand down my stomach, finally grasping my neglected cock. I moaned as I gripped my shaft, my thumb spreading precum and the last bit of lube across the head. I began to jack it hard and fast, matching the pace with which I was riding the dildo. Pleasure bubbled under my skin like magma waiting to erupt from a volcano. The dildo's ridges and rounded head rubbed over my prostate with every move I made, dragging a stream of moans from me.

I was so close, my whole body pulled taut as I stood on the brink of a precipice, waiting to be hurled over the edge. I just needed a tiny bit more…

In my imagination, Leo gripped my hips with one hand, the other pinching my nipple as he thrust up into me, pulling me down onto his thick cock as my own hand worked my dick, twisting over the head in just the right way.

"Come for me, Jay," fantasy Leo said. So I did.

"Leo," I cried, my body momentarily frozen as pleasure overtook me. Thick streaks of cum shot from my cock, painting my hand, my abdomen, and even the sheets. I felt my channel squeezing the dildo, milking every drop of pleasure from its bulbous, ridged shaft. I collapsed onto the bed, gasping for air as the last shockwaves of my orgasm rolled through me.

Holy shit. I couldn't remember the last time I'd come that hard or that much.

I gently eased the dildo from my hole, dropping it beside me and wiping my hand on the sheet. I knew I needed to clean up, but sleep was once again reaching for me, and my orgasm had left me completely boneless and exhausted. I didn't want to wake up crusty, but just the idea of moving made me shudder.

On the count of three, I'd get up. It wouldn't take long.
One. Two.
Three…


I woke up several hours later to the soft jingling of my alarm, half stuck to the sheets with dried cum and a fuzzy brain. I couldn't quite remember why I felt so gross, and why my beloved dildo was bumping against my thigh.

"Ew, gross." I rolled over, hoping to separate myself from the sheets as bits and pieces of memory crawled back into my mind. I remembered having a sexy dream. A very sexy dream if what I remembered was true.

A little smiled played over my lips as I remembered waking up desperate to be fucked and filled, hence the reason George was in bed with me rather than in his basket. I remembered the fucking amazing orgasm I'd had from riding the dildo's thick shaft while I played with my nipples and my cock.

In my sleep-addled state, the only thing I couldn't remember was who I'd been dreaming about. I was sure it would come back to me. It had probably been Jason Lu, my favourite actor from the paranormal drama I'd been binging lately. It wouldn't be the first time I'd had a sex dream about him.

Heaving myself out of bed, I stripped off the sheets and hauled myself—and George—into the bathroom. Grabbing the small bottle of toy cleaner I kept in there, I quickly washed the dildo before climbing into the shower. I sighed happily as the hot water hit my muscles. It wasn't the most powerful shower in the world, but it was enough to help wash away the remains of my night and soothe my sore shoulders.

As I ran my hands across my body and between my cheeks the memory of who I'd been fantasising about resurfaced alongside the ghost of a moan and the recollection of firm fingers on my skin.

Holy crap. I'd had a sex dream about Leo.

## CHAPTER SEVEN

*Pansy — Thoughtful reflection, Merriment*

**Jay**

No, no, no, no. *No.* This could not be happening. I wasn't supposed to be having sex dreams about Leo. No matter how gorgeous or handsome or downright sexy I found him. This could not be happening.

Technically, there was nothing I could do about it now, and I'd obviously enjoyed it, given the evidence in my washing machine. The only problem was that I didn't know how to deal with this. Having sex dreams about actors you thought were cute was very different than having sex dreams about local florists you thought were cute. Mostly because I'd have to look the latter in the face again.

I'd told myself I just wanted to be friends with Leo, but evidently my brain hadn't gotten the message. Either that or it had decided to ignore the memo and go straight for Edward's sex-only approach.

I stuffed the last of my toast into my mouth and grabbed my phone off the side, pulling up the message thread I had with Edward. I needed to talk to him about this. He'd always been my sounding board, and even though I was dreading what might come out of his mouth, I desperately needed his advice.

JAY *Please come to the shop ASAP!!!*
JAY *Also bring drinks*
JAY *And maybe cake*
EDWARD *I take it there's some sort of emergency?*
EDWARD *I'll be there in twenty. Do you need gin?*
JAY *It's eight thirty in the morning!*
JAY *But I'm not saying no for later*

I rubbed my eyes, trying not to smudge my glasses. There was nothing more I could do until Edward arrived, so I made my way down to the shop and tried to busy myself by setting up for the day and organising the paperwork I needed to sort through. I pulled open my ancient laptop and began to work through my stock list, putting together an order to be placed with the wholesalers. Just the idea of opening a box of new books was soothing. There was something about it that made my heart happy.

I was halfway through my list when there was a tapping noise at the door. I looked up to see Edward on the other side of the left-hand window, holding up two takeaway cups and a brown paper bag.

"What's the emergency?" he asked as soon as I'd unlocked the door and ushered him inside. He handed me one of the takeaway cups and the brown paper bag. The cup contained a frothy vanilla latte, which was my go-to treat drink. And inside the paper bag was a large, warm cinnamon bun, covered in cream cheese icing. I'd already had one breakfast, but I wasn't going to say no to a second.

"So, um, last night," I said, perching myself on the padded stool behind the counter and taking the bun out of the bag, "I kinda had a sex dream. About Leo."

Edward's face went from mildly interested to intrigued in less than a second. He'd always had an expressive face, and these days I knew how to read every single look. The tiny pinch between his eyebrows meant he was dying to ask for more details, and if the dream hadn't been about someone we both knew, I would have told him. We'd never kept secrets from each other.

"Why is that a problem?" He sipped his coffee, his finger playing with the gold edging on his frock coat. It was nearly floor length and black with gold detailing. He'd seen something similar on an anime character and had decided to make one for himself. Edward was the only person I knew who could pull off something so dramatic before nine on a Thursday. He was like a walking gothic vampire fantasy. "You like Leo."

"Yes, but..." I tried to find the right words, but my tongue wouldn't cooperate. "But I don't want to date anyone. And I don't want to have sex with him."

"Well, clearly part of you does." I glared at him and took a bite of my second breakfast. Fuck, I loved cinnamon buns.

Edward shook his head, his pale hair fanning out in waves. "Don't look at me like that. It's not a bad thing, you know. To be attracted to people again."

"I'm attracted to Jason Lu from *Celestials*."

"Yes, but you're never going to meet him, are you?"

"I might. There's rumours the cast of *Celestials* is coming to London Comic Con at some point. I could go for a meet-and-greet, and he could fall desperately in love with me." I grinned, but I knew I was clutching at straws.

"Don't be obtuse. I meant men you've met. Men that you could conceivably have a relationship with."

I felt panic rising in my throat. I knew Edward was right, but that made it all the more terrifying. I'd sworn off relationships when I'd left London last year, and just the thought of another one filled me with dread.

"But I don't… I don't want that." My voice cracked. "I can't, Edward. I can't go through that again. I just know it would end badly." My shoulders began to shake, and I put my hand on the counter to steady myself. I heard my pulse in my ears, and from somewhere Edward made a soft, distressed sound before his arm wrapped around my shoulders and pulled me into his chest.

"It's okay," he said as his fingers stroked through my hair. "Look, I know things ended badly with the dickwad who shall henceforth remain nameless, but not all men are like him."

"I know." I sighed against Edward's surprisingly solid frame. "I just… It was my fault everything went wrong, and I can't risk that happening again. Not with someone I really like."

"I'm sorry. I think I went temporarily deaf. Can you repeat the first part of that?" Edward's voice was deathly cold, like the frozen planes of the arctic tundra.

"It was my fault everything went wrong."

"Jacob Morris you look at me right now." Edward's fingers grasped my chin, and I found myself looking up into his piercing silver-blue eyes. "What that dickwad did was not your fault. It was not your fault that he ruined a seven-year relationship because he couldn't keep his dick in his trousers. And it was absolutely not your fault that he broke your trust and betrayed you by sleeping with someone who called themself your best friend. You were never the one at fault."

"Yeah, but I worked such long hours that I drove him to it. I neglected him and our relationship."

"And who pushed you into taking that promotion? Who told you he was happy with you working those hours? Who never said a fucking thing about being unhappy?"

"Kieran." I sighed, and Edward placed a little kiss on my forehead.

"Exactly. It wasn't your fault at all, no matter what that twat said. If he had a problem, he should have talked to you rather than falling into bed with someone else and blaming you for it. You can't trip and fall into somebody's ass."

"I know." And deep in my heart I really did know. I'd been over this in my head enough times to logically know I wasn't really the one at fault here. What had happened with Kieran wasn't how functional adults handled relationships. But it was one thing to tell myself that and another to believe it.

That was why I didn't want to date again. Not yet. My heart still wasn't ready to be open with someone, and I couldn't risk giving it to someone who was going to break it again. I still felt fragile as if I'd only been stuck back together with Blu-Tack.

"What if I'm never ready?" I asked, my voice so deathly quiet I could barely hear myself. I leant against Edward's chest so I didn't have to look at him. "What if my heart never heals? What if I'm alone forever?"

"Darling, you are far too wonderful not to find someone who loves you." There was a warm, cosy certainty to his voice. "One day, you're going to meet a man who recognises just how truly amazing you are, and who's going to love every single inch of you and everything about you. Even that you work too much, think tea needs a minimum of six sugars, and continue to wear that dreadful red hoodie, even though it's got holes in it."

"Hey, I like this hoodie!" I sat up and tugged at the sleeves, pulling them over my hands and slotting my thumbs into the holes I'd created. It was the sort of thing I'd started doing during my emo teenage phase, and I'd never really grown out of it.

"You could at least buy a new one. This one looks like it belongs to some sort of skulking teenager."

"That's because it once did."

Edward squinted at me, his lips pursed as if he wanted to say something but had decided now wasn't the time. Instead, he took a deep breath and raised an eyebrow. "I know I've said this before, and I'm going to say it again.

You like Leo, and since you're adamant about not dating, why not just try to be friends with him. You have his number. Why don't you message him? See if he wants to hang out or ask him about the book he's reading. Just because your brain wants to bone him doesn't mean you have to act on it. And if you have the dream again, enjoy it for what it is: a fantasy."

I nodded, but I couldn't stop my cheeks from heating as my brain casually dropped memories from the night before in front of me. The way I'd fantasised about Leo touching me, fucking me, wanting me. It was almost too much.

My heart and my head were already at war, and I didn't know which side I wanted to win.

I didn't have time to figure it out either, because Edward's face suddenly broke out into a wide grin. It was the sort of smile that I knew was going to cause me a headache.

"By the way, darling, I have something to distract you."

"Oh?" Edward's idea of a distraction was never a good one. The last time he'd offered to distract me, it had cost me over a thousand pounds, and I'd ended up with an enormous tattoo on my back. Not that I could be too mad. I loved my backpiece.

"So, you know how I'm sort-of helping out with the organisation of the Impulsion Steampunk Festival at the end of April?"

"Yes?" I vaguely remembered Edward mentioning something about it, but that had been several months ago. I'd been far too distracted with the shop to keep tabs on

Edward's never-ending list of things he was involved in. I had no idea how he found time to do everything.

"Good. Well, one of our venues fell through for the workshops. Apparently, they're having some renovations done, although why they didn't get them done over the winter is beyond me."

"Edward!"

"Oh yes, anyway, I volunteered The Lost World."

"I'm sorry?" I stared at him, stunned. "You did what?"

"I volunteered the shop to host some of the workshops." Edward beamed at me. "It'll be perfect. There's plenty of space downstairs, and you already have tables and chairs. Plus we'll be able to offer you a small fee for the space, and it'll bring lots of customers in too."

I groaned, scrubbing my face with my hands. That was all I needed; to be dragged into the organisation of something else. I could barely manage to keep myself coordinated, let alone a whole weekend of workshops. That was Edward though. He'd always been a look before you leap person.

"I promise, you won't have to do anything. I'll help set everything up and if anyone has any questions, they can ask me. All you have to do is provide the space," Edward said, a tiny note of pleading in his voice.

"Ugh, fine. But only because I love you." And because Edward had already done so much for me. I'd be a real asshole if I didn't help him out the one time he asked.

"You're a star. It's going to be amazing." Edward pressed a kiss to my temple before launching into a long explanation of what workshops they were running and who'd be involved.

I sighed and nodded, sipping the last of my vanilla latte, even though it was cold, a new layer of stress settling on top of the already precariously stacked pile. I wasn't sure how long it would be before it came crashing down around me.

## CHAPTER EIGHT

*Alstroemeria — Devotion, Wealth, Prosperity, Fortune*

**Leo**

I HUMMED to myself as I arranged some stocks alongside some white alstroemeria, loving the slightly wild and charming look the flowers had when slotted in beside some delicate bits of foliage. It was the sort of bouquet that looked like it had been picked from some country cottage garden and should be in a jug on a kitchen windowsill somewhere, looking out over rolling hills.

Much as I loved doing interesting, dramatic things with flowers, I had a soft spot for these sorts of arrangements. They reminded me of summers spent with my gran and the way my grandad would bring her bunches of wildflowers from his allotment. Those flowers were so full of love and devotion. It was why I'd chosen stocks and alstroemeria for this bouquet when I'd been putting it together. Both of them had devotion, affection, and beauty amongst their meanings, and it had nudged at a warm, little, nostalgic spot in my heart.

Rolling my shoulders, I heard something pop in my spine. That probably meant I'd been here for too long. I'd told Emily I was planning on staying late to finish up some orders, but I wasn't sure what time it was now. As I glanced across the workroom to the clock on the wall, my mouth twisted in surprise. It was twenty past eight, which was at least an hour later than I'd intended to stay. I was surprised Angie hadn't come to find me, but when I stuck my head around the door, she was curled up in her bed, snoring happily.

I'd taken to keeping some dog food here and giving her dinner in the workroom on the nights I wanted to stay late. Since she'd been fed and been out, she'd have been content to stay here for hours.

Not that that was a good thing. I was supposed to be making more time for myself and trying to get out of the habit of working twenty-four-seven. I'd made a promise to myself that I was going to aim for more balance this year. So far it was not going well.

"Come on. Time to go home," I said, crouching down to stroke her head. My knees clicked, and I winced. I'd definitely been in one position for too long. Angie opened one eye and regarded me as if debating whether or not to ignore me and go back to sleep.

"Come on." I chuckled, standing up to pull my coat on before grabbing hers and holding it up. The early mornings and late nights could get very chilly, and I didn't want to risk her getting cold. Angie sighed and heaved herself out of her bed, walking two steps before plopping down at my feet. Clearly I wasn't worth the energy.

I fastened her coat, grabbed my keys, and did a quick sweep of everything before flicking off the lights, heading out the front door, and locking it behind me. The streets were quiet, and the biting wind that had nipped at my exposed skin that morning hadn't eased up during the day. Dark clouds skittered across the sky, threatening rain or maybe even snow. Not that it mattered, since I didn't want to be out in either.

Giving a little whistle to Angie, I started up the hill, walking as fast as my legs would carry me. Now that my body realised what time it was, my stomach was starting to complain that I hadn't eaten recently. Not since the couple of biscuits Emily had left me with a cup of tea mid-afternoon.

I racked my brain trying to figure out what I could make for dinner that wouldn't take long. I had some leftover chilli in the freezer, but that was about it. It looked like it was either going to be pasta or takeaway, unless I stopped by the Co-op on the way home to grab a ready meal.

As I rounded the bend and walked past the next line of shops, something caught my attention. There was a single light on in The Lost World, creating a dull glow through the window. I paused, trying to remember if Jay had said he had any events on that evening.

We'd been messaging back and forth for a couple of weeks, mostly sharing random Dungeons and Dragons memes and chatting about books. He'd reached out the day after the first games night to ask what I'd thought about our first D&D session, and I'd wondered if it had been that obvious I'd been nervous. Still, I'd been touched that he'd asked.

I'd thought that would be it, but then he'd asked what I was reading. All it had taken was one message about the chapter I was reading in *Gideon the Ninth* and we'd spent the whole evening chatting about it.

It was nice to have someone to talk to, someone who shared similar interests, someone I didn't feel I was imposing on, like I sometimes did with Emily. She spent all day putting up with me; I doubted she wanted to do it in the evenings too, no matter what she said. And it had been fun to chat with Jay during the chaos of this week. Valentine's Day had been yesterday, but the busier days were always the two or three leading up to it when everyone suddenly remembered they needed to order flowers. Today had been almost back to normal, except for a few harried customers who'd clearly forgotten to get anything and were now trying to make it up.

Since I couldn't recall Jay mentioning any events, I assumed he was working late. An uneasy feeling settled in my stomach. I knew exactly what it was like during those first few months of running a new business when nothing outside of work seemed to exist. That included things like food and sleep. I'd run myself ragged in that first six months, refusing to take breaks and working non-stop until I'd reached the point of no return. I'd found a bit of balance eventually but still not as much as I needed.

I'd be the first to admit I worked too much. Emily was

always pestering me about taking time for myself, and she was the reason I was trying to get out more. After Christmas she'd not-so-subtly suggested I needed to find a hobby that wasn't related to flowers and take better care of myself. I'd had to admit she was right.

I stared at the door of The Lost World. If Jay was anything like me, then getting lost in work meant forgetting about everything else. I wondered if Jay had had anything to eat or if he'd had a break at all today. Would it be too much of me to knock and ask? I didn't want to overstep, but I thought we were sort of friends and I didn't want him to fall into the same traps that I had. I wouldn't wish that level of exhaustion on anyone.

Before I could second guess myself, I raised my hand and knocked on the shop door.

There was a clang and the sound of swearing, and I winced. Then I heard keys turning and a bolt being drawn back.

"Leo?" Jay looked slightly confused as he poked his head around the door, his hair sticking up at odd angles.

"Sorry, I was just walking home, and I saw the shop's light on. I figured you were working late, and I just wanted to check that you were okay." Now that I'd said it out loud, it sounded fucking ridiculous. Jay was a grown man. He didn't need me checking up on him like some overbearing parent. My intentions were good but that didn't mean I wouldn't look like a patronising arsehole.

"What time is it?" Jay asked.

"Um, about half eight or quarter to nine?"

"Shit! I thought it was only about seven." He chuckled

and shook his head. "Do you wanna come in? It's fucking freezing out there. Unless you need to get home?"

"I've got Angie. Is that okay?" Angie whined from beside me and a grin broke out on Jay's face.

"Of course. Come in." The shop was still warm, and Jay bolted the door behind us. Angie was clearly happy to be inside again because she sighed before pottering off to explore, probably in the hope she'd find something edible.

"I got lost in paperwork," Jay said, gesturing to the counter where there was a laptop and a little desk lamp set up. I nodded because I knew that feeling all too well. "I don't have a desk upstairs, and I know if I try to do the work on my sofa, I'll just get distracted by the TV." He grinned. "Netflix just got the latest series of *Celestials*, and I'm obsessed."

"I've never seen it," I admitted. "I don't really get a lot of time for TV, and when I do, I tend to comfort watch. I'm currently rewatching *Last Call*." Jay looked at me blankly, and I grinned. "It's this super cheesy eighties cop show set in New York about this guy who runs a bar and solves crimes with his best friend who happens to be a cop. They've all got sunglasses, bad hair, and terrible catch-phrases. I think you'd love it."

"Wow." Jay snorted. "That sounds like the best and worst thing ever, so it's totally going on my to watch list. I can't believe you haven't watched *Celestials* though. I'd have thought it would be right up your street."

"What's it about?" I heard the name, and now that I thought about it, I'd seen its title card pop up in my recommended viewing on Netflix.

"Okay, so, it's about these two brothers and their sister who are these beings called celestials, and they're supposed to defend the world against evil and keep it in balance, but then everything starts going wrong!" Jay was practically fizzing with excitement, like a can of Coke that'd been shaken and was ready to explode as soon as you pressed the tab. "It's kinda tropey. I mean it's got all the supernatural tropes you could ever want—vampires, werewolves, fae, demons—but it's super fun. Plus it's got like two, potentially three, canon queer couples, and I fucking love it. Like one of the brothers is gay and he falls in love with this man who's supposed to be his mortal enemy. The mortal enemy is played by Jason Lu, and honestly, he's the hottest of them all. Anyway, they have to try and navigate that because they love each other so fucking much! Also, they're hot as fuck, and they even have a couple of sex scenes. Well, I mean what passes for sex scenes on a TV show that's barely a fifteen."

"Spoilers." I chuckled.

"Were you gonna watch it?"

"I might. You've made it sound pretty good."

"Do you wanna watch some now?" Jay asked, pulling his lip ring with his teeth. I must have paused a fraction too long, distracted by his movement, because he continued. "I mean it's totally up to you, but I'm currently renting the flat upstairs, and if you're not busy, maybe we could order pizza and watch a couple of episodes? No pressure, obviously. I mean you're totally welcome to tell me to fuck off if I'm overstepping."

"That sounds great," I said, finally managing to get

words in before he took the offer back. The idea of spending time with Jay made something flicker in my chest that I didn't want to ignore. "Would you mind starting at the beginning?"

"Of course not! I could watch it a million times and never get bored. And I promise not to talk too much either. Edward always says I'm a nightmare to watch films with because I chat constantly."

I threw my head back and laughed because it was something I could picture as clear as day. It was probably cute as fuck as well. I wondered whether I'd end up watching the show or whether I'd spend most of my time watching him. "Well, you'll be better company than Angie. She just snores and farts."

Jay snorted, walking over to the counter to grab his laptop. "Do you want to order pizza now?"

"Sure."

Half an hour later, I was relaxing on the squishy grey sofa in Jay's flat with Angie lying at my feet, and two large pizza boxes rested on the coffee table in front of me. Jay sat at the other end of the sofa, flicking through Netflix to find the first episode of *Celestials*. He'd been surprisingly easy-going when it had come to picking pizza toppings. Or maybe it was just because I usually only ordered pizza when my brother came to visit, and he and I had very different tastes. Despite the fact he was a chef, I'd still never managed to convince him that pineapple belonged on pizza.

"Do you want me to explain anything before hand, or should I just start it?" Jay asked, pulling up the episode.

"I'm sure I can pick it up." I gave him a little smile as I reached for the pizza box, offering him a slice. "But you should definitely point out who the hot brother is, just so I know who to focus on."

"They're all hot. Seriously. This show is filled with beautiful people. It's unrealistic."

"So you're just going to torment my poor bisexual heart then?"

Jay laughed. "Yeah, pretty much."

Ten minutes into the episode, I realised Jay was right. The whole cast was beautiful.

One of the brothers was blond with a sharp interesting face and piercing green eyes. The other had dark hair swept back off his face and intense dark eyes that seemed to sear into my soul. Both were obviously muscular but not so much that it was off putting. It just made me want to run my hands across the dark-haired guy's broad shoulders. Their sister was just as beautiful with shapely curves that had been poured into a skintight dress followed by ripped jeans and a vest top. She'd looked stunning in both outfits and my poor little bisexual heart really was suffering.

It didn't help that we then got a glimpse of the dark-haired brother's mortal enemy and love interest. He was so sexy I thought I might die. He had golden skin and enticing eyes lined with kohl, and silver rings glittered on his perfect fingers.

"See? I told you they were hot," Jay said, smirking at me as I turned to look at him. "Especially Jason, right? I would totally say yes." He picked up another slice of pizza, and I couldn't help noticing how long and slim and perfect his fingers were too.

I chuckled. "Was I staring?"

"More like you wanted to climb through the TV and then climb him." I felt my skin prickling with embarrassment, and I'd never been more glad my beard covered half my face. I reached for another piece of pizza in the hope that Jay wouldn't be able to see my blush. But it didn't seem to bother him.

"Don't worry. I feel exactly the same. You should follow him on Instagram. He has a habit of posting shirtless selfies. In fact, you should follow all of them." He pulled his phone out of his hoodie pocket, and I was sure I'd find links to their profiles on our message thread as soon as I opened it later.

I turned back to the TV, quickly finding myself lost in the rest of the episode. Like Jay had said, it was a bit tropey and over the top, but it was fun, and I couldn't help but be drawn into the story. When the episode finished, Jay turned to me and grinned, holding out the remote and raising his eyebrow, the question obvious on his face.

I nodded, leaning back onto the sofa and reaching up to untie my hair. Since it was so long and thick, I usually spent all day with it in some sort of loose bun to keep it out of my face, but I let it down as soon as I finished work. At the moment, it reached down to my chest, which was the perfect length for me. I ran my fingers through it, even though that would make it go wild and puffy because I'd washed it that morning and it hadn't dried before I'd had to leave. Emily always called my hair my lion's mane, and right now it probably looked like one.

Beside me, Jay let out a little noise. I glanced at him, and then at the TV. He was staring at me, and I couldn't work out if I'd done something wrong or if I'd missed something important. Knowing how much he loved the show, it was probably the second.

"Did I miss something?"

"N-no, sorry," he said, shaking his head and glancing away quickly. It was like he'd been caught doing something he shouldn't have, but I wasn't really sure what that was. "My, um, my back's a little sore from sitting hunched over the laptop earlier, and it just popped. I have really shitty posture."

"Do you need some painkillers?"

"No, it's fine." He waved his hand, brushing off my concern.

"It's probably a good thing you don't work a desk job then."

"Yeah, my old job killed my spine. I don't recommend sitting at a desk for twelve hours a day in a really shitty desk chair. It doesn't end well."

"What did you used to do?" I asked. I'd never had an office job, and I'd never wanted one either. I'd always been good at practical things, so I'd figured out quite young that I wanted to do something with my hands. In my teenage mind, that equated to rock star. It was only after several failed attempts at learning to play the drums and then the guitar that I'd decided it maybe wasn't for me. I'd ended up going to university to study biology, mostly because I enjoyed doing the practicals, and I hadn't known what else to do with myself at the time. Three years had easily convinced me that academics wasn't for me.

"I worked in London as a graphic designer for a marketing company."

"That's a bit different from running a bookstore in Lincoln. This place is tiny compared to London!"

"Yeah, just a bit."

"What made you make the change?" There was a moment of silence, and I suddenly realised I might have stumbled onto something I shouldn't have. People made dramatic life changes for different reasons, but that didn't mean they always wanted to talk about them. Given that Jay wasn't really looking at me, his eyes focused somewhere between the TV and the wall, I guessed it hadn't been a good thing at the time.

"I was working long hours and even though it was everything I thought I'd ever wanted, I guess my heart just wasn't in it." He paused, worrying his lip ring with his teeth. "And then my long-term boyfriend cheated on me with someone I thought was my friend. After that, I just couldn't face staying in London."

"Shit. I'm so sorry."

"It's okay. We'd been having problems. I'd been working all the time, and I guess that was the final straw." He sighed. "Turns out, Kieran was more of an asshole than I thought he was."

"Holy shit." I wanted to reach out, pull him into a hug, and keep him wrapped in my arms. I couldn't imagine how hard it would be to have your whole life come crumbling down all at once. To have everything you'd ever wanted poisoned and rotted by someone who was supposed to love you. "That must have been really hard."

"It was fine," Jay said with a shrug. I wondered if he actually felt like that or whether he just didn't want me to make a big deal out of it. "Some people have it worse. Kieran wasn't anything more than your standard heartbreaking douchebag."

"That doesn't matter. He still hurt you." My hand stretched out across the cushion between us, bridging the divide. I grasped his shoulder gently. Jay stiffened and then relaxed, taking a deep breath and giving me a small smile. "And problems or not, it sounds like he was a coward. He shouldn't have treated you like that."

"How do you know I didn't deserve it?"

I paused. Did Jay really believe that? What had his ex said to him to make Jay think that could possibly be true? Anger bubbled up in my stomach, and I had to push it down.

"First of all, nobody deserves to be treated like that. You're a good person, Jay. You deserve so much more than that."

"Thanks." Jay's smile flickered. "It's been a year. I don't know why I'm still hung up on it."

"You're still grieving the end of the relationship. These things take time I've been told."

"No tragic heartbreak for you, then?"

"Not really." I released his shoulder, resting my hand on the cushion between us. "I've had a few relationships, but nobody who ever stuck. I work a lot, so I'm always busy, and I'm not the most sociable man. A lot of people don't want that." Not to mention I sometimes came off as gruff and unlikeable. Someone had once described me as a marshmallow with a concrete exterior. But I'd found most people didn't want to look beyond the concrete. After a few bad experiences, I'd given up trying. I'd always been the sort of person to fall for someone quickly, and more than once I'd found myself caught out, planning for a relationship that hadn't lasted a month. In the process, I'd given away too many pieces of myself. They hadn't been tragic breakups, not in the same way Jay's seemed to have been. But each one had chipped away a little more of me, until I'd decided it was easier to throw myself into work rather than risk another accusation of not trying hard enough.

"I get that." Jay chuckled darkly, shaking his head. "There's always so much to do."

"Especially if you're starting up by yourself."

"Yeah." Jay nodded. "Edward helped me write the business plan so I could get the loan for the shop, and he invested a chunk of money in it too. But he's got his own business to run. He helps out whenever he's bored or has some free time, but he's not really staff, and I don't have the money to hire anyone right now. So long hours it is."

"You should remember to take care of yourself though," I said. "Burnout is a real thing, especially when you're trying to do everything on your own. Make sure you take time off. And eat too."

"Speaking from experience?"

"Yeah. The first year I opened Wild Things, it was just me. I kept the shop open by myself, and I'd get up at five to go buy or receive flowers or make orders, do deliveries, keep the shop open and then stay late to do any more orders or paperwork. I was fucking exhausted, and when my brother came to visit, he made me realise I needed a break." I chuckled at the memory. "Aaron's not exactly subtle and he made it clear that if I didn't start looking after myself, I was going to make myself ill. That's the polite version anyway." My brother wasn't the most eloquent man —he'd give Gordon Ramsey a run for his money most days. "So I started closing the shop on Mondays, to at least give myself one day off, and then eventually I was able to hire Emily to give me a hand on five of the other days. I still work too much, but at least its manageable now."

Jay's hand was resting on the cushion, not quite next to mine, but close enough to touch. I nudged it gently, feeling the warmth of his skin against mine, and something sparked along my hand, like a sharp nip of static electricity. "I know how hard it is, and I don't want to see you struggle like I did. Promise me you'll take care of yourself."

"I will. I promise." Jay's fingers brushed against mine again, sending tingles up my arm, then he interlaced his little finger with mine.

## CHAPTER NINE

*Sweet William — Grant me one smile*

**Jay**

"A MAN APPEARS through the door of the pub, dressed in a dark cloak. Hunter and Snorri, you're busy playing cards, and you notice something out of the corner of your eye, but it's not enough to distract you. Ustri, you're still deep in conversation with the potential rebels, and Castien, you're too busy sitting at the bar trying to fix your lute and—"

"Doing vocal warmups," I said, attempting to do some very off-key scales while Edward fixed me with a piercing look. Mostly because I couldn't sing for shit. Beside me, Leo chuckled softly.

"Doing your terrible vocal warmups," Edward continued. He turned to Leo, a dangerous smile curling at his lips. That usually meant we were in trouble. "But, Kruk, you do notice the man, and you also notice that he's heading towards the piano…"

"Oh no," Leo said, sounding slightly exasperated already.

"Oh yes, and he's pushed his hood back to reveal a rather gleeful looking old man."

It was game night again, and we were halfway through our Dungeons and Dragons session for the evening. Edward had decided to switch things up and had us running the local tavern for the night, complete with a set of house-rules which I knew he was going to spend all evening trying to break. So far, we'd had a bar fight, some people plotting to start a rebellion, and someone attempting to distribute pamphlets. Although that hadn't been helped by Daniel's character, Ustri, sitting down and engaging them in a long conversation about their cause.

The last thing we needed was to accidentally start an uprising. Especially since my character, Castien, had also gotten into a very heated argument with someone when I'd attempted to start singing… which may or may not have been the cause of the bar fight. It had ended with Leo's character, Kruk, leaping over the bar to my defence and throwing the instigator out. I had to admit it was a pretty charming gesture, and my walking disaster of an elven bard may have found it quite attractive.

Now it seemed like the one person who wasn't allowed to play the bar piano had just turned up. I wondered if I could challenge him to some sort of sing off. True, I had a shocking voice and Edward's was lovely, but since it would be the dice rolls that made the decision, it couldn't hurt to try.

"Are you going to sing?" Leo asked, leaning down to whisper in my ear. "It might distract him."

"I might. Would you like a tuneless rendition of the Spice Girls or Queen?"

"Does it come with dancing too?"

"It does now." I threw my head back dramatically, striking a pose.

"Spice Girls then." Leo chuckled. "You get his attention. I'll do the rest. It's time the world heard my true genius. Whether they want to or not."

Leo snorted and turned back to Edward and the rest of the group, a wry smile on his lips. "Hey, you. What do you think you're doing?"

An hour later, when we'd semi-successfully finished running the tavern for the evening—we'd only broken two tables and quashed the rebellion to Daniel's chagrin—the session wound down and people began drifting home.

Edward volunteered to man the door to save me having to run up and down the stairs to unlock it every time someone wanted to leave. I began wiping down the tables and folding them away. We usually had one table out permanently, so people could sit and read or draw or write, but the rest were just cheap folding card tables I'd gotten at a car boot sale. I usually stacked them in the little corner cupboard, along with the hoover and some basic cleaning supplies. It took a bit of Tetris-ing to get them all in, and I often had to shove the door shut, but once they were in, they were in.

I had to admit, as much as I didn't want to think about it, this space would be perfect for the steampunk festival workshops. Especially as we could easily adapt it based on what each session needed.

"Is there anything I can help with?" I looked up to find Leo watching me, a charming but uncertain smile on his face. It had only been a few days since he'd ended up on my sofa eating pizza, watching *Celestials,* and listening to me unintentionally pour my soul out. And holding hands.

I'd gone to bed that night full of panic that I might have fucked everything up, despite the fact that Leo hadn't seemed upset, at least not with me anyway. After a pitiful three hours of sleep and a lot of attempts to tell myself it was fine, I'd ended up texting him to apologise for rambling at him.

But he'd replied saying I hadn't rambled, and he'd had a great evening. Then he'd turned up when I opened the shop with a little bouquet of yellow roses. He'd even taken the thorns off them. Probably because he'd known I was likely to stab myself with them. The roses had sat on the counter for the past three days, in the vase he'd given me at the grand opening, and every time I looked at them, I felt a funny lurching in my chest.

"It's fine," I said, attempting to fold one of the tables. I was still half looking at Leo though, and the table slipped from my fingers and dropped onto my foot. "Mother fishcakes!"

I cringed, squeezing my eyes tightly as my toes

throbbed. The table wasn't the heaviest thing in the world, but it had landed awkwardly on my foot, and I was only wearing Vans. I'd always been clumsy as fuck, and my knees were covered in scars from falling over on the playground or out of trees as a kid. It hadn't gotten any better as I'd gotten older, except these days it was more dropping heavy things onto myself or tripping downstairs. And there'd been one memorable trip to Accident and Emergency when I'd gotten glass in my foot.

"Are you okay?" Leo asked.

"'M fine." I shoved the table off my toes. "Totally fine."

"Sit down for a minute." Leo's voice was gentle but firm. I opened my eyes to see him standing right in front of me, looking down with eyes full of worry. It was moments like this, when we stood close, that I realised how much taller he was than me. I barely made five foot six on a good day because I was a complete short arse, and Leo must have been well over six feet. My face was eye level with his chest, and I was trying not to focus on the way his body sat under the thick, knitted jumper he was wearing, or how beautifully broad his shoulders were, or how I just wanted him to wrap his arms around me.

Leo put his hand on my arm, gently steering me into a chair before kneeling in front of me. "Is it okay if I take your shoe off?"

"You don't have to. It's really not that bad. It just stings a little." I looked away, trying not to squirm in my seat while my face and neck grew impossibly hot. "I just banged it."

"True, but I'd rather check they're not bleeding or obviously broken."

"Okay."

Leo gave me a little smile and eased off my shoe. I probably should have been embarrassed I was wearing pink socks with little avocados all over them, but I thought they were cute. Apparently, so did Leo.

"Are those avocados dancing?" He sounded amused as he gently tugged at my sock, and I felt the warm, rough touch of his fingers against my skin. This should not be making me feel the way it did—embarrassed, awkward, and almost turned on. Apparently, my body had decided that any touch from Leo was a good one, even if it came from him trying to check for broken toes.

"Y-yeah. I've got another pair with doughnuts on."

"They're cute. Like you." Leo stilled, and my heart stopped. I wanted to say something, but I had no idea what it should be. My brain seemed to have frozen, and all I was getting were fucking error messages.

"I'm sorry. I shouldn't have said that," Leo said, clearing his throat, his eyes still fixed on my foot. "I didn't mean to make you uncomfortable."

"No, it's fine. I mean, you didn't make me uncomfortable. I don't mind that you said that. I, um, thank you."

"You're welcome." Leo slid his hand gently over my skin and although it was sore, the pain eased with every passing second. When I glanced down, the skin on my toes was a little pink, but I doubted I'd have anything more than a bruise by tomorrow morning. "Does it hurt?"

"A little, but not much. I think it's just bruised."

"Do you have any ice packs?"

"Um, maybe? There are some frozen peas in my freezer."

"I'll take you upstairs, and we can find them."

"No, it's fine. You don't need to do that. It's hardly hurting now." I wiggled my toes in an attempt to get him to believe me, and although they tingled a little, it wasn't that sore. "See?"

Leo frowned, but gave in. "Alright. But you sit here. I'll put the tables away."

I wasn't going to argue with him, so I sat and watched as he carefully folded the tables and stacked the chairs, neatly pushing them into the cupboard. Maybe I'd get him to do this every week if he could put the tables away without having to elbow them into place.

Reaching for my sock, I pulled the pink material over my foot, my eyes catching on the little avocados. They were cute, and so was I. At least according to Leo. I wasn't sure what to do about that.

I couldn't deny how those words had made me feel. Or how I felt about Leo. How could I when my pulse raced and my skin tingled every time I looked at him? When all I wanted was to spend hours curled up on my sofa with him and Angie, watching endless episodes of *Celestials* or talking for hours so I could unravel every little mystery that made Leo the person he was.

I kept telling myself I hardly knew him, that this was just simple infatuation and that I should get over it. I didn't want to date, and I needed to stick with that. But every time I thought those words my resolve weakened a little. It was like chipping away at a block of marble, but I wasn't sure what I'd find underneath. Part of me wanted to find a new determination to say no, but the rest of me knew I was being stupid. I still had my emotional shields up as if I expected my heart to be attacked at any second, but perhaps Leo was different.

Perhaps Leo would be the one who put it back together.

It felt like I was rolling a die. I just didn't know whether I was going to get a one or a twenty or whether I wanted to succeed or fail. Maybe I just had to take the risk. After all, some dungeons contained gold and some contained traps. You never knew which you would get until you opened the door.

"You okay, Jay?" Leo was watching me from beside the closed cupboard door, and I realised I'd been staring off into space, lost in my thoughts.

"Yeah, just thinking." I tugged my sock on and pushed my foot into my shoe. I wobbled as I stood, mostly because the shoe was only half-on. Leo moved in an instant, putting out his hand to steady me. I tried to ignore the tingle that ran across my skin, but it was impossible. I swallowed, looking up at him.

There was hardly an inch between us.

"Thanks for your help. I don't usually get the tables put away that easily."

"You're welcome."

"And for the record, I think you're cute too. Well, I guess handsome is probably a better word, but I mean…" My voice trailed off as Leo's hand gently cupped my jaw. I shivered, even though I wasn't cold.

"You're adorable too." Leo tilted his head, pulling me towards him gently, and I went without resistance. I felt his breath ghosting across my face. My heart was racing so fast I felt dizzy, and I wanted him to kiss me more than anything.

"Darling, are you oka—oh shit!" Edward's voice was accompanied by the thudding of footsteps. The moment shattered like glass on a stone floor. Leo released my face and stepped back, eyes wide and cheeks pink as if he couldn't believe what he'd almost done.

"I... I'm... thanks for a great evening." He grabbed his coat from the back of a nearby chair where he'd set it down. "I'll see you later."

I watched helplessly as Leo disappeared up the stairs, my mouth open in shock, not able to truly process what had just happened.

## CHAPTER TEN

*Rose (Thornless) — Love at first sight*

**Jay**

MY HEAD WAS POUNDING and my eye twitched as I rolled over in bed. I groaned as I threw my arm over my eyes, willing myself to go back to sleep. But that wasn't happening, no matter how much I pleaded with my brain to please, please shut down.

I rolled over again, sinking my head into the pillow before giving up and reaching for my phone to check the time. Nearly half four in the morning. Great. So far I was running on about two hours of sleep, and I was starting to severely doubt I'd get any more before my alarm went off at seven. It looked like I was going to be spending my day downing giant coffees and Monster energy drinks to keep myself upright and smiling. There was nothing like being a grumpy asshole to drive off potential customers, and the bookshop needed every sale it could get.

All I could think about was last night. The way Leo had looked at me, the way he'd cupped my face and pulled me close, the way he'd looked into my eyes and made me feel like I'd just had a hot chocolate, warmed from the inside out. It was the strangest feeling, and I didn't quite know how to describe it. All I knew was I wanted to feel it again.

I knew if Edward hadn't interrupted us, we would have kissed, and I couldn't stop thinking about what it would be like. No matter how hard I tried to dismiss the thoughts, my mind lingered on my desire to feel Leo's lips against mine.

I was going to fucking straight up murder Edward.

He'd sworn he hadn't done it on purpose. He said he hadn't even realised Leo was still downstairs. I was sure he was lying. Leo and I had been talking, and I was convinced Edward had heard me drop the table on my foot. But apparently not. Now I had to imagine the press of Leo's lips, rather than knowing what they felt like against mine.

My resolve to avoid dating fractured even further.

Was it so bad to want one tiny taste, one tiny hint of what Leo's mouth could do to me?

It wasn't like I wanted anyone else. If I went out to a club or a bar, I wouldn't be interested in picking anyone up. Leo belonged in a separate space than everyone else, one that included him and only him. Maybe Jason Lu, but that was just unrealistic. I just had to figure out what I wanted to do about my interest in Leo.

I had to roll the dice and make a choice.

Sighing, I heaved myself out of bed. Since sleep wasn't forthcoming, I figured I might as well do something useful with my time. Grabbing my laptop, I propped myself up on a couple of pillows and began reviewing my spreadsheets and plans for the next couple of months.

I'd always wanted to introduce events early on in the shop's life because it would be a great way to embed it into the local community. The only problems were the costs associated with keeping the shop open late and actually organising the events. I'd get some money from hosting the steampunk festival workshops, but I wouldn't get that until closer to the time. Being a one-man operation was all well and good until I needed to be in three places at once. I was going to need to figure out a way to do it during the festival, despite Edward's insistence that he'd be around to help. Unless he had a secret clone stashed away somewhere I didn't know about.

The game nights were going well though, which was a good start. My next goal was to introduce a few author events, and for that I really needed to get more familiar with Twitter so I could connect with them.

I'd always struggled with being an active Twitter user, mostly because I found it a hellsite to be avoided at all costs, but there was a huge author and indie-bookstore community. I just wasn't the greatest social media person. I'd never really seen the need for it, apart from keeping up with the occasional friend from university or high school. Most of my friends came from fandom worlds on Tumblr, and that was about the only platform I still used. I couldn't even remember the last time I'd logged in to Facebook.

I was trying my best, and so far, the shop had a couple of hundred Twitter followers, which was better than nothing. I was well aware followers didn't necessarily translate into customers and sales. Especially since The Lost World didn't currently have any sort of online ordering system.

I guessed I could do it via email and PayPal. I knew a couple of the bookshops I followed allowed customers to order like that. It was something I needed to investigate further, and I made a mental note to add it to my ever-growing to-do list.

Maybe I'd ask Edward to give me a crash course in social media as recompense for ruining my almost kiss. Maybe he'd see how bad I was at it and take it over for me. Although that would probably make me feel horribly guilty. Edward was one of the UK's most successful cosplayers and costume makers with hundreds of thousands of fans worldwide. He didn't have time to run my social media accounts as well. He spent enough time on his own.

I wondered if Leo had a Twitter or Instagram for Wild Things. My mind began to wander, imagining Leo taking snapshots of his work or artfully arranging flowers for photos, his tattooed hands moving with precision and skill. He seemed like someone who'd apply that sort of focus to anything he cared about whether that was making a bouquet or making love…

"Snap out of it!" I shook my head and rubbed my eyes. I needed to make a list. That would give me something to focus on that wasn't the sexy, tattooed florist who seemed to fill every second of my conscious, and unconscious, life.

A tiny, optimistic part of my brain kept trying to tell me this was exactly the push I needed. If I couldn't stop thinking about Leo, then clearly it was a sign that I needed to go for it. But five in the morning was definitely not the time to do anything about it.

Ten, though, that was more reasonable. At least, that's what I told myself as I walked down Steep Hill clutching the brown bag of bakery goodies and two hot chocolates wedged into a little cardboard tray.

A familiar electronic beep sounded as I pushed open the door to Wild Things, letting the scent of flowers and fresh greenery envelop me. Leo stood at the counter, chatting with an old man who was holding a bouquet of what looked like wildflowers. It reminded me of the sort of thing my granny had always had on her kitchen windowsill.

I watched Leo, noticing tiny details I'd never seen before. Like how loose strands of hair framed his face as they fell from his bun, how his eyes danced as he talked about different types of perennials, and how his hands moved as he spoke. Leo was a man of few words, but it was clear he was passionate about what he did. You could see it radiating out of every fibre of his being.

Eventually, the old man said his goodbyes and waved at Angie over the counter, giving me a cheery smile as he pottered out of the shop.

"That's Albert," Leo said. It was like he was a mind

reader, and I wondered if it should bother me that he knew the answers to questions I hadn't even asked. It didn't though. Leo seemed to be able to read people like open books, his quiet observation giving him insight I'd never been able to see. "He comes in every Thursday to buy flowers for his wife, Mary. They've been married for sixty years."

"That's so sweet. Romance is alive and well in Lincoln then."

Leo chuckled, then yawned. I suddenly felt guilty, wondering if I'd kept him awake in the same way he'd kept me from sleeping. That was a ridiculous idea though, so I brushed it aside. "Here," I said, putting the brown paper bag and one of the hot chocolates on the counter. "This is for you."

"Thank you." He opened the bag, his eyes widening in a delighted expression I'd never seen on him before. It sent my pulse skyrocketing and happiness skittering through my chest. "I love cinnamon buns." There was a little whining noise from behind the counter. Leo looked down. "No, not for you. For me."

"I'm sorry, I should have brought her something."

"No, she doesn't need any more treats. Albert always brings her something, so I know she's not hungry."

"Aren't dogs always hungry?"

"True." He picked up the takeaway cup, taking a sip and then another straight away. "Hot chocolate?"

"Yeah. It's cold, and I didn't know if you preferred tea or coffee. So I got hot chocolate instead. I'm sorry. Should I have gotten something else?"

"No. It's perfect." Leo's eyes twinkled as he sipped his hot chocolate. One hand moved to brush a stray piece of hair out of his face. There was silence between us, but it didn't feel awkward or strained, more like one of those warm, comfortable silences where both parties were content. I wondered whether I should bring up last night and what had happened, but I was afraid of making things awkward.

Leo yawned again, and another little wave of guilt lapped at me. "Are you okay?"

"Yeah. Just had to get up early to go to one of my wholesalers. It's over near Spalding, and I had to get up at four to be there when they opened. They offer delivery, but when I can I like to go myself, although I usually come back with more than I intended." He shook his head, cradling his drink like it was the most precious thing in the world. Given the amount of sugar that was in it, it probably was. "You'd have thought the early mornings would get easier after five years, but they never do."

"I'm sorry. I shouldn't have kept you so late," I said. "You really didn't have to stay to help clean up. Especially if you had to get up so early."

"Don't worry about it. How's your foot?"

"It's good. Just a little bruised." I held out my foot and wiggled it, even though he couldn't see anything under the old, checkered Converse I was wearing. "Nothing that hasn't happened before. I didn't even break anything this time."

"This time?" Leo raised an eyebrow.

"Oh, well, I mean..." I stammered, not meeting Leo's

gaze. "I mean, I might have dropped a lamp on my foot once and broken my toe. And there was the time I was cooking in bare feet and dropped a glass and cut my foot open. I have to tell you, A&E nurses are very lovely when they have to dig glass out of your foot, even when you throw up."

"A lamp?" There was a friendly, teasing note in his tone.

"In my defence, it was one of those desk lamps with the solid base. It really fucking hurts when they land on you."

"I think I'll stay and help with clean up again then. I don't want to hear you've squashed your fingers in a table."

"That would be gruesome but absolutely something I'd do. You should have seen me trying to build the bookcases for the shop. Poor Edward eventually got so sick of me catching myself on nails and dropping shelves on my feet that he made me sit and watch while he built them. It's a good thing he's never asked me to sew anything because I can guarantee I'd put my finger through the machine." I sighed, remembering the fraught exasperation on Edward's face when he'd finally snapped somewhere around bookcase number three. "Oh, Edward makes cosplay costumes, along with doing a million other fandom things. He's amazing, you should check out his Instagram," I added, seeing the look of confusion on Leo's face. He nodded.

"So, I was, er, I was wondering," I continued. "I don't know how busy you are, and you can totally say no, but I was just thinking this morning… would you like to come round again at some point? Maybe watch some more *Celestials*? Or we could start that show you told me about. And maybe we could get takeout again, or I could make dinner. I mean I'm not the best, but I can make the basics. Do you like curry? I had a housemate at uni who taught me her mum's recipes. I'm not as good as her, but I'm not terrible. And—"

"Jay," Leo said, gently interrupting me before I babbled for another hour. "That sounds good. I'd like that."

# CHAPTER ELEVEN

*Daffodil — Regard, Unrequited love, Respect*

**Leo**

I took a deep breath and knocked on the door of The Lost World, looking around the empty street as if I expected someone to be watching me. I had no idea what I was doing, but Jay had looked so earnest when he'd invited me round the other day that I couldn't say no to him. I was already in far too deep to make any rational decisions.

So here I was, spending my Saturday night being sociable.

Emily's jaw had hit the floor when I'd told her, and I'd wanted to laugh. I knew she'd assumed I was going to spend my evening either working or binge-watching something on Netflix. I'd expected to be doing the same. I couldn't remember the last time someone had invited me to hang out.

I didn't think this was a "Netflix and chill" kind of situation, but since we hadn't talked about our almost kiss at games night, I had no clue what I was supposed to do now. Was I supposed to bring it up, or was I supposed to pretend it hadn't happened?

I didn't want Jay to feel pressured into anything he wasn't ready for. From the sound of it, he'd had a pretty shitty experience with his ex-boyfriend. And it also sounded like he was reluctant to try dating again. I'd probably feel the same if I were him.

"Hey, you made it! And you're right on time." Jay pulled the shop door open, a beaming smile on his face. "No Angie today?"

"No, I took her home." The last thing I needed if something happened between Jay and I was an excitable Angie trying to climb onto our laps. She liked being the centre of attention.

"If you were worried she wouldn't be welcome, please know she always has an open invitation. I love her cute, squishy face."

"I'll bring her next time." Something bubbled in my chest as Jay talked about Angie. She was family to me, and I wanted him to love her as much as I did. Somehow, I didn't think I had anything to worry about, and that made the funny knot in my stomach, the one that always seemed to appear around Jay, twist tighter.

"These are for you," I added, holding out the little bunch of daffodils I'd brought with me. "They should bloom in the next few days. I only got them yesterday and they were freshly picked then."

"They're beautiful. I love daffodils." Jay's eyes lit up with an emotion I couldn't place, and he rocked a half step closer on the balls of his feet. "They're one of my favourites."

"Mine too." He was so close I could reach out and touch his chest or even run my finger along his jaw. Temptation surged in my chest. All it would take was one movement. But then I remembered what I'd been thinking about while I stood on the stoop. "You'll have to let me know what other flowers you like."

"Yeah... yeah, I will." He sounded almost disappointed as he turned away and walked through the shop, snapping the moment like a thread. Was I supposed to have kissed him?

"Dinner shouldn't be too long. Do you want to watch more *Celestials*? Or do you want to show me some of *Last Call*? I have to say the idea of cheesy cops solving murders sounds appealing."

I followed him through the store and up the stairs, trying not to dwell on what had just happened. "You mean one cheesy cop and one cheesy barman."

"Double the amount of cheese? Count me in!" He paused on the stairs, just two above me. It made him fractionally taller for a moment. A playful smile danced across his lips, and there was a gleam in his eyes.

"I'm not sure you're prepared for the amount of cheese you're about to witness."

"Bring it on. I can handle cheese. I once marathoned the entirety of *Xena: Warrior Princess* in a week."

"That's a lot of cheese," I said, folding my arms, unable to stop myself from smiling.

"See? I'm perfectly prepared. I am a cheese master!" He waved his arms airily then wobbled. "Oops! Okay, time for dinner. So, I'm not as good a cook as Georgie was, but it's her mum's recipe and she said they were idiot proof."

The curry was delicious, and Jay had even made fresh naan to go with it. They were light and pillowy soft, and I could have eaten a thousand of them. Well maybe not quite that many, since Jay had also bought a raspberry cheesecake for pudding.

"You're spoiling me," I said as he handed me a bowl of cheesecake before flopping down on the sofa next to me.

"Technically, I'm spoiling me too. I don't usually cook like this for just me. I am king of pasta, noodles, and batch cooking, and that's only because I was terrible at making single portions when I started living by myself." He stabbed at his own piece of cheesecake. "When I first moved up here, I lived with Edward. Now, don't get me wrong, I love the man, and I would do anything for him, but his house is the literal embodiment of chaos."

"That bad?"

"Oh yeah! His spare room, well one of them, is technically his workspace, so there's bits of costume all over the place, sewing dummies and a couple of props too. He's got this giant pair of mechanical wings in there. That was the room I slept in because it still had a bed. The other spare room had been converted into a studio for filming because he has a YouTube channel as part of his cosplay job, and it was just easier to leave all the cameras and lights set up in there." The more Jay revealed about Edward, the more I thought I was going to have to Google him. Out of curiosity more than anything. I knew there were full-time cosplayers out there, but I didn't know anything about them.

"How long did you stay there?"

"Until the start of January when the shop was nearly finished. We went back to my dad's for Christmas. I dragged Edward to make sure he'd actually take a break and enjoy himself. He doesn't have the best relationship with his parents." Jay's face creased for a moment, like he was worried he'd said too much. I wasn't going to pry though. He and Edward were obviously close, and I respected that.

"Shall we watch another episode?" I asked, gently steering the conversation away from something that might make him uncomfortable.

"Definitely. You were right, this show is epically cheesy. I mean, it's almost like a car crash in slow motion, but I can't quite tear my eyes away. Like I don't get why they're always wearing sunglasses, especially when they're indoors? It makes zero fucking sense."

"Just roll with it," I said with a chuckle. "I think you'll like this one. It involves a murder on a golf course."

"Wait, are there even any golf courses in New York?"

"I don't know. You'd have to Google it. I think the show was mostly shot in LA."

"Let's be grateful they didn't try to set it in London. All the characters would have bad cockney accents and somehow the queen would be involved." Jay was still grumbling happily when the opening credits rolled over the pre-credits scene where the two main characters had been enjoying a day off and discovered a brutally murdered corpse on the ninth tee. I had no idea why the local police department would let one cop and his best friend, who was a barman, investigate a case on their turf, but I'd learnt it was best not to pick holes in this show. The second you looked too closely at it, it crumbled into dust.

We ended up watching another three episodes mostly because the second one was part of a two-parter, and the first episode finished on such a weird cliffhanger we had to watch the second. Although we'd started the night at opposite ends of the sofa, the longer we sat there the closer we'd gotten.

When Jay had bought the cheesecake, he'd sat down a little closer than he had before. And when I'd returned with some more drinks, I'd sat a little closer to the middle. He'd shifted in his seat several times, each one bringing him towards me. I wasn't even sure he realised he was doing it. Now, at the end of the third episode, there were barely six inches between us.

All I wanted to do was put my hand out and draw him into my side. Or tilt his head up for a kiss.

But I knew we needed to talk. We couldn't keep pretending there was nothing between us or ignoring what had happened on Wednesday. I needed to know where we stood before I did anything.

The episode drew to a close.

"We need to talk," I said. Jay's lip twitched, highlighting

the ring. I swallowed, wishing I'd had the sense to think through everything I'd wanted to say before we got here. "I hope I didn't make you feel uncomfortable the other night."

"Y-you didn't."

"Okay. Well, I... I just wanted you to know that I don't want to push you. You told me about your ex and that you're still working through that. I don't want you to feel like you have to rush into anything here. If you just want to be friends, then that's fine. If you want more, I'd like that. But if not, I won't hold it against you." I tried to give him a smile, but it felt awkward. I had no idea if I'd said the right things. This was why I stuck to saying very little. At least then I couldn't get it wrong.

"Thanks." Jay twisted his fingers in his lap, teeth pulling on his bottom lip. "I just... I'm sorry if you thought I was leading you on. I know I'm a little bit of a mess right now."

"It's okay." I put my hand out, resting it on his thigh. I'd wanted the gesture to be platonic, or maybe friendly, but I didn't think it had come off that way. I moved my hand again, dropping it onto the sofa. "I'll still be here if you ever decide you want more, no matter how long it takes."

"And what if I never figure it out?"

"Then we can just be friends and watch too much bad television together." I gave him a smile and Jay chuckled.

"You really weren't kidding when you said this show was cheesy."

"I warned you."

"I kinda love it though, like it's so bad it's good. I kinda just want to watch the rest of the season just to see what happens. I mean, it's gotta get better, right?"

"Define better," I said, giving him a wry smile. "I think after a while you just care less and watch it purely for the terrible drama and bad puns."

"Yeah, I can see that." He sighed and looked up at me. There was worry and sadness lingering behind his eyes, and I wished I knew how to take it away. If I could, I'd do so in a heartbeat. I just wanted Jay to be happy, whether that was with me or on his own. If anyone deserved to be happy, it was him. "Are we okay?"

"Yeah, we're good."

"And you're sure you'd be okay if… if nothing happened?" he asked, pulling on his lip ring again.

"Of course. I like you for you. I'm not going to stop being your friend just because you're not interested in dating. I'm not a dickhead."

"Okay." Jay nodded, and it looked like he actually believed me.

I was telling the truth. I would be his friend, no matter what happened. He was funny and interesting to be around, and I loved listening to him talk about anything and everything. He could talk to me about the weather and I'd still be fascinated by him.

So why, hours later when I was lying in bed, staring up at the ceiling, could I feel nothing but a heavy weight on my chest and a sinking feeling of loneliness.

## CHAPTER TWELVE

*Daisy — Loyal love, Gentleness, Innocence*

**Leo**

MOTHER'S DAY was three weeks away, on the last Sunday in March, and I already had more orders than I knew what to do with. I knew I should be grateful for the extra business, but as I put the phone down after talking to my latest customer and looked down my list of orders, I knew I was going to be pulling some very late nights just to get everything done.

This was everything I'd been working towards for the past five years, and although it had been touch-and-go at times, making Wild Things flourish had been my greatest accomplishment. Three years ago, I'd never have imagined being this busy, and even last year I'd never even considered we'd be so rushed off our feet we were starting to need an extra pair of hands.

Emily and I could only do so much, and I didn't want to turn away orders if I could help it. And since I'd decided I needed to start focusing on having a life outside of work, I didn't want to fall back into my old habits of pushing myself to exhaustion. My dream had been to make this shop a success, and now I wanted to focus on some of the areas of my life I'd sorely neglected.

Maybe it was seriously time to think about hiring a third member of staff. Just someone part-time who'd be able to help me with the orders so Emily and I weren't permanently chasing our tails. And it would give me an extra pair of hands if Emily needed time off or had family things to deal with. I didn't want her to feel obligated to be here if her family needed her. I sighed, rubbing the bridge of my nose. It was definitely something I needed to think about. Otherwise I was going to spend a whole week pulling all-nighters, and being tired made my work sloppy. I could always tell when I'd been tired while making an arrangement, and I didn't want my customers to have shitty looking bouquets because I couldn't manage my business properly. Plus it was a sure way to lose customers. One bad review was all it took these days.

That settled it. I needed to hire someone.

The idea of having someone new around the shop made me nervous, but that was something I'd have to deal with. I couldn't let my business suffer because I got anxious around new people. Besides, if I could survive bringing Emily in—someone who was my polar opposite—then I could manage this. I wondered if I still had the job description from when I'd hired Emily. Although maybe it would just be better to rewrite it. Emily would definitely have some ideas about the sort of person we should look for, and I wanted her to feel included. Besides, she was so much better with people than I was.

I heard the front door buzz and Emily chatting with someone, but I wasn't really listening. I was too focused on my ever-growing to-do list.

"Hey, Mr. Lion… Leoooo," Emily's voice prodded me out of my thoughts. I looked up to find her smirking at me from the doorframe. "You have a visitor."

"Who?"

"Why don't you come and find out?"

"I don't have time for this, Em."

"Don't be such a cranky-pants," she said, then she turned to the other person. "He's not usually this mardy. He just hasn't had lunch today. Even though I told him he needed to eat something."

I sighed and rolled my chair back, striding towards the door. I didn't have any appointments booked for today, and I had no idea why Emily wasn't telling me who it was.

"Seriously, Em, I'm…" I froze. Standing on the other side of the counter was Jay, looking awkwardly at the floor. Shit. "Jay."

"I'm sorry, you're really busy. Would it be better if I came back later? Or I can just send you a text."

"No. It's fine. I'm just… mardy." From beside me, Emily snorted. I'd just admitted she was right, and I knew she'd be using it against me for months. I was never going to be able to deny it. "Everything okay?"

"Yeah, I just… I wondered if you wanted to grab lunch?

Just quickly. I know you've been really busy lately, and you mentioned barely getting to have a lunch break the other day, so I figured I'd come by and see if you wanted to get a sandwich." He was so adorable, standing there in his well-worn red hoodie, tugging at the sleeves with his thumbs, his dark curls sticking out at angles from the spring breeze. I wanted to run my fingers through them.

"He'd love to," Emily said before I could open my mouth. "Go on. Get your coat and get out of here. I don't want to see you for an hour."

"Are you my mum?"

"No, just someone who'd like to not get her head bitten off by a grumpy lion this afternoon. Now shoo."

I did as I was told, grabbing my battered leather jacket off the coat rack and pulling my beanie over my bun. Angie looked up from her basket for a second, but since she showed zero inclination to move, I decided to leave her where she was. Maybe I'd stop at the little bakery at the top of the hill on the way back and get her a doggy doughnut as a treat.

I followed Jay out into the street, pulling my jacket around me a little tighter as the breeze nipped at my skin. Being on top of a hill in a largely flat county made it all the worse when cold winds blew in.

"I'm sorry," he said as soon as the door closed. "If you're busy, you really don't have to come with me. I can feign a work emergency. I mean, I left Edward in charge of the shop for an hour, so it's probably not that far off the mark."

"It's fine. Honestly. I just had a stressful morning. The

break will do me good." I smiled down at him, hoping it would wipe the nervous crinkle off his face. Everything had felt so fragile between us since our almost kiss the other week, like an egg hovering on the edge of a kitchen counter. One wrong move, even a small one, would see it smashed on the floor.

I'd hoped things would get better when we had dinner the other night, but there was a good chance I'd made things worse. I was fine with us just being friends, but I wasn't quite sure where Jay stood.

Maybe it would have been better if I'd told Jay exactly how I felt, that I thought he was gorgeous and adorable and just bloody amazing. I could listen to him talk for hours and never get bored. I loved the fact he was chatty. His clumsiness was endearing, even if I was half-terrified he was going to fall down the stairs in his shop and break at least one limb. Maybe two.

But I wasn't good with words. I doubted I'd ever be able to tell him all those things, not without stumbling over half of them. And anyway, I didn't want to put any pressure on him. I'd told him so, and I intended to keep my word.

"Are you okay?" Jay asked, giving me a little half smile. "You seem a little lost in thought. Something on your mind?"

"Just thinking about work," I lied. "Sorry."

"Don't worry about it. I totally get it. Now, where do you want to get lunch?" We'd been ambling slowly down the hill without any destination in mind, but now that Jay had asked, I had the perfect place in mind.

"Have you been to Rosy's?"

"No? Where's that?"

"It's just down here." I pointed down Steep Hill and we continued on down the narrow, cobbled street. The urge to reach out and take his hand in mine was ridiculous, but instead, I shoved my hands deeper into my jacket pockets. "It's a tiny vintage tea-shop. They do great food and homemade cakes."

"Sounds perfect! Don't let me forget to take some cake back for Edward. He'll spend the whole afternoon sighing forlornly if he finds out I had cake without him."

I chuckled. "I'll remind you."

I almost had to duck to get through the low café door, and although a couple of tables were occupied, there was a spare one up a little set of steps, tucked into the corner. Emily had first brought me here a few years ago, and ever since we'd been coming here for what she dubbed "team-meetings", which were basically just an excuse to have tea and cake. The shop had a warm, cosy feel with its mismatched vintage china and softly playing big band music.

We ordered some sandwiches and drinks, and Jay took a moment to examine the old photographs that were tucked under the glass tabletop. Sitting so close together, it almost felt like we were on a date.

I almost would have called it one, if it hadn't been for our conversation. Since then we'd chatted on and off, mostly about new books and Jay's enthusiasm over the *Celestials* renewal.

"Any reason you're so busy?" Jay asked eventually.

"Mother's Day is at the end of the month, and people are being very organised this year."

"That makes sense. Well, I suppose it makes sense if you want to get things sorted. Sorry, now I'm not making sense."

"No, I know what you mean."

"I always forget about Mother's Day," he said, running his finger around the edge of his floral teacup. "My mum died when I was six. I don't really remember her, so it's okay."

"I'm sorry."

"It's fine," he said, giving me a little smile. "I grew up with my dad, and he was a great parent. He's a really nice guy as well. I think you'd like him. He's the reason I read so much. Our house was always full of books, like so full you'd trip over them all the time. Although last time I spoke to him, he'd taken up gardening as a hobby. Probably so he can buy more books. Last year he promised he wouldn't buy any more books unless they were absolutely necessary, but he'll need to read up on his new hobby." Jay chuckled fondly and shook his head.

Our conversation paused as the cafe owner, a woman named Linda, set down two huge sandwiches in front of us, complete with crisps and coleslaw. Jay stared.

"You know, when you said vintage teashop, I was imagining delicate sandwiches and mini cakes, not this."

"Bless you, love," Linda said, giving him a wide smile. "Can't be having with small portions."

"Jay's from London," I said, unable to resist teasing him. Linda pulled a face but kept smiling.

"No wonder you're surprised, duck."

"By the way Linda, I have more daffodils in if you want any. And some tulips."

"Thank you. I'll send Phil up to get some when he gets back." She patted my arm and left us alone. Jay picked up half his cheese and pickle sandwich, eyes wide behind his glasses. To be fair, the sandwich was the size of a doorstop.

"At least I won't need dinner."

We chatted on throughout lunch, mostly about our D&D campaign and what we thought Edward had planned for us. He hadn't dropped any hints, but we both suspected he'd be sending us out on our main quest soon enough, and it was fun to swap outrageous conspiracy theories about what we thought we'd have to do.

"Edward has a habit of writing in insanely dramatic reveals and backstory moments, so prepare for that," Jay said as he picked the last of his crisps off his plate. "They're always really good though. Like proper rip your heart out stuff, so that's fun."

"Does everyone have to have a tragic backstory?"

"Of course! The more tropey and tragic the better." I laughed because I definitely hadn't invented a tragic backstory for Kruk. I'd always gone simple in terms of background, so I was curious to see what Jay had come up with for Castien.

We decided to order some cake, although that might have been a mistake because Linda's slices of cake were about the same size as her sandwiches. They were delicious though, and she even warmed up my piece of chocolate fudge cake and gave me a little jug of cream to go with it. Emily was going to be so jealous when I told her.

Jay only managed about half of his piece of Bakewell tart, so Linda put it in a box alongside a giant slice of lemon and poppyseed cake for Edward, handing them to him in a brown paper bag.

I almost wished I didn't have to go back to work. It had been nice to have a break from the stress and to get out for a bit. I glanced at my watch and realised I still had twenty minutes left. Emily had booted me out for an hour, and she'd meant it.

"I still have twenty minutes before I have to go back to the shop," I said as we stepped out into the street. The wind had eased slightly, and the early March sunshine warmed my cheeks. "Do you want to go for a walk?"

"Sure! Lead on."

We made our way slowly back up the hill, stopping now and then to peer into shop windows. It was strange walking past Wild Things without going in, but Jay was already three steps in front of me, gazing at a display in the nearby sweet shop and waving for my attention.

When we reached the top of the hill, we paused for a second, catching our breaths. "If we hadn't just had cake, I'd buy you an ice cream," I said, pointing at the little walk-in, walk-out ice cream shop on the far corner.

"Oh man! We're totally getting ice cream next time," Jay said. His skin was flushed, and his curls were wild. He looked so fucking gorgeous that all I wanted to do was kiss him.

I cleared my throat, hoping it would clear my mind at the same time. "Do you want to walk around the cathedral?"

Jay nodded, pushing his hair out of his eyes, and the two of us walked along the cobbled road and under the arch that preceded the cathedral. The light danced across the honey-coloured stonework, highlighting the carvings and gargoyles. I paused for a minute, my eyes roaming over the intricately carved arches and the great towers beyond.

"It's a beautiful building," Jay said from beside me, his voice soft. "I've never really looked closely at it before. I've always been too busy."

"You should go inside one day. It's very pretty. And you have to find the Imp."

"The Imp?" Jay gave me a confused smile. I turned and began leading him around the cathedral, following the little path that ran all the way around the outside. I sometimes walked Angie around here during the day because it was far enough to allow us to stretch our legs without keeping us away from the shop for too long.

"Yeah, there's a carved imp high up inside. It's a little grotesque, but it's the symbol of Lincoln."

"That's awesome. I'll have to go find it. My dad and I used to spend ages poking around cathedrals and old castles when I was a kid since it was a good rainy day or holiday activity. And then we'd usually find these tiny, old second-hand bookstores. Y'know the ones with so many books it's almost dangerous? Where you can find pretty much anything if you dig hard enough. I always hoped one of the bookstore owners would turn out to be a wizard or something and send me on an adventure. Or I'd find a magical book that would take me to another world. I, er, I was kind of a dorky kid."

I smiled. "My brother, his best friend, Ben, and I once spent an entire summer building a secret fort and pretending to be knights who were also international super spies. We roped the dog in as our sidekick. But if he didn't want to play, we pretended he was our arch nemesis instead."

"Oh my fucking God, that's so cute! Is your brother older than you? Younger? I bet you were super adorable."

"He's a year older than me. Our birthdays are exactly two weeks apart. My mum told me she wanted two kids close in age because we'd always have someone to play with." It had been both a blessing and a curse to be so close in age to Aaron, and we'd had some serious falling outs in our teenage years. He was a chef now, which suited him perfectly because he had a tendency to be a bit of a hot-headed asshole at times. I still loved him though.

Jay peppered me with more questions as we walked around the cathedral, mostly about my family and growing up in Yorkshire. I didn't mind, and it was nice to talk to him about them. I was usually a very private person, which came with the territory of being quiet and grumpy, but there was something warm and refreshing about sharing my story with Jay.

Maybe it was because I thought he actually cared. That he wasn't just asking these questions because he had to, but because he genuinely wanted to get to know me. I'd never really had anyone try that before, even in my past relationships.

Jay didn't seem put off by my short answers; he just

moved on to the next question, chattering nineteen to the dozen and mixing in his own anecdotes and tangents.

He paused, and I realised we were nearly back at the front of the cathedral. A sudden pang of sadness struck me. I didn't want the moment to end. I wanted to live in it for just a little longer, letting it seep into my bones and warm me from the inside.

"Everything okay?" I asked. Jay was half a step in front of me. He pivoted, looking up at me with a soft smile.

"Yeah, everything's great." He inched a little closer, and I swallowed, my tongue darting out to lick my lips. "Can I ask you one more question?"

"Sure."

"Do you still want to kiss me?"

## CHAPTER THIRTEEN

*Violet (White) — Let's take a chance*

**Jay**

My heart hammered in my chest as I waited for his answer. It felt like I could hardly breathe. Leo stared at me for a second, his amber eyes gazing into mine, then he nodded.

"Yes. I do."

Warmth, coupled with sheer relief, enveloped me, and I stepped closer to him, still clutching the paper bag filled with cake. If I looked down, I knew my knuckles would be white. Leo's hand reached out, gently cradling my jaw, and a little shiver ran over my skin. We were as close as we had been in the basement of The Lost World, but this time, there would be no interfering friends to stop this from happening. I didn't care if anyone saw us. I needed him to kiss me more than I'd ever needed anything before.

I pushed onto my toes, tilting my head as he drew me

towards him. His lips were warm and firm against mine, and I sighed into the kiss, melting against him as his other hand wrapped around my waist. Sparks danced across my skin, and in an instant, I felt more alive than I had in years. How could one kiss make me feel this way? How could one man change everything?

I wanted to stay in this moment forever, even though I knew it couldn't last. The kiss broke but neither of us moved. Leo's eyes searched my face, trying to gauge my reaction.

All I could think to do was kiss him again.

Hints of chocolate lingered on his lips, and I pushed my tongue against the seam of his mouth. Heat flared in my veins. The same heat I'd felt that night I'd dreamt about him inside me. His mouth teased my lip ring, sending a jolt through me. I let out a tiny moan, and Leo's hand tightened on my waist. He broke the kiss, desire dancing in his eyes.

"We probably shouldn't do this here," he said. "I don't think the cathedral staff would be impressed by us making out outside their building."

"Probably not." My skin was tingling, and I was pretty sure I was the same colour as my hoodie. "But I do want to do it again. Soon. And a lot. Yeah, definitely a lot."

Leo chuckled. "Me too."

"Really?" I surprised myself by asking. Apparently, my brain hadn't quite accepted that Leo wanted to kiss me, despite the fact he'd been doing it not thirty seconds before.

"Yes. You're really cute."

"I-I'm not."

"Yes. You are."

"So, um, what... what do you want to do now?" My mind was suddenly swirling with a thousand thoughts as I wondered what we should do next. I had no idea what you were supposed to do at the start of a relationship. I'd been with Kieran for seven years, and we'd met at university and had spent most of the beginning of our relationship either in bed or eating takeaway and playing video games. We hadn't gone on a proper date for at least six months.

And that was assuming that Leo wanted a relationship. I mean, all signs pointed to yes and he'd practically written it in neon lights the other night, but that still wasn't enough for my anxious brain.

Leo checked his watch. I wondered if the twenty minutes were up and if he would have to go straight back to work. Shit. I'd totally fucked this up. I was going to spend the rest of the afternoon trying not to think about him.

"Let's walk around once more, and we can talk."

"Are you sure? I don't want you to get in trouble with Emily."

"She'll live," he said, lips twitching. "Will Edward be okay?"

"Well, if he's already caused complete and utter chaos, then it doesn't really matter either way. And I have bribery if he starts moaning." I held up the cake bag. "Although he said he was procrastinating on a project because he's got some really fiddly detail work to do, so I'm sure he'd be happy to skive off for as long as possible."

"Sounds good." Leo turned to follow the path back the way we'd come. It had been quiet on the way around, and hopefully we would still have privacy on the way back. He held out his hand, and I took a breath.

I didn't want to be held back anymore. I wanted this.

I slipped my fingers into his, feeling the warmth of his skin against mine and the callouses on his palm.

We walked a little way in silence, just getting used to the feeling. It felt strange to hold someone's hand again, and I hadn't realised it was something I'd missed. Kieran and I had drifted further and further apart in the last year we'd been dating, and he'd been reluctant to hold my hand when we did spend time together. It was only now that I was beginning to appreciate how touch-starved I'd been.

"So," I said as we rounded the far corner of the cathedral, "what do you want to do now? Are we dating? Do you want to date? Or did you just want a casual thing? Sorry, I'm really bad at this. I'm out of practice with this whole dating thing… Do we need to define if it's just us? I mean, if you want to keep it light and see other people, you could totally do that. I just—"

"Jay," Leo interjected gently. He pulled gently on my hand, bringing us to a stop. "Yes, I want to date you. No, I don't want to see anyone else." He kissed me, the touch of his lips melting my worries away. "You don't need to panic."

"Sorry, I'm terrible for that. Panicking, I mean. Edward always says I overthink things."

"It's okay. I do it too."

"You do?"

"Yes."

"Oh." I pushed my glasses up my nose, even though

they hadn't slipped. It was a relief to know that he might have some idea what I was going through. Leo started walking again, and I followed, my hand still tucked into his.

"We can take this as slow or as fast as you want," Leo said. "And I promise to talk to you. I'll always be open with you."

The statement was casual but sincere as if it were a given and something I should just expect, but hearing Leo lay things out was comforting. "Thanks. I promise that too."

We finished our circuit of the cathedral and began walking back towards Steep Hill and the realm of reality. It had been so nice to escape into our own personal bubble for an hour that I almost didn't want to go back. Still, I didn't want to leave Edward alone for too long. An hour might not be that much time in the grand scheme of things, but I'd seen him do more with less.

"So," I said as we turned down the hill, "when can I see you again? Have you got a busy week or weekend? Is that too soon?"

"Saturday. Let's go out on Saturday."

"Okay. I can do that. Is there anything you want to do? I can see what's showing at the Odeon? Are you a film person, or is that too cheesy for a first date?"

"It's not too cheesy, and I like films." Leo stopped, and I realised we were outside The Lost World. "Will you let me surprise you?"

"Um, yeah. Sure. That, er, that would be really nice."

"Good." He drew me close and my heartbeat kicked up another notch. "I'm going to kiss you again now."

The kiss left me spinning, and when he left, after promising to message me, I stumbled back in through the bookshop door. My whole world had been turned upside down, and I wondered if Leo knew how much he'd affected me.

There was a cough from behind me, and I realised I was standing in the middle of the shop staring into space like I'd just had some sort of vision. I blinked and spun slowly on the spot.

Edward sat behind the counter, his platinum hair tied up in an elegant half-up, half-down topknot. He peered at me over the rim of a duck-egg-blue teacup. There was a teapot on the counter as well as a sugar bowl and milk jug. They were all a similar blue colour with gold detailing across them and around the rim and a suspiciously perfect match to the embroidered frock coat Edward was currently wearing.

"Did you have fun? I'm assuming so since your very suave florist gave you a goodbye kiss." There was a playful smile on his lips as he reached for one of the ginger biscuits he had laid out on a little plate. "I'm glad you finally decided to take my advice. You two are adorable together, and I have to say your new beau is incredibly handsome."

"Edward," I said before he could get any further. I was still staring at the new crockery that had suddenly appeared in my bookshop. "Where the fuck did you get that tea set?"

## CHAPTER FOURTEEN

*Spearmint — Warm sentiment*

**Jay**

BY THE TIME Saturday evening rolled around, I was a fucking mess.

I had no idea whether I was doing the right thing by going out with Leo. My brain was even starting to doubt that kissing him had been a good idea, even if it had felt amazing at the time. Leo had said we'd take it slow and talk to each other, like adults in a relationship should. But, as Leo knew, I'd been burned before, and those scars hadn't quite healed. They still pulled, reminding me of their presence and the reason they were there.

Sure, you started off with the intention of talking to each other and being open about what was bothering you, but the next minute they were complaining about the promotion they'd encouraged you to take while banging your best friend behind your back.

I took a deep breath, fiddling with the cuffs of my shirt for the hundredth time. Leo wasn't Kieran, and I had to remember that.

Leo hadn't even told me what we were doing this evening, although he had promised to keep it simple. Like he'd subconsciously known I was nervous. Or maybe it wasn't subconscious at all, given how much I'd rambled at him the other day. Either way, I was grateful. He'd gone as far as asking what sort of food I liked and if I had any allergies, but that was it.

I grabbed my phone off my bed, checking the time again. I still had fifteen minutes before Leo was supposed to pick me up. Maybe it would be better if I waited in the shop... at least then there was less chance I'd fall trying to get down the stairs quickly. Although maybe that would make me look desperate... and I didn't want to come across as weird or clingy. But I also didn't want Leo to think I didn't care. Because I did. Almost too much.

As if some sort of "Jay is panicking" signal had lit up the sky, my phone buzzed and Edward's name, along with the ostentatious picture he'd assigned himself, filled the screen.

"Hey," I said, scooping up my jacket and tucking my phone under my ear so I could put it on.

"You're panicking, darling," Edward said without so much as a hello. "I can sense it from here."

"How did you know? Did you suddenly develop psychic powers? I mean, I'd be very impressed if you have, although I'm sure you could think of more productive things to use them for."

"I have my ways, but mostly I figured it out because you've sent me twenty snaps in the last thirty minutes asking if you looked okay when I know for a fact you're wearing the same shirt in all of them. Although I noticed you're wearing the nice jumper I bought for you instead of that abominable old hoodie."

"It's a date. I thought I should look nice. Was that wrong? Am I overdressed?"

"Jay." Edward's voice was calm but firm, the sort of tone that brooked no argument. "You're not overdressed. You look very sexy. Leo is going to love it." I nodded, even though Edward couldn't see me. Not unless he'd suddenly developed super sight as well. "Take a deep breath for me. I promise it's going to be absolutely fine. In fact, it's going to be more than fine. It's going to be fabulous."

"I'm so fucking nervous. What if I totally fuck this up?" I paced my bedroom floor, pausing briefly to triple check my appearance in my wardrobe mirror. My carefully styled hair had already started to go askew. Maybe it would be easier if I just shaved it all off. Meh, that would probably make my head look like a weird egg.

"You're not going to fuck this up, darling. I promise. Leo already likes you just the way you are. Just be yourself. That's all you need to do."

"Thanks, babe. What would I do without you?"

"Be at least fifty-seven per cent less fabulous," Edward said, and I snorted, shaking my head. "Now, walk carefully down the stairs and wait for your beau. And when I say carefully, I do mean it, darling. I'd rather your date didn't end up with you in A&E."

"I'd argue that I'm not that bad, but we both know that's not true. Thanks for calling. I love you."

"I love you too. Have fun."

I hung up, slipped my phone into the back pocket of my jeans, and grabbed my keys. I locked my flat door, which had a separate lock from the shop, and then headed slowly down the stairs. As I reached the shop floor, there was a sharp rap on the door. Peering through the window, I could see Leo waiting on the street, wrapped in his customary leather jacket. My chest fluttered, excitement wriggling through me.

That was new, but now wasn't the time to dwell on it. Even if I did want to do a ridiculous happy dance across the shop, complete with badly done cartwheels.

I unlocked the door and opened it, stepping out into the street. "Hey, right on time." I relocked the door and turned, allowing myself a moment to look at him. Leo was wearing a pair of snug-fitting jeans I hadn't seen before and polished brown boots. His jacket was half-done up over a navy shirt that seemed to be moulded to his broad form.

Fuck. I wanted to tell him to forget the whole dinner thing and drag him back inside. My sexually deprived lizard brain was determined to remind me of each and every tiny detail of my Leo sex dream.

Except Leo had spent time preparing this date, and I wasn't going to ruin his hard work. Plus, while part of my brain was on board with the whole "take Leo inside and let him bang your brains out" scenario, I knew the rest of me was too chicken to go through with it.

"You look good," Leo said. He stepped closer, and I couldn't resist reaching out with one hand to gently grasp the front of his jacket, closing the distance between us.

"So do you." I tilted my head, and Leo's lips brushed against mine in a sweet kiss that made me immediately want so much more. I stepped back, trying to clear my head. "So, where are we going?"

"Dinner." There was a hint of a playful smile behind his beard. "I booked us a table at Thailand No.1."

"Ohhh, it's really nice there! Have you been before?"

Leo shook his head, and we turned to start walking towards the Bailgate area at the top of the hill where a collection of shops, pubs, and restaurants decorated the street. "No, but I've been told it's good."

"Emily?"

"Yeah. She and Daniel go there a lot."

I smiled. "Daniel came into the shop yesterday to get some more dice, and we ended up chatting for ages about board games and movies, like the new one that's just come out, *Empire of Dust*. I really want to see it at some point, but it's hard to find the time, y'know?"

"You might be in luck then," Leo said as we crossed the crossroads at the top of the hill, passing the cathedral. Spotlights bathed the stone in a soft golden glow that made it look utterly mesmerising.

"Wait? Did you send Daniel to spy on me?" My lips curled into a smile, and I nudged Leo playfully. I didn't want him to think it was a bad thing if he had. It was cute.

I'd never been on a date with anyone who had tried so hard before.

"Not deliberately." Leo gave a little snort. "He came to pick Emily up and said you'd been chatting. He might have mentioned you wanted to see the film, and I might have booked tickets."

"Seriously? That's amazing. Thank you." A spark of excitement zipped through me, replacing my nerves. "I can't wait! I've wanted to see it ever since I saw the trailer. Edward's going to be so jealous when he finds out. I know he wants to do a cosplay of one of the characters for the May Comic Con in London, and he's desperate to go see it."

"I hope I haven't started a war," Leo said.

"Nah, it's fine. He'll get over it. I'll take him to see it on Monday if I can get tickets. I think I've got a Meerkat Movies code I can use." We chatted about the movie a little as we continued up the road until we caught sight of our destination.

The front of the restaurant was painted deep purple and delicious, spicy scents wafted out when we pulled open the door. I fucking loved Thai food. Leo spoke to the waitress, and she led us to a little table near the front. It was tucked in beside the window, and there was enough space between it and the other table in the alcove to not feel overcrowded. She left us with menus and promised to come back in a minute to take our drinks order, but by that point I wasn't really listening because Leo had slipped off his jacket, and his shirt sleeves were rolled up to his elbows.

I was dead.

Literally dead.

I dropped into the seat opposite him in the most inelegant way possible, nearly falling off the other side of the chair in the process. Leo didn't say anything, for which I was really fucking grateful. I was going to assume he hadn't noticed, or if he had, he was too polite to mention it.

It wasn't my fault I was ridiculously distracted by the beautiful lines and colours of his tattoos and the way his shirt hugged his broad shoulders and biceps. I wondered if Leo worked out or if floristry just gave you those sorts of muscles. Were flowers heavy? Books definitely were, and Sod's Law meant they got even heavier just as the bottom tried to drop out of the box or as you were trying to carry a stack downstairs. I'd learnt that the hard way.

I shook my head. It was not the time to think about work.

The waitress came back, and Leo and I each ordered a beer. Luckily he asked for a couple more minutes when it came to food, since I hadn't even looked at the menu.

"What are you getting?" I asked, my eyes scanning down the menu. Bingo, they had massaman curry. That was me sorted. "Do you want to get starters? Is this where we get into some sort of awkward situation where we realise one of us believes in sharing starters and the other is a 'touch my food, feel my fork' kinda person?"

Leo chuckled. "I'm not that bad. Except if you try to take my onion rings. They're mine."

"Why onion rings?" There was definitely a story there. I leant over the table, resting my chin in my hands. "Just because they're your favourites? I mean, if it were chips I'd totally agree, but onion rings are a new one."

"You don't usually get many," Leo said, "and if I only get two of them, I want both."

"That's totally fair. It's like those people who ask to try something of yours and then take a huge bite! I had a boyfriend in high school who did that, and honest to God, I could've fucking murdered him."

"Where do you think the onion ring thing came from?" Leo's eyebrow twitched, along with his lip. "I went on a date with a woman once and she tried to steal my onion rings before I'd even touched my plate, even though she'd said she didn't want her own. Apparently, she thought it was cute to share food on a date."

"No! That's amazing. Well, it's amazing for me to listen to your torment though I'm sure it was terrible for you. What did you do?"

"I suggested she order her own, then politely declined a second date."

"Sounds like you dodged a bullet there."

"That's nothing compared to this vegan guy I went out for coffee with last year. He spent the whole time loudly berating everyone for not drinking soy milk, then got into an argument with one of the baristas."

"Holy shit! What did you do?" I couldn't stop grinning at Leo's misery. It was probably mean of me to be glad none of those dates had worked out, but I was really glad they hadn't.

"I left. And deleted all the dating apps off my phone."

"Yeah... I've managed to avoid those. Although Edward tried to install Grindr on my phone for 'funsies'. That didn't last long." It had lasted all of two minutes once I'd realised what he'd done. Edward said it could help me blow off steam, but he'd dropped it surprisingly quickly when I'd threatened to auction off a date with him to his fans for charity. For someone so extroverted, Edward was surprisingly private. I relayed this story to Leo, watching a little smile curl onto his lips that had my stomach tying itself in knots.

"Well," Leo said, laying his hand out on the table in invitation. Tentatively, I slipped my fingers into his, letting the warmth of his skin soothe the last dregs of my nerves. "You weren't ready. There's nothing wrong with that."

He smiled at me, and for the first time in a long time, I felt totally relaxed.

The waitress returned a minute later, and we ordered, even settling on a platter of starters to share. Our conversation turned to the new book Leo was reading, another one I'd recommended to him, and then onto our favourite fictional characters. I'd never dreamt of spending an entire evening happily discussing books with someone, but we hadn't moved on from the topic by the time we'd finished our mains. I'd thought Leo would get bored of my rambling, but he listened carefully, asking questions and adding his own comments. Everything he said was measured and considered while I jumped from thought to thought, my brain burbling like a river at full flow. It didn't seem to bother him though. At least I hoped it didn't.

"Do you want pudding here?" Leo asked as I finished my point about why I really wanted to see Garth Nix's Old Kingdom novels adapted for TV because they were bloody awesome. "Or do you want to get something at the cinema?"

"I'm definitely up for getting popcorn. And Minstrels too." Leo looked at me, his eyebrow half-raised. "Oh my God, have you never done that? You have to mix them together, then you get all the chocolaty goodness alongside your popcorn! We have to do that now. I'm not letting you go another day without experiencing that. You do like Minstrels, right? And popcorn? It would be really awkward if you hate them and I'm determined to make you try them together."

"I do. I've just never had them together. I'm willing to try though." The weird fluttery feeling that had been bubbling away in my chest for the whole evening kicked in again. I didn't think this was anxiety though. This was different. I couldn't explain it, but it didn't quite come with the heart-stopping terror I associated with feeling anxious. It was strange how being with Leo made me feel both completely at peace and utterly alive. I was filled with a wild exhilaration that was as beautiful as it was unfamiliar.

We decided to walk through the city to the cinema. There were a few people around, but most were clustered around the myriad restaurants since it was too cold to sit in the beer gardens. As we walked back down to the cathedral and the top of Steep Hill, I felt Leo's fingers brush against mine.

The city spread out like a blanket of darkness beneath us, dotted with lights, and a cool spring breeze brushed at my skin. And as we laced our fingers together, it felt like anything was possible.

## CHAPTER FIFTEEN

*Iris (Yellow) — Passion*

**Leo**

IT WAS strange how one date could change everything.

I'd been floating on a high for seven days since my first date with Jay. Even though work was progressively getting more stressful, it didn't seem to be bothering me as much as it had just a few days previously. I had a list of things to do that seemed to get longer with every minute, but I didn't feel like I was about to explode every time I looked at it. I'd even made time to write a new job advert and stick it up online. Emily was keeping an eye on the responses and bouncing any she thought weren't worth my time, but we'd already had a couple of applications that looked promising.

I heard the clink of keys from the front of the shop and looked up from my workbench where I was working on a personal project.

"Good morning," I called.

"Good morning?" Emily said, a note of disbelief in her voice. She stuck her head around the door. "You're very chirpy this morning. What the hell happened? Did you get abducted by aliens last night? Did you get laid? Is that why you're so happy."

"Am I not allowed to be happy?"

"Well, yes, but I've known you for five years and not once have you greeted me with such blatant enthusiasm. Especially not at seven thirty on a Saturday morning. Hence the sex or alien abduction theory. Although my money is definitely on the second. I'm sure you've had sex since I've known you, and it's never made you this happy. I definitely think you've been replaced by a replicant. One that hasn't quite mastered your personality yet."

"You've never seen *Blade Runner*, have you?" I asked, chuckling to myself as I turned back to the bouquet I had on the bench in front of me.

"Damn. Caught out! Daniel tried to get me to watch it last night because it's his favourite, but I fell asleep halfway through. Although I will say, Harrison Ford was very handsome in his youth. I wouldn't have said no."

"Are you done with the conspiracy theories then?"

"Eh, I think so." She grinned, shedding her coat and scarf. "But you still haven't explained why you're so, so… chipper this morning."

"Do I need a reason?"

"Well, no. But you know me, I like to be nosey."

"I'm sorry to disappoint you, but there isn't some epic reason."

"Boo! You're so mean. Isn't he mean, Angie? Not telling us why he's so happy. Yes! Such a mean daddy, not telling us." I heard Angie making happy snuffling noises as her tail thudded on the door frame.

"Stop bringing my dog into this."

"Now he's mean and demanding. Yes, he is. So mean and grumpy," Emily said, clearly still talking to Angie, who sneezed. "See? Angie agrees with me."

I sighed. I was clearly outnumbered in this situation. I felt like it was a low blow to bring my dog into this since she'd take the side of anyone she thought would give her food.

"I'm serious, there's no real reason. I'm just happy."

It had been just over a week since Jay and I had first kissed and a week since our first date. He'd been so nervous about it, and I'd wanted him to have a good experience, even if I wasn't the best person to plan the ultimate romantic night.

Dinner had been amazing though. I'd never felt that sort of connection with anyone, and we'd hardly stopped talking. Jay had been so excited to see *Empires of Dust* too, and I was glad I'd booked tickets because the cinema had been packed.

From what I'd seen of it, the film had been really good, but I wouldn't have been able to answer any questions about it. I'd spent just as much time watching Jay out of the corner of my eye as I had watching the spaceship battles. I'd loved watching Jay's face light up as he became more and more engrossed in the story. We'd ended up holding hands on the armrest between us, and all I'd been able to focus on was how warm his skin was against mine.

Since then, we hadn't seen each other much except briefly at game night. We'd both been busy with our respective businesses, but we'd kept up a steady stream of messages. I was hoping we'd be able to go out again soon. Or maybe I could invite him to dinner at my house instead. I'd been to his flat several times, but I had a giant couch and an even bigger bed…

I shook my head. We hadn't talked about sex, even though it was getting harder not to think about what Jay might have under the red hoodie and the dark skinny jeans he always wore. He'd mentioned having tattoos before, and I desperately wanted to know what they looked like.

I may have had several fantasies about what his lip piercing would feel like against my cock. I loved feeling it against my lips whenever I kissed him, but I desperately wanted to feel it on the rest of my body.

"Well good," Emily said, interrupting my thoughts, which were becoming rapidly unsuitable for work. "I'm glad you're happy. It looks good on you." I heard her flick the kettle on and felt her presence beside me, peering over my shoulder. That was the problem when your employee was nearly as tall as you were. You couldn't hide anything. "That's pretty. Who is it for?"

I didn't say anything. The flowers were for Jay, a nice little reminder I was thinking of him. I couldn't do romantic words, but I could do flowers, and hopefully that would be enough. Jay always seemed to like it when I sent flowers.

"The silent treatment, eh? These aren't a regular order

are they…yellow irises… tulips…" She gasped dramatically. "Oh my God, these are for Jay, aren't they? You're so cute! Look at you making romantic flower arrangements for him. I love it."

I kept my mouth shut and continued working. I knew anything I said would be held against me, not in a bad way but in an excitable Emily way. She kept chatting away about how cute we were as she made tea and shoved a tin of biscuits under my nose. I thought for a moment she was going to keep it up all morning, but eventually she settled on singing along quietly to the radio when she realised I wasn't talking.

I finished up the flowers for Jay, putting them carefully to one side to deliver later, and began working through some orders while making a mental list of everything I needed to get next time I went to the wholesaler. Like most Saturdays, the day flew by. It was only when one of my regulars, Angela, made an offhand comment about meeting her friends for an afternoon coffee and catch up, that I finally looked up at the clock.

It was nearly three. That explained why my stomach had been complaining at me for the past two hours. All I'd done was eat biscuits whenever Emily pushed the tin at me.

"Have you had lunch?" I asked, sticking my head around the workroom door where Emily was wrapping ribbon around a walk-in order.

"Yeah. A couple of hours ago. While you were talking to Sue about the flowers for her grandson's christening." She squinted at me, a frown deepening between her eyebrows. "Why? Have you?"

"No."

"Why didn't you say something?" Emily snipped the ribbon with force, then pointed at Jay's flowers, which were tucked away in a cool corner. "Take your flowers to your boyfriend and go get a sandwich. Now."

"You know, sometimes I think you forget I'm your boss," I said, sounding grumpier than I felt. In truth, Emily kept my head screwed on the right way.

"I don't forget. You're just a bit useless sometimes."

"Charming."

"You know it's the truth."

I did. Which was why I didn't say anything. Instead, I grabbed my jacket and the flowers before heading out the front door, nearly walking smack into someone coming the other way.

"Sorry," I said, pausing to let them come through. It was a lady named Helen Barnes, who often popped in to order a variety of arrangements for the large house she owned in one of the nearby villages. I'd only been there a couple of times when Daniel and I were doing deliveries.

"You're in a rush today, Leo," she said, giving me a warm smile. Helen was a genuinely charming person who always seemed to have time for everyone. I was just hoping I could get away without being drawn into a long conversation. "Last minute delivery?"

"Sort of." I gave her a half smile and hoped she wouldn't ask who the arrangement was for. "If you let Emily know if there's anything specific you want in your next arrangements, I'll see what I can get. This time of year

I can get a bit of a wider selection. Some very pretty sweet peas and lily of the valley should be available."

"Thank you. That would be perfect. I was looking for something softer and perhaps a little more unstructured for a change."

"I can do that."

"Excellent. I'll speak to Emily. I'll let you get on, or I'll keep you all afternoon."

"Cheers," I said, gently pushing the door closed behind her as she stepped through. It appeared that holding the flowers had given me a good out. Perhaps I should carry plants everywhere if it kept people from trying to talk to me.

It only took me a couple minutes to reach The Lost World, and I was pleased to see the shop was busy. Jay had mentioned having several very quiet days this week, and quiet days didn't pay the bills. He was currently chatting animatedly with a lesbian couple I knew fairly well while placing books in a paper bag. One of the women was carrying a toddler, who was staring and reaching for the glittering display of dice Jay had built on the end of the counter. The dice were very pretty, in a myriad of colours and patterns, some of them laced through with glitter. A set made with a swirling mix of pink, purple, and blue caught my eye. Maybe it was time I treated myself to some new dice.

I waited patiently, holding my flowers in one hand while my eyes drifted towards the new release bookcase. I kept telling myself I had enough books at home and didn't have enough time to read what I already had. Still, there were a couple of covers that caught my eye, and it wouldn't hurt just to look.

By the time Jay was free, I'd found two new books to buy and one to come back for at a later date.

"Hey," Jay said, sliding around the counter, a wide grin on his face. "Long time, no see."

"Hey." I tilted my head down to catch his lips in a soft kiss. "These are for you." I offered him the bouquet, loving the way his smile widened. It was like I'd given him the most precious thing on earth.

"Holy shit, Leo! These are beautiful. What's the occasion?"

"No occasion. I just wanted to bring you flowers."

"I love them." Jay stepped closer, rolling onto his tiptoes to press a quick kiss to my cheek. My skin burned where his lips touched me, like a brand I knew I'd feel for hours. "You spoil me." He carried them around the counter, laying them gently on the surface while he searched underneath, presumably for the vase I'd given him.

"Ah shit." His scrunched-up face appeared again, and he pushed his glasses up his nose with one hand while his teeth toyed with his lip ring. I recognised it as his thinking face. It was the same adorable expression he wore during D&D when he was plotting his next action or working out which badly sung song would annoy Edward the most. "I think I left it upstairs. Hang on two seconds."

Jay extracted himself from the counter again, dashing over to the stairs leading to the basement room, before practically throwing himself down them. I was half expecting to hear a crash. But nothing happened, and two minutes later Jay reappeared, looking red in the face and out of breath.

"O-okay, Edward's going to get the vase," he panted. I stared at him and made a noise through my lips as I nodded. I wasn't sure I trusted myself to speak when my brain had taken the liberty of imagining Jay red and panting in a totally different situation. Like spread out on my bed.

Bloody hell, my imagination was trying to kill me by sending all the blood in my body rushing south at once.

"So," Jay continued, unaware of exactly what he was doing to me. "How're you? Busy day?"

"Yeah. Very busy actually. I only just escaped."

"Did you forget to eat lunch again?" He frowned, but it was paired with a playful smile.

"I didn't forget. I just didn't get a chance."

"Tomayto, tomatoh," Jay said. "Do you have plans tonight?"

"Um, no not really." Was he asking me because he was curious, or was he asking because he wanted to have plans with me?

"Want to come back later, binge watch a ton of *Last Call*, and eat your weight in pasta with me? I have garlic bread in the freezer if that sweetens the deal."

I didn't need garlic bread to sweeten the deal. I'd been in from the moment he'd started the sentence.

"Sure." I smirked. "I told you you'd like *Last Call*."

"I don't know if it's like or more can't tear my eyes away from the car crash I'm witnessing." He sighed, leaning on the edge of the counter. It stretched his slim body out and the edge of his hoodie rode up around his hips, taking his t-shirt with it. There was a flash of pale skin and dark ink. My fingers itched to reach out and touch, to lift the material farther and see the treasures that lay beneath etched into Jay's skin. "Oh, by the way, I have something to show you! I think you'll be proud of me."

Jay spun around, leaning over the counter. His black jeans hugged the curves of his arse. As he bent over, his hoodie rode up even farther, revealing the edges of what could be a large back piece. It looked like vines twisted into a frame. My curiosity demanded to see more, but it wasn't like I could ask Jay to strip off in the middle of his shop. Maybe we'd get to that later...

"Here!" Jay thrust a notebook into my hands, startling me out of my thoughts. I looked down to see a list of days and opening times in spidery handwriting. One thing immediately caught my eye.

"You're closing Mondays?"

"Yep." Jay grinned, leaning forward and pointing at the list. "And I'm only opening Tuesday afternoons. Plus, I'm adjusting the rest of the times so they're more mid-morning to late afternoon. I'm thinking six-ish so people still have time to pop in after work. And on Wednesdays, I'm thinking about staying open until six thirty when game night starts because it'll just be easier that way." He looked up at me, eyes anxious behind his frames. I wasn't sure why he wanted my approval. He didn't need it. But I was proud of him for putting himself first for a change.

"I think it'll work well," I said, handing the notebook back to him with a smile.

"I think so too. Mondays are always really quiet anyway, and closing on Tuesday morning means I can get my paperwork and orders done instead of squeezing it in whenever I get a spare five minutes. Plus, it'll save on my bills too. I hope. Maybe then I'll be able to get the website and webstore working properly." He sighed and rubbed his face. I could see the stress etched into his features and the dark smudges underneath his eyes. "I was chatting with another small bookstore owner in York on Twitter, and they said they do a ton of online business, so I really need to get that sorted. I've been putting it off because I'm rubbish with coding, but it's going to have to be sooner rather than later at this point."

"Let me know if I can help," I said. "I don't want you to exhaust yourself."

"Thanks. I'll be fine though. At least now I'll have some time to sleep."

I wasn't sure I believed him, but I didn't want to bring it up. There wasn't time to anyway. A moment later, Edward appeared, his face like thunder and clutching the vase in one hand and his phone in the other.

"That motherfucking bastard," he said, venom in every syllable. He shoved the vase into Jay's arms, barely looking up. "I'll fucking kill him. In fact, I'm going to poke needles into his eyes."

"Has the mortal enemy struck again?" Jay asked, grinning. Then he looked down at the vase and shook his head. "Babe, you could have put water in the vase."

"I was busy, darling. And you didn't ask for water, just the vase."

"Why would I want a vase without water?"

"I thought it was rude to ask."

Jay chuckled, placing the vase on the counter and gently scooping the bouquet into it. He looked up at me, clearly noting the confusion on my face because he said, "Edward has a mortal enemy. 'The Masked Gentleman'. He's another cosplayer, and he and Edward loathe each other."

"Loathe isn't a strong enough word," Edward muttered. "I detest this man with every fibre of my physical being. And my spiritual being too. He is the bane of my existence, and if murder were legal, I would shoot him on sight."

"Could you perhaps tone down the murderous rhetoric in the middle of my shop?" Jay asked, although there was no force behind his words. I got the feeling the whole situation amused him.

"Apologies, darling, but this time that repugnant putrescence has gone too far."

"How?" I asked, looking between the pair of them. Jay shrugged. He was clearly just as much in the dark as I was.

"I posted a photo of Prince Ailluen from *Empire of Dust* and said I was working on his second court look for May. Today, he posted a photo of his worktable where he'd laid out pieces from Duke Iestyn's costume. From the same scene as mine." Edward looked between Jay and I, expectation clear on his face. I got the feeling Edward thought we'd understand his point, but Jay looked just as confused as I felt.

"Babe, just explain."

Edward sighed dramatically, rolling his eyes. "Ailluen and Iestyn are secret lovers, remember? And the two costumes are from the scene where they steal a moment together and declare their undying love for each other. It's just before they have sex in the bath."

"Ohhh." Jay grinned mischievously. "That scene was really hot."

"That's not the point," Edward said, frustration clear in his voice. "He's doing the costume of my *lover*. Our fans are going to wonder if we're together. In fact, they already do." He thrust his phone under our noses, pointing at the stream of Instagram comments with one of his neatly manicured fingers. There were a lot of emojis. "And they're already asking if we'll take pictures together or do photo ops as a pair. This is a disaster!" Edward pouted. "The sneaking toad already said yes."

"It won't be that bad," Jay said. "And everyone knows you're a better costume maker, and you're prettier."

"You're very sweet, darling."

"I am. You know he's just trying to get under your skin, and you're letting him. Just be the bigger person here." Edward opened his mouth, and Jay shot him a look. "Without turning it into a competition."

"You ruin all my fun, you know." Edward sighed dramatically, looking at me as if hoping I'd sympathise or take his side. I was still a bit confused by what I'd just witnessed, so there was no way I was taking sides.

"Babe, can you watch the counter for two seconds while I go and get some water?" Jay asked, picking up the vase.

"Of course," Edward said sweetly, cutting off his muttering about someone—Lewis maybe—being upset with him. Not that I knew who Lewis was. I was just focused on the note in Edward's tone that made me slightly worried. As soon as Jay was out of earshot, Edward turned to me, and I suddenly felt like I was being eyed up by a cheetah. "So… those flowers are very pretty. Did I see tulips and irises in there?"

"Yes." I had an idea what he was digging at, but I wasn't going to show it. "They look good together, and the colours are nice and vibrant."

"Yes… they are…" Edward stared at me. In his heeled boots we were eye to eye, and his silver-blue eyes were uncomfortably sharp. It felt like he was pressing a sword to my ribcage. "I will only tell you this once because once will be enough. Jacob is my best friend, and I would do anything to protect him. If you hurt him, I can guarantee you will live to regret it."

"Understood."

"Good. I think you're good for him." Edward tapped his chin thoughtfully with one finger. "I haven't seen Jay like this in a long time. When he talks about you, he's… different." Edward smiled, but it looked almost sad, like he was remembering something he'd rather forget. Then he shook his head and his smile widened. I felt the sword ease from my ribs.

"It's like he's remembering how to be happy again."

## CHAPTER SIXTEEN

*Jasmine (Spanish) — Sensuality*

## Jay

IT WAS eleven o'clock on a Friday night and I was bored.

I was supposed to be trying to get some sleep so I'd be nice and rested for seeing Leo tomorrow. But so far anticipation was having the opposite effect on me. I was completely wired and horny as fuck.

Leo and I had agreed to take things slowly, and I'd been grateful for that. I'd been apprehensive about anything to do with a relationship, and I hadn't wanted to rush into anything. I was still nervous but mostly about being a shitty boyfriend. But the more time I spent with Leo, and the more hours we spent messaging about everything and nothing, the more assured I felt. Leo had promised he'd always be honest with me, and I trusted him. I knew he wouldn't hurt me. Not intentionally anyway. If anything, I was more worried that I'd do something stupid.

I rolled over in bed and groaned, throwing my arm over my face dramatically.

Contrary to my worries, other desires were starting to make themselves abundantly clear. Namely the fact that I desperately wanted to get laid.

I'd been hoping Leo and I could have a little fun when he'd come to watch *Celestials* last week, but that had been an utter fail. Part of me had wondered if it was a mistake to have dinner first, but my exhaustion and hunger after a stressful week had overruled my libido. As soon as I'd finished eating, I'd realised I was too full and sleepy to do anything except use Leo as a pillow.

And now I was paying the price.

My hand and my dildo had seen more action this week than they had in months, and I was desperate to swap them out for Leo's tongue and cock. I groaned again, my dick hardening as my imagination began to suggest all the delicious things Leo might do to me as soon as he got the chance.

My fingers slipped beneath the duvet and under the waistband of my boxers.

"Shit," I groaned as I gripped my cock. I rubbed my thumb over the silky head, teasing the slit. Sometimes I'd take my time and drag my jerk off sessions out until I was panting and desperate. This was not going to be one of those times.

I threw my head back into the pillow, biting my lip as I jacked myself hard and fast. It was a little dry, but I wasn't going to stop to grab the lube. I almost liked the slight bite of abrasion. Besides, I was too lost in fantasies of Leo to care.

Leo on his arms above me, kissing me senseless as he pushed his cock inside me. Leo lying between my legs with his lips stretched around my cock. Leo sucking hickeys into the soft skin of my inner thigh, his beard scratching against the skin and making me whine with pleasure. Leo underneath me, clutching the sheets while I fucked him, his mouth slack and eyes closed.

"Oh shit. Fuck!" The words were gasped out breathlessly as I came, cum spilling over my fist and into my boxers. I lay still, my heartbeat pulsing in my ears as my chest heaved. A smile spread across my face, and I let out a low chuckle. At least now I might be tired enough to sleep.

I pulled my hand out of my boxers, wiping my fingers on the material. They needed a wash now anyway, and I couldn't be asked to get out of bed to go to the bathroom. That was probably gross, but I didn't care. It wasn't like anyone could see me.

I shucked off my underwear and kicked them out from under the duvet onto the floor beside me. My phone was beside the bed, and I tapped the screen, checking to see just how late it was. Except I didn't look at the clock because there was a WhatsApp message from Leo and that was far more interesting.

LEO *Why am I still awake?*
JAY *Is it the same reason as me?*
LEO *Which is?*

JAY *I was jerking off. Thinking about you*

There was a slight pause in the response, but at the top of the screen I could see the green text telling me Leo was typing. Either I was going to get an essay, or he didn't know what to say. I bit my lip, wondering for a second if I'd overstepped. Sure, Leo was my boyfriend and clearly found me attractive, but that didn't mean I hadn't gone too far. Knowing me I was bound to have gotten it wrong.

LEO *Shit. I wish I could see that. I bet you look fucking gorgeous when you come*
JAY *Maybe you'll get lucky tomorrow ;) If you want that?*
LEO *Yeah, I really do*
LEO *Do you?*
JAY *YES lol*
JAY *I may have jerked off a lot this week. My poor dildo hasn't seen this much action in months*
JAY *I need to replace it with something more realistic*
LEO *Fuck yes. Tomorrow, I promise*
LEO *One day will you show me your toy?*
JAY *Would you like that?*
LEO *Yeah, I bet you'd look sexy as fuck riding it while I watch you*
JAY *Shit*
JAY *We're doing that at some point lol*
JAY *I need it*
LEO *So do I*
LEO *God, I'm so horny now*
JAY *And I'm sleepy lol*
LEO *Go to sleep then*

JAY *Are you gonna get yourself off?*
LEO *Maybe =P*
LEO *Or maybe I'll save my load for you*
JAY *Oh God. You are not helping this sleep thing*
LEO *Sorry*
JAY *No, you're not*
LEO *You're right. I'm not*
LEO *But you should still go to sleep. You might need that energy tomorrow*
JAY *No I WILL need that energy tomorrow ;)*
JAY *Goodnight x*
LEO *Sweet dreams xx*

I smiled as I looked at his last message and the little kisses that filled my whole body with warmth. Anticipation thrummed through me and I couldn't wait for tomorrow evening when I could finally find out exactly what was under Leo's clothes.

I yawned and stretched, sleep finally reaching for me. Rolling over, I snuggled under the duvet, a smile on my face as I drifted into unconsciousness.

## CHAPTER SEVENTEEN

*Rose (Coral) — Desire*

**Leo**

"Jacob Hayden Morris, give me that damn hoodie right now!"

"No! There's nothing wrong with it."

"There's a bloody great hole in the back. I am not letting you go out dressed like that, and I will use force if necessary."

"No."

"Yes."

"No!"

"Yes!"

I froze in the doorway of The Lost World, staring at the scene in front of me. Jay and Edward stood in the middle of the first room, half-wrapped in each other's arms. It looked like Edward had finally snapped and decided to bin Jay's beloved red hoodie. I could almost see his point, given that the hoodie had definitely seen better days, but considering I still wore cosy, old jumpers my gran had knitted for me that were just as frayed, I didn't think I was in a position to judge.

I coughed and the pair of them sprang apart like two startled cats.

"Thank fuck," Jay said. "Leo, can you please tell Edward to get his thieving paws off my clothes."

"Leo, can you please tell your boyfriend he cannot wear that thing around customers anymore. Especially since he ripped a giant hole in it this afternoon."

"I never said I was going to wear it in the store." Jay made a face and stuck his tongue out. "I was just going to wear it at home."

"And out on your date," Edward retorted.

"I was going to get another one."

"Llama!"

"I'm not llama-ering."

"You are a llama, sir!"

I had no idea why they were suddenly talking about llamas. It was like dealing with two five-year-olds hopped up on sugar.

"Ugh, fine. Have it your way!" Jay said, rolling his eyes. He unzipped the hoodie and pulled it off, hurling it dramatically at Edward's face. I'd have been tempted to laugh, except I was too busy staring.

In the weeks I'd known him, I'd never seen Jay without

that hoodie or a jumper on. He'd pushed his sleeves up occasionally, but only part of the way up his forearms. And now he stood there in a tight black t-shirt that looked more like a second skin. It wasn't just the t-shirt that was drawing my attention; it was the colourful ink spilling from under his sleeves and down his arms. Both of his upper arms seemed to be covered in a myriad of beautiful pieces that ended at his elbows.

Bloody hell. I knew Jay had tattoos. The little glimpses I'd seen here and there had told me that, but I'd never thought he had so many. My cock throbbed in my jeans, tightening them considerably.

Jay turned and my heart stopped. Through the tight material of his t-shirt, I could see the outline of two bars. Jay had his nipples pierced.

It was official: my brain had stopped functioning. And so had the rest of me.

Jay said something, but it went in one ear and out the other.

"Sorry. I missed that," I said. Jay raised an eyebrow and shot me a playful grin.

"I said, I'll just go grab my stuff and get rid of the pest and then we can go."

We'd agreed Jay would come to my house for our weekly binge-watch session this week. It was the first time he'd come to mine, and he was going to stay the night.

Last time I'd been to Jay's, we'd eaten so much pasta and garlic bread we'd both fallen asleep on the sofa before we'd gotten to anything more than a little light making out. By the time I'd woken up, it had been nearly eleven, and

Jay had been passed out on my lap, curled up and snoring. I'd covered him in a blanket, snuck out, and locked up behind me, sticking the keys through the shop letterbox. I'd been tempted to stay, but Angie would desperately need to go out, and she'd never forgive me if I delayed her breakfast.

That was the problem with being so busy. I rarely had the energy to do anything else, and feeding me a good meal was a sure-fire way to have me dead to the world in twenty minutes. Tonight, I was desperately hoping to change that.

We'd agreed to take our relationship slowly, but we were both getting to the point where we wanted more. It felt like there was a permanent itch under my skin, and no amount of jerking off in the shower or before bed was helping.

Neither was the memory of the messages Jay had sent me last night. They'd been burning a hole in my mind since I'd woken up, and it had taken all my willpower not to jerk off, imagining sinking into Jay's perfect arse while he moaned underneath me. Just the thought of them had my libido skyrocketing.

I cleared my throat. "Sounds good."

Jay stuck his tongue out at Edward again before making for the ascending stairs. Edward returned the gesture, then chuckled. He was still holding the hoodie, examining the hole in the back of it.

"I thought I'd be able to fix it," he said, without looking up, "but it's so frayed I'd have to patch it, and considering it's a Primark hoodie worth a tenner, it doesn't seem worth it." He shook his head and gave me a rueful smile. "I'll have to get him a new one."

"I may have already done that," I said sheepishly. I'd wanted to surprise Jay with it later, but now seemed like as good a time as any to show him. I'd always been terrible at keeping secrets from people I liked. Emily always said I wore my heart on my sleeve, but most people didn't get close enough to notice.

"Oh? You have?" Edward's smile was somewhere between wolfish and charming. It was a little unnerving.

"Yeah. He messaged me to say he'd ripped it, and I went into town at lunch." I swung my backpack off my shoulders, unzipping one of the many pockets to pull out the paper Primark bag that I'd neatly folded in there.

"Aren't you an angel?" His smile softened into something fonder. Then he snapped his fingers, his eyes lighting up. "By the way, now that I have you captive, there's something I need to ask you."

"That sounds ominous," I said with a low chuckle.

"It's not a bad thing, I promise. I'm helping to organise the Impulsion Steampunk Festival this year and I wanted to pick your brain."

"Er, sure." I'd been to the festival several times for a wander around the stalls, and I'd chatted to plenty of the folks attending. It was a hugely popular event, one that drew people in from all over Europe, and it had always been a good weekend for Wild Things. Emily kept saying we should have a little stall and sell 'love language' bouquets and favours, but since there were only two of us, we'd never had the staff to make it work.

"We're looking for a couple of people to run workshops, and I wondered if you'd be interested. I know it's not technically steampunk, but the Victorians did some interesting things with flowers, and I thought it might be right up your street. Plus the workshops are being held here so you wouldn't need to come far." He gestured around the shop. I swallowed.

Edward hadn't specifically said floriography, but I knew that was what he meant. A bolt of fear slid down my spine. Did he know what the flowers I sent to Jay meant? I'd been making him arrangements weekly, and now I was terrified that someone might realise exactly what I was saying.

Then again, plenty of people knew the language of flowers existed without knowing what the meanings were. Except for maybe red roses, and I was more subtle than that.

Edward was giving me another charming smile.

"Sure. I could do that," I said before my brain could come up with a reason to say no.

"Wonderful! It's the last weekend in April so make sure to add it to your diary. I'll make sure you get all the details in the next couple of weeks. If there are any problems, just let me know. Now, where is that beautiful boy of yours?" Edward walked over to the stairs, leaning against the banister as he called up. "Darling, are you ready?"

"Just a second." There was an almighty crash from the floor above us, and Edward and I winced simultaneously.

"Don't break anything," Edward said. "Neither of us want to cart you to A&E."

"I'm not going to break anything," Jay said, brushing off

Edward's concerns from the top of the stairs. He did descend them slowly though, which was a start. He was carrying a duffel bag over one shoulder and had pulled on a large, black hoodie as well as his jacket. "See? I can climb stairs."

"I'd accept that if you hadn't fallen up those stairs this morning." Edward pointed to the stairs that led to the lower floor. "And you can't deny it because I watched you do it."

Jay flushed but didn't say anything. Instead he turned to me. "Ready to go? Where's Angie?"

"She's at home. I dropped her back and gave her dinner." I looked at the Primark bag in my hand, wondering for a moment if I'd overstepped. "This, um, this is for you."

"You didn't have to get me anything. You're always spoiling me, and I feel guilty because I never get you anything." Jay took the bag, leaning up to press a kiss to my lips. He wobbled, and I reached out my hand to steady him, my fingers brushing the edge of his hoodie as I gently gripped his hip.

"It's fine."

"I'll make it up to you later," he whispered before kissing me again. This kiss was fiercer, his tongue pushing into my mouth, taking what he wanted. Fuck, I couldn't wait to pull him into my lap or stretch him out over something soft. The sudden, simmering tension between us suggested we might not get any further than the sofa. I'd have to shut Angie in the kitchen first.

It was like we'd been holding back, stretching our restraint like an elastic band, and it had finally snapped.

Behind us, Edward coughed. We broke apart. Jay's face was deep pink, and his chest was heaving, which really wasn't helping my self-control. I just wanted to pick him up and put him on the counter, throw his legs over my shoulders and fuck him until he couldn't remember his own name.

I couldn't wait to have him inside me either.

When it came to sex, I'd always been vers. I just hoped Jay felt the same. It was something we should probably talk about.

"As charming as watching you two suck face is, I'm going to go home and pretend I'm not horribly single."

"Awww. You could message The Masked Gentleman."

"I'd rather stick needles in my eyes."

"Some people are into that," Jay teased. Edward just raised his middle finger.

"Do fuck off, darling."

"I'm planning on it." Jay grinned, his attention returning to the bag in his hand. "I'm just going to open my present first. Although, considering it's in a Primark bag I'm assuming it's not some sort of sex toy. Unless Primark have started making them now?" Edward snorted behind him. "Well you never know. They sell so much other random stuff. They might have started making dildos."

"And on that delightful note, I'm leaving," Edward said, making for the door, calling over his shoulder. "Thanks for your help, Leo. Remember to use condoms."

The door clicked shut behind him, leaving Jay and I

alone. My pulse quickened, and my tongue darted out to wet my lips. It would only take two steps to lock the door...

But I'd much rather our first time together was on something soft where I didn't have to rush. And I didn't have to think about getting home to let the dog out.

"Do I want to know what he asked you?" Jay asked.

"He asked me about doing some workshops at Impulsion."

Jay sighed. "Oh my God! He's such a menace, honestly. First he roped me in, now you. He'll be dragging Emily and Daniel in next."

"I think they'd enjoy that. Emily keeps talking about making a dress for it. And Daniel wants to wear a top hat."

"Don't tell Edward. We'll never hear the end of it." He chuckled and shook his head. "So, where were we?" He looked down at the bag and then up at me, his lips curling into a hungry smile. "Oh, yes. I'm going to open this, and then we're going to yours where you're going to fuck me." It was as if Jay had read my mind, and I wasn't going to keep him waiting. I nodded, pressing a final kiss to his lips. Jay stepped back, opening the bag.

"I had to guess on size," I said. "If you don't like it, I can take it back."

"Y-you got me a new one?" Jay was staring at the new hoodie in his hands, running his fingers across the vibrant red fabric. It was as similar as I could get to the old one, and I didn't think it was too far off.

"You said it ripped, and I know how much you loved it." I shrugged as if it were nothing, even if both of us knew that it wasn't. Something caught inside me as Jay looked up at me, a new feeling—unfamiliar—in my chest.

Whatever this was between us had already begun to blossom into something beautiful.

"Take me home," Jay whispered, pressing up against me. "I need you."

## CHAPTER EIGHTEEN

*Poppy (Red) — Pleasure*

**Jay**

I PROBABLY SHOULD HAVE BEEN nervous about going to Leo's in some way, but all I felt was need burning a hole inside my chest. I wanted this more than I'd ever wanted anything, especially after our conversation last night, and my patience was getting stretched thinner and thinner with every passing minute.

And if the heat rolling off Leo and the dark flare in his eyes meant anything, then he felt the same. I was so thankful I'd remembered to put on nice underwear when I'd nipped upstairs to grab a clean hoodie. Comfy boxers with a hole in the thigh were not what I wanted to be wearing when I finally got naked with the delicious man currently holding my hand.

Leo was practically dragging me along the pavement. I

chuckled to myself and wondered if we should've gotten a taxi instead. Although at this pace we'd have beaten a car. Leo's house was in the north of Lincoln, in a newer estate towards the edge of the city. He'd said it was usually about a half an hour walk, but it might take us closer to forty minutes because he walked faster than I did. Now I was thinking we might make it in twenty. I wasn't going to have any soles left on my shoes. Not that I was complaining. The sooner we got to Leo's, the sooner we could finally get naked.

Leo's house was a cute little semi-detached townhouse made of red brick. There were lavender bushes lining the short path to the dark green front door, which stupidly made me think of Bag End. This was really not the time to be thinking about *The Hobbit*. Stupid nerd brain.

Angie crowded us as soon as we walked in the door, bouncing around our feet. Her tail was wagging so hard it made her whole body shake, which was so fucking adorable I couldn't resist stopping to coo at her.

"I'll just put her in the kitchen," Leo said. He pointed to a door on the left. "The living room is through there. Make yourself at home."

I kicked off my shoes, anticipation building under my skin. I dumped my duffel bag on the floor by the stairs, then thought better about it and pushed it surreptitiously closer to the living room. I'd stuck a bottle of lube and a box of Durex in the top of it, just in case Leo didn't have any.

I poked my head around the living room door and gasped. The room was the full length of the house, split into a living and dining room. It was mostly painted a soft grey with one long wall a deep, rich navy. A round mirror hung over a fireplace and the walls were dotted with large prints. The curtains were already closed, and the whole room was lit by lamplight. There were several long, trailing plants on various surfaces that gave it a wild, cosy feel. It was a room I instantly felt at home in. Especially when I noticed the sizeable IKEA Kallax unit which had shelves overflowing with books and board games and some tiny nerdy trinkets. Little Funko Pops of Alucard and Trevor Belmont from Netflix's version of *Castlevania* were perched next to a couple of books on tropical plants.

"You found Alucard," Leo said. I turned to see him leaning against the doorway, arms folded casually. He'd lost his leather jacket and his jumper, revealing a loose, dark t-shirt. He looked so utterly perfect and at home in this space.

"I always thought Edward looked like Alucard, especially when he wears his black and gold frock coat."

"Does that make you Trevor then?"

"We snipe at each other enough." I chuckled.

"You do." Leo pushed off the door frame, making his way over to the huge, navy corner sofa that was tucked against the two walls nearest the door. The sofa was dotted with cushions and I knew they were going to end up all over the floor. At least they were going to if I had my way.

He sprawled over the corner section, spreading his legs and resting one on the sofa. The look on his face was hungry and inviting. A lion waiting for his prey. And I was an oh-so-willing victim.

I sauntered over to him, watching the heat flare in his

eyes. His tongue darted out to lick his perfect, plump lips. Fuck, I needed to feel them against me. Feel the scratch of his beard on my skin from my neck to my thighs. A note of nervousness fluttered in my chest, and I exhaled as I reached him.

"Are you okay?" He held out his hand, a questioning look on his face. The fact that he wanted me to be comfortable washed all my lingering doubts away. I knew being with him would be amazing, and that he'd take care of me.

"Yeah," I said, curling my lips into a wry smile. I took his hand and climbed into his lap, straddling his broad thighs. "I'm great."

"Sure?"

"Yeah." I leant down, taking his lips in a deep kiss and brushing my tongue against his lips. His hands ran slowly up my thighs, settling on my hips. Leo's fingers snaked under the bottom of my t-shirt, stroking over the skin underneath as we kissed. The frantic urgency that had been there earlier had faded, replaced with an intense heat and a deep-seated need. His mouth explored mine, drawing a moan out from deep in my chest. Oh fuck, could Leo kiss.

Leo's stiff cock was straining at his jeans, brushing against mine. I moaned again, his name dripping from my lips. His fingers tightened on my hips. I gasped as he lifted me, flipping us over so I was lying on the sofa with him above me. Delight and desire surged through me, followed by anticipation. Leo dipped his head, his lips trailing kisses down my neck. His beard brushed against the sensitive skin, sending little shivers through me.

I reached for my hoodie, frantically tugging at the zip.

Leo realised what I was doing and sat back, his hands taking over. I sat up and he pulled my hoodie off, throwing it onto the floor, then he reached for my t-shirt. His eyes locked with mine. I smirked and shrugged my shirt off. Leo let out a little growl that went straight to my cock.

"Fuck." His fingers skated across my abdomen and up my chest, reverently tracing the lines of tattoos. There were two large mandalas running across my pecs and chest. Down my left side was a colourful galaxy that seemed to pour out of the pages of a book, while the bottom of my right ribcage was scattered with lines of text and some flowers. I hadn't filled my front as much as my back. I'd have to show him that later.

I gasped as Leo tilted his head and ran his tongue across my chest to my nipples. Slowly, he flicked the end of one of the piercings, and I bucked my chest up, desperately wanting more. Leo chuckled darkly. Then he did it again, this time on the other end of the piercing.

"Shit, y-yes." I'd forgotten how good it felt when someone else played with them. "I-I, ah, I love ha-aving them sucked." My voice caught in my throat as I struggled to form a complete sentence. That did not bode well for the future. If Leo could do this with just his tongue on my nipples, I wasn't sure what would happen when he got rid of my jeans. There was a very real possibility I might explode. Spontaneous human combustion wasn't supposed to be an actual thing, but I was starting to wonder if I'd be the exception.

Leo made a deep noise in the back of his throat that was

so much sexier than it needed to be. Then he sucked one of my nipples into his mouth, and I stopped functioning. His tongue caressed the bar as he sucked, shooting pleasure straight through me. I writhed underneath him as he took me apart, moving from one nipple to the other and then back again, always changing just before I reached the point of oversensitivity. I wasn't sure how he knew where that line was, but he knew. And I was too drunk on pleasure to care.

When he sat back on his knees, there was a pleased smirk on his face and my nipples were red and swollen. I'd have said something, but I was way past coherency at that point. This man was going to utterly wreck me, and I couldn't wait.

"Take… Fuck, words… Take your shirt off. Please."

Leo said nothing. He just fixed me with a hungry smile, stood, and dropped his t-shirt onto the floor. Any commonsense I'd momentarily regained was instantly lost at the sight of Leo's broad, hairy chest covered in ink and the dark trail of hair than ran down over his stomach and into his jeans, which were sitting *very* low on his hips.

"You, um, you should take your jeans off too. They look a little, er… tight?"

Leo chuckled and reached for his leather belt, unbuckling it before popping the buttons and lowering the zip. He slid them over his thighs, leaving him in just a skin-tight pair of navy boxers which were already straining. Holy fucking hell. Apparently, Leo was big *everywhere*. I wasn't going to complain though. After all, I was the one who owned a giant, fantasy dildo.

I stared, mouth agape. Leo seemed to take my silence for hesitance.

"Still okay? Do you want to stop? Or go upstairs?"

"Yes, no, and definitely not. In that order. You are going to fuck me. Right now. Unless of course you're worried about making a mess on the sofa, which I can understand because it's a very nice sofa. Very comfy too."

"Then I'd better take off your jeans," Leo said, bending down to run his hands up my thighs. I spread them instinctively. I was already desperate for him. His fingers reached for my jeans, making short work of the buttons before tugging them down, taking my neon-blue briefs with them and leaving me spread out and naked in front of him. If I'd known he wasn't going to be seeing them, I wouldn't have bothered changing my underwear.

"Fuck, you're gorgeous," Leo continued tracing his fingers over my skin and the random fandom tattoo on my hip. He brought his lips to mine, taking my mouth in a heated kiss.

"Not as gorgeous as you." A random part of me hoped Leo wasn't too hung up on size because my dick was definitely on the average side. I was what you'd describe as thoroughly proportional for my height.

"We'll have to agree to disagree." Leo knelt in front of me, and I sat up. I kissed him again, wrapping my hands around his shoulders and my legs around his waist. His body was pressed against mine. I'd never anticipated how slow things would be between us. I didn't want to go faster though. I wanted to live in this moment forever.

"There are supplies in my bag." I whispered in between kisses. "It's just by the door."

Leo gave me a sly smile, and I knew he'd already noticed it as he'd come into the room. He broke away, standing and stepping over to the door to grab the bag. He unzipped it, pulling out the lube and the box of condoms and throwing them down on the sofa next to me.

He dropped back down to his knees, pushing my thighs apart and trailing kisses down the inside of them, his beard scratching the skin perfectly. I groaned as he nipped at my thigh, throwing my head back into the cushions. Leo spread my legs wider, his mouth trailing across my skin. I gasped as his tongue swiped across my hole. I hadn't been rimmed in so long, I'd forgotten just how fucking good it felt.

Leo's tongue was talented as he worked me open with it, sending spasms of pleasure jerking through me. His fingers wrapped around my cock, stroking it slowly as he worked his mouth over the sensitive skin of my hole. The dual sensations were driving me wild, but selfishly, I wanted more.

"Leo," I said, the word hanging desperately in the air. "Wait. I-I want… I want to suck you."

Leo looked up at me from between my thighs, his eyes dark with lust. "Are you sure?"

"Yes, I'm fucking sure." I pushed myself into a seated position, even though my muscles felt like jelly. That had happened a lot faster than I'd thought it would. Spinning myself around, I lay down on the L-shaped side of the sofa. Leo seemed to get where I was going. He picked up the bottle of lube and drizzled some onto his fingers as he stood, moving closer to me. Anticipation thrummed across my skin. I swallowed.

Leo grasped his thick cock between his fingers, angling it towards me. I wrapped my lips around him, groaning as he filled my mouth. My lips stretched around him perfectly, and I flicked my tongue across the swollen head, loving the way Leo moaned. I'd debated about getting my tongue pierced for years, and now I really wished I'd gone through with it.

I moaned around Leo as I felt his fingers between my thighs, pressing at my hole. He pushed a thick finger into me, and I groaned again. Fuck, this was perfect. I loved the way he was filling me. This was so much better than I'd ever imagined.

I sucked him hard as he began to work me open, but fuck it was hard to concentrate. His fingers were as talented as his tongue, and soon I was nothing more than a moaning, desperate mess with a mouth full of cock. I looked up at Leo, and he smirked down at me. There was hunger and desire written across his face, but there was something softer there too. Something warm and achingly sweet. He was the perfect combination of everything I'd ever wanted.

"You're so beautiful," Leo said, his other hand coming down to stroke my hair. "I want you so much."

"I want you too," I said, releasing his cock and pumping it with my hand. He was slick and hot and so fucking hard. I couldn't wait to take him inside me. Leo slipped his fingers out of me and turned, sitting on the sofa, cock jutting out. Waiting for me.

Leo reached for the box of condoms beside him, took one out, and rolled it over his perfect cock.

He crooked his finger, and I grinned, rolled over, and hopped off the sofa. It took me two steps to be back in his lap, my mouth against his. I reached around, grasping his cock and lining it up with my hole.

"Slowly," he said. "I don't want to hurt you."

"You won't. I can take it."

"Slowly." Leo's tone brooked no argument. "My beautiful boy." He kissed me again, tongue caressing my lips as I began to sink down onto him. I gasped as his cock breached me because holy fuck, he was big. But he felt so fucking good stretching me wide. It was like all my fantasies come to life. Except that this was a million times hotter than the sex dream I'd had.

Leo's hands gripped my hips, his thumbs rubbing soothing circles over my hip bones as I slowly took him inside me. I paused a couple of times, letting my body adjust. Taking a real dick over a dildo was a bit of a change of pace, but I wasn't complaining. Dildos didn't come with soft words of desire or gentle touches, which was what I'd missed most about being with a partner. I groaned as Leo bottomed out, my breath coming in pants and sweat already beading across my forehead.

"Fuck. You feel so good." I wiggled my hips experimentally. A little sigh of pleasure slipped from my lips.

"You look so good on my cock. So fucking perfect for me." Leo trailed one hand lightly across my abdomen and up to my nipple. He traced his finger across the swollen nub, caressing the bar and sending a surge of pleasure through me. Leo grinned, his finger moving across to the other. God, this man was going to be the death of me. The coroner's report was just going to read "Cause of death: fucking amazing sex".

And this was just the first time. What was it going to be like when we got to know each other's bodies, when we knew exactly where to touch and lick and suck? It was going to be incredible.

I groaned as Leo played with my nipples, my hips beginning to roll. I rode him slowly, testing and teasing, but soon it wasn't enough. I needed more. My hands rested on his chest, using them as an anchor so I could ride him harder. My thighs began to shake as I bounced on his cock, pleasure burning through me.

Every movement sent his cock sliding across my prostate, and it was too good to last long. I reached for my cock, wrapping my fingers around my aching shaft as Leo flicked my nipples. His pupils were blown wide, his mouth slack, and I knew if I came, he wouldn't be far behind me.

"I, I'm..."

"Come for me," Leo growled. "I'm right behind you."

I pumped my cock, sliding deep onto Leo for one final time before my orgasm exploded out of me. Pleasure washed across my skin, and I felt my whole body contract as I cried out. Leo grabbed my hips, thrusting desperately up into me until he came with a shout, his cock pulsing inside me.

I threw my hands out, steadying myself on his chest while I tried to remember how to breathe. I got the suspicious feeling I wouldn't have any idea how to use my legs. My brain hadn't come back online yet either.

Leo's chest rose and fell under my fingers. There was a soft smile on his face, full of an affection I'd never seen before. It warmed my heart, melting it like the centre of a perfectly toasted marshmallow.

And I knew right then that whatever happened, I'd never be able to let Leo go.

# CHAPTER NINETEEN

*Tulip — Love and passion*

**Leo**

THE JINGLING tone of my alarm nudged me from sleep much sooner than I'd hoped. It felt like it had only been five minutes since I'd finally drifted off.

Jay and I had stumbled into bed around eleven after a couple of episodes of *Celestials* and some late-night Chinese food. We hadn't done a lot of sleeping though. Now that we'd had a taste of each other, we couldn't seem to get enough.

Halfway through the last episode we'd started, Jay had climbed into my lap again and we started making out. We'd given up on the episode ten minutes later, and I'd carried him upstairs, dropping him onto my giant bed before stripping him naked and fucking him deep and slow.

We had drifted off after that, but I think somewhere in

the early morning I'd woken up to find myself grinding against him, Jay's arse pressed against my cock. I'd thought he'd be too sore for anything, and I'd been embarrassed at how horny I suddenly was. But Jay had just wrapped my arm tighter around him and whispered how much he wanted me. I'd ended up reaching for the supplies and sliding back inside him, rocking my hips while he moaned and grasped at my arms until he'd come all over my fist.

I felt like I was nineteen again, a mess of wild desire and desperation.

I reached for my phone, blearily swiping at the screen until it went quiet. At least it was Sunday and the shop didn't open until ten. I sat up, stretching my arms above my head and listening to my joints pop.

Jay was spread out on his stomach next to me, one arm hugging his pillow. The duvet was wrapped around his waist, and the soft pre-dawn light sneaking in around the edge of the curtains highlighted the outline of his back piece.

It was an illustration of The Hanged Man that I'd seen in tarot decks. The wooden branches stretched across his shoulders, while the man stretched down his spine. The whole thing was framed by woven branches, leaves and flowers. I'd examined it in more detail last night and it was one of the most stunning tattoos I'd ever seen. It must have taken hours to complete. I wondered if it would be too nosey to ask when he'd had it done, or why. I knew tarot cards all had meanings, but my knowledge was incredibly rough. All I could remember was that the Death card didn't mean death.

As I watched him, Jay gave a little snuffly snore and rolled toward me. He looked so adorable in sleep, and I wanted to watch him for hours. But if I did, I'd have a very grumpy Staffy and a string of nosey messages from Emily.

Sighing to myself, I slid out of bed, reaching for the t-shirt I'd discarded last night and a pair of comfy joggers I wore around the house from the nearby armchair. I ran my hands through my hair, deciding against pulling it up, mostly because I couldn't remember where my hair bobble had ended up.

I pottered downstairs to the kitchen, opening the door to find Angie sulking in her bed. I clearly hadn't been forgiven for banishing her from my bedroom. Apparently, her luxury dog bed wasn't as good as spreading out over mine.

I flicked the kettle on before shooing Angie outside. She gave me a disgruntled sniff as she went, and I raised an eyebrow, wondering how on earth I'd managed to raise such an entitled animal. At least I wasn't one of those people who bought Waitrose rotisserie chickens for their dog. Or fillet steak from the meat counter. Angie was spoilt, but she wasn't *that* spoilt. Not yet anyway.

She was still sulking when she came back in and stared disdainfully at her breakfast. Then she sniffed again and went back to bed, curling up with her back to me. I chuckled and finished mixing two cups of tea, hoping I'd remembered how Jay liked his. The last thing I wanted was to upset both of the important creatures in my life. Although I thought Jay was more likely to forgive me.

Jay was still asleep when I got back upstairs. He'd rolled even farther onto my side, his face buried in my pillows.

Something tugged inside my chest, a feeling I'd never had before. I'd fallen hard and fast in the past, but this felt different. It felt… right. I knew it was early, and that Jay had been burned by a bad relationship, but I couldn't help the way I felt.

For so long I'd looked for someone who wasn't afraid to see me as me. Who took me for the man I was, not the man they wanted me to be. Maybe I'd been looking in the wrong places all along. Maybe I'd been looking for the wrong person.

This time it felt like things would be different.

It gave me hope.

I put the mugs on my bedside table and gently nudged Jay across the bed. He made a soft grumbling noise, then blinked sleepily.

"Mornin'," I said, leaning down to give him a kiss. He gave me a drowsy smile that made my heart melt a little further.

"Hey." He frowned, squinting at me. I wondered how much he could see without his glasses. "Are you dressed? Did I oversleep?"

"No, you're fine." I pointed to the mugs of tea beside me. "I made tea and put Angie out. She's sulking."

"Why? What did you do?" Jay sat up and gave me a curious smile. He reached for his glasses and slid them onto his nose.

"I love how you assume I did something," I said dryly before handing him his mug. "Let me know if I made it wrong."

"It'll be fine. I'm not as picky as some people." He took

a little sip and sighed happily. "And I'm assuming you did something because I'm like ninety-nine percent sure you did."

I chuckled. "She's just cross because she had to sleep downstairs. She usually sleeps up here." I was suddenly worried Jay would think that was weird. I'd definitely met people in the past who thought dogs shouldn't be anywhere near bedrooms. "Don't worry. I changed the sheets."

"Aww, I'd be cross too," Jay said. "Banished to the kitchen because Daddy wanted to get laid."

"It's not like she sleeps on the bloody floor. She's got a seventy-quid bed to sleep in."

"Yeah, but it's not the same as curling up with you."

"She doesn't curl. She sprawls," I said, sipping my tea. "There's a reason I have such a big bed. I only get a tiny bit of it."

"She can't be that bad."

"She can come stay with you then. You can be pushed out of bed and listen to her snore."

Jay laughed. "On second thought, I think I'm okay."

"Thought so."

"This bed is super comfortable," he said, sighing again and snuggling against the pillows, looking up at me with a smile. "Plus it comes with great company. Very sexy. Would stay again."

"Dork." I chuckled.

"Oh, one hundred percent. And you love it." He tilted his head up, pulling a ridiculous duck face and begging for a kiss. I couldn't resist. Even if he did look ridiculous, he was my ridiculous.

"Mmm, I don't suppose we have time for something fun?" Jay murmured against my lips, his mouth curling into a devious smile. "I'm assuming at some point you'll turf me out of bed to go to work. What's the time anyway?"

"About half seven?"

"Ugh! Why so early?"

I shook my head, unable to stop myself from smiling at him. "I usually go in at about eight on Sundays. Gives me a chance to finish orders before the shop opens."

"At ten." He wrinkled his face. I think he was going for annoyed, but he just looked like a bunny with a wiffly nose.

"You're welcome to stay here," I said, kissing his cheek. "I can leave you a set of keys."

"It's okay. I'll go to The Lost World and make a start on the stock count so I don't have to do it on my day off. Speaking of day off, what are you doing tomorrow? Want to bring Angie and come to mine for a bit? My bed might not be as big and comfy, but it is a bed."

"You're incorrigible."

"You say that, but I bet you wouldn't turn your nose up at seeing my dildo." His voice trailed off, leaving the suggestion hanging in the air. I had to admit I was intrigued.

"That can be arranged."

"Good." Jay's face relaxed as if he'd been expecting me to turn him down or say something about him having toys. Virtually every partner I'd ever had had had a selection of sex toys, and I'd always enjoyed watching them use them.

There was something incredibly hot about watching someone show you *exactly* how they liked to get off.

I kissed him again, then I put my mug down and reached for him, letting him put his tea down before I drew him into my arms. I wrapped my arms around him, and we slid down to the mattress, our bodies intertwined while our lips slowly explored.

Desire burned in my chest, not quite as fierce and wild as last night, but still hotter than I'd ever experienced. Nothing seemed to satiate it, and all I could do was temper it for a while until the need grew too great again. It was like a wildfire, sweeping through the desolate landscape that had been my romantic life, clearing the remnants that had been left behind by previous loves. My craving for Jay was all encompassing. I wanted him more than anything. It should have been terrifying, and if I was being objective, I would have questioned how quickly I'd been swept away by this man.

But I didn't want to be objective, and I didn't want to question how I was feeling because I was already well on my way to falling in love with him. I wanted to bask in this moment for as long as possible.

I was all too aware of how fragile these moments were.

I could only hope it would last.

"So..." Jay's mouth was soft and swollen, his cheeks dusted pink. "You never answered my question."

"What question was that?"

"Do we have time for something fun?" He pressed his body against mine, and I felt his hard cock pressing against my hip. "If we desperately need to get up, we could always combine it with a shower. I've always liked giving head in the shower, and I definitely haven't had enough chances to get my mouth on you." I moaned, and Jay chuckled darkly. "I'm going to take that as a yes then."

His hand reached for my cock, but I grasped his wrist. "I think you'll like my shower," I said, trying to keep my voice casual. It was impossible though. "Want to see?"

Jay kissed me again, tongue sliding against my lips. "Show me."

# CHAPTER TWENTY

*Gooseberry — Anticipation*

**Jay**

MY GOOD MOOD lasted until the post arrived on Monday morning.

I'd floated through the rest of Sunday on a little cloud of candy-floss happiness: fluffy, sweet, and almost a little sickly. By the time I'd crawled into bed on Sunday night, I was quite sure I'd never been as cheerful as this. Or at least I hadn't been for a very, very long time, which probably said a lot about my relationship with Kieran.

I'd slept like a log and spent the first part of Monday morning pottering around my flat doing long neglected housework and belting out songs I hadn't listened to in years thanks to the random Spotify mix I'd selected. It had been a great morning until I'd gone down to the shop and seen the letter from the council with a red urgent stamp on the front.

With confusion, I ripped it open, staring at the notice for overdue business rates, which was backdated. By two months. Fuck! How had I missed two fucking payments?

I was sure I'd set up a direct debit to pay the fees monthly. I'd put it into my enormous budget spreadsheet, and when I'd checked my business account the other day, the amount of money left made me think I'd paid it. I grabbed my laptop and fired up the elderly machine, logging into my online banking as fast as possible. There was no need to panic. All I needed to do was check the payments had gone out and then I could ring the council and tell them they'd made a mistake. These kinds of things happened. It was just a simple processing error.

Except it wasn't a bloody mistake.

Because the fucking direct debit had never been set up.

Bollocks. Bloody blue bollocks.

I looked at the letter, noticing the nice, large, bold number I owed the council. The letter said I had to pay within seven days, or they would take action against me. There was also a "helpful" telephone number so I could call someone in case there was a problem.

Yeah, the problem was that I didn't currently have enough money to pay the bill.

I should have set up the fucking online shop months ago. Maybe then I wouldn't be struggling as much as I was. Sure, the shop had a few regular customers, but three or four regulars were not going to pay my bills for much longer, especially with the cost of business rates on top of stock and electricity and internet and all the other random bills I had to pay. And that was without taking a salary for myself.

I was lucky I still had some savings to live on. I'd always been fairly frugal, mostly because London had been so fucking expensive. I was sure I'd need some money for a rainy day. A couple of years ago, the last of my grandparents had passed on, leaving me nearly half their estate. I'd saved a lot of the money, using some of it to clear my overdraft and credit cards and some for tattoos, but I'd put a huge chunk of it into an ISA so I could save for a house deposit. The money was locked in there for at least five years, and I still had a couple to go before I could touch it.

It looked like the last of my liquid savings would be going to keeping my business afloat. My only other option was to take out another business loan, but since I already had one, I doubted I'd get another.

Ah fucking hell. I had to start repaying that soon too.

I'd used some of my savings, a small loan, and what Edward had called an "investment gift" to get the shop started, furnished, and stocked. I'd thought it would be plenty—it had allowed me to pay for a year's lease upfront—but I'd apparently forgotten about the rest of my bills.

I groaned and scrubbed my hands over my face, sending my glasses flying across the counter. Whatever. I'd get them later. I flopped my head down on the counter, letting out another overdramatic groan. This was just my fucking luck, wasn't it? Everything was going great for once, so the universe decided to shoot down my little balloon of happiness. I wondered if there was some sort of cosmic prize for ruining my life. Like a giant, star-filled teddy bear.

Visions of alien funfairs danced across my imagination. Clearly my brain had decided it would be best to ignore the problem. At least for the moment. I had seven days. I could figure something out... I hoped.

I just needed to build the online shop and get some serious social media presence. And some orders. And some more regular customers.

Y'know, small, simple things that would be super easy to sort.

There went all my days off—and my evenings—for the foreseeable future.

My head throbbed and my chest tightened, my stomach sinking faster than a lead balloon. What the fuck was I going to do about Leo? We'd just gotten to a fun, sexy place, and I genuinely loved spending time with him. I didn't want that to go south just because I had work problems. I'd been there once before and knew exactly how that turned out. I was not going there again.

Still... Mother's Day was this weekend, and Leo had a lot of orders to do. And then we'd be into April, and I was sure he'd get busier as we got further and further into spring. He'd already mentioned that he was looking to hire another member of staff to help him out. It wasn't like we'd get to spend a ton of time together anyway if we were busy, and he knew I wanted to do the online shop... I didn't need to tell him what was going on with the money or that I had a ton of stuff to do. I just had to get through the next couple of weeks and then the steampunk weekend, and everything would be fine.

If I was lucky.

And if I were being honest, luck hadn't been on my side lately. I wasn't exactly Domino.

Meh, it would be fine. I wasn't going to give up now. I'd worked too damn hard to get this far, and I wasn't going to let go of my dream over some silly mistake. Even if the insidious weasels in my brain were beginning to whisper that it would be easier to give up and admit I couldn't do this. Like I couldn't make things work in London. Like I couldn't make a relationship work either.

A sharp knock at the door cut off the muttering of the brain weasels, and I was glad of the interruption. I retrieved my glasses off the counter and shoved the council letter underneath it before grabbing my keys. I was really hoping it was Leo because I could use the distraction.

I'd teased him about showing him my fantasy dildo, but now I was thinking that might not be such a bad idea, especially since Leo's eyes had lit up when I'd mentioned it. I craved the boneless, floating feeling I got from a hard fuck and an intense release. The idea solidified in my mind, freezing out my worries about the shop. I'd come back to them later, and maybe my brain would come up with a solution while I was too fucked out to care.

As soon as I opened the door, Angie bounded inside, her tail wagging so fast it was almost a blur. I chuckled, leaning down to scratch behind her ears, loving the way she pressed into my touch. Clearly, I wasn't being blamed for her night in the kitchen.

Leo's face was fixed on her. He looked utterly unimpressed.

"I take it you still haven't been forgiven?" I asked, giving him a wry grin.

"No."

"Wow. For a dog, she can really hold a grudge. I thought you'd be forgiven as soon as she wanted treats."

Leo shut the door, bolting it behind him. "So did I. But apparently that's not how this works."

"Awww, are you punishing him?" I asked Angie, who just wagged her tail harder, giving me a sweet, Staffy smile before licking my hand. "I think the answer is yes."

Leo grumbled quietly, but there was a warmth in his eyes. I grinned at him. "Don't worry. I'll give you plenty of attention."

"Oh? Does this have anything to do with what you mentioned yesterday?"

"Maaaybe." I straightened up, turning to head towards the stairs. "Why don't you follow me and find out?"

I started walking, swaying my hips in the most ridiculous way. As I got to the stairs, I wondered if Leo was actually following me, but one cursory glance over my shoulder had me realising he was too busy watching my ass as I walked away. A shiver of anticipation ran down my spine, and Leo's eyes locked with mine. I saw the hunger burning inside them.

I giggled, trying to rush up the stairs, my heart racing. What was it about the idea of him suddenly catching me, taking me upstairs, laying me out, and claiming me as his? There was something utterly primal about it that set my body on fire, sparks igniting in my nerves.

Leo's footsteps sounded behind me, and I let out a high-pitched squeak as his arms wrapped around me, pulling me close.

"You're teasing me." His voice was a low growl that made me melt against him, boneless and needy.

"A-and if I was? What are you going to do about it?" Leo spun me in his arms. He had one eyebrow raised as if he were wondering what to do. I smirked. "Whatever you're planning to do, I'd do it."

"Or what?"

"Who knows?" I left the teasing challenge hanging in the air. I had no idea what I'd do, but just the idea of doing *something* was enough for me. There was something about Leo that turned me on in ways I'd never experienced before. I rested my palms on his chest, standing on my toes to bring my mouth closer to his. "But you should definitely take me upstairs and let me show you my favourite toy. I bet you'd love to watch me play with it."

Leo growled, his hands gripping my waist. I gasped as he lifted me, my legs instinctively wrapping around him. His mouth met mine in a possessive kiss and everything inside me melted. All my fears, all my worries, and all my problems seemed to vanish as if Leo was a knight in shining armour who'd come to banish my demons. I knew they'd be back later, but for now this was enough.

Leo broke the kiss, then he carried me upstairs.

## CHAPTER TWENTY-ONE

*Lavender — Loyalty, Love, Devotion*

**Leo**

I DROPPED Jay onto his bed, listening to him laugh as he bounced onto the mattress while I shut the door behind us, leaving Angie in the hallway. She'd probably end up curled on Jay's sofa.

"So," Jay said, staring up at me with come-hither eyes as he stretched out on the sheets. "What are you going to do now?"

"First, I'm going to get you naked." A smile played on my lips at the delight that flitted across Jay's face. I crouched at the end of the bed, gently easing off his Vans and chuckling at the little cups of coffee decorating his socks. Then I slowly ran my hands up his legs, caressing his thighs as I reached the waistband of his skinny jeans. I opened the button and zip and tugged them off, throwing them onto the floor. A low rumble echoed through my chest as I looked at him, spread out in his tight, red briefs that were already stretched over his erection. I stood and reached for his hand, pulling him into a seated position so I could unzip his hoodie and pull his t-shirt over his head.

"You are so fucking sexy," I said, leaning in and kissing him possessively.

"What are you going to do now?" Jay broke the kiss, looking up at me, his glasses slightly askew. I gently slid them off his nose, then folded them on top of the nearby chest of drawers.

"Now, I want to watch you play with your toy. And after that, I'm going to fuck you." Jay shivered, pulling on his lip ring as he looked up at me. He already knew how to push all my buttons.

"There's something you should know." There was a blush creeping over his cheeks. "My, um, my favourite dildo, the one I always use, it's not exactly… traditional."

"Oh?" I was intrigued now. I'd seen alternative dildos on the internet before, and now I was curious to see exactly what Jay meant. I had an inkling of an idea though. "Is it a fantasy one? Like a tentacle or one of those with a knot."

"Um, it's a fantasy one, but it's not a tentacle. It's just, er, quite big." He smiled and his shoulders relaxed. I hadn't realised how tense he was. "I was tempted by the tentacle ones, but I could only afford one, and I didn't want to get one I wasn't completely sure about."

This conversation had only served to intrigue me even further. I tilted my head down and kissed him. "Maybe tentacles for your birthday."

"Tease! Now get naked and sit on the bed," Jay said, sliding away from me and patting the mattress. He watched me strip, a hungry smile on his lips. I'd always been ambivalent about my body. It did the job, and I liked all my tattoos and the way they looked on me. But Jay made me feel… sexy. The way his eyes seared into my skin, made me want to melt. But it was more than that. It was the fact that I wasn't just a piece of meat to him. He was interested in who I was on the inside as well as what I looked like on the outside.

I sat on the bed, propping myself up on Jay's pillows. I stretched my legs out in front of me, my hand resting on my thigh. I was tempted to start stroking my cock, but if I started now, I'd never last, and I wanted to give Jay my full attention.

Jay was hanging half-off the bed, rummaging in something I couldn't see. It was cute watching his arse wiggle as he moved. I wanted to reach out and squeeze it. He had such a perfect little butt, and I wanted to play with it. He threw a dildo onto the bed along with a bottle of lube.

He hadn't been lying. It was large. I couldn't wait to see it buried inside him.

He was going to look amazing all stretched and full.

"So, this is it. It was called "The Gorgon", but I call it George. Which sounds really weird when I say it out loud," Jay said as he crawled backwards on the bed. I suppressed a laugh. It was like he was introducing me to a friend in the pub, not his favourite sex toy.

"He's impressive. I can't wait to watch you take him."

Jay's skin flushed coral all the way down his chest. "Show me how you touch yourself."

Jay winked and licked his lips before stretching out next to me. He stripped his briefs off and chucked them onto the floor. His cock was hard and leaking against his abdomen, but Jay didn't reach for it. Instead, he ghosted his fingers across his nipples, teasing the bars. I fucking loved that he had pierced nipples. I wanted to suck and lick and tease them for hours. I wondered if he'd ever be able to come from nipple play…

I watched him, never taking my eyes off him as his touch got harder, little moans ghosting across his lips. My cock throbbed against my hip, demanding my attention. I ignored it, focusing my attention on the beautiful man on the bed next to me, but it was getting hard to resist. Especially when Jay slid his fingers down his stomach and wrapped one hand around his dick, pumping it slowly. He looked over at me, locking our gazes together as he moaned, louder this time. The sound went straight to my cock.

"Touch yourself," Jay gasped. "Want to watch you."

That was all I needed to hear.

I groaned as my fingers gripped my cock, my thumb smearing the little bit of precum across the head. The friction was just on the right side of rough and it sent little rolls of pleasure through me, like the distant rumbles of thunder that heralded a storm.

Beside me, Jay clicked open the bottle of lube, drizzling a little onto his fingers. He smirked and reached over, grasping my cock and slicking it with lube. "I had too much," he said, giving me a little smile that undid me from the inside out. "I thought I'd share."

I leant down and kissed him, my tongue pressing into his mouth. "That's very generous of you."

"I know." He winked. "I love watching you jerk off. You look so fucking hot."

"So do you." I kissed him again.

Jay blushed deeper, then he slipped a hand between his legs, drawing his thighs up and spreading them wide. He groaned, and I assumed he was touching his hole. I sat up, changing my angle so I could watch him. I wanted to see him finger himself, working his arse open for his toy.

"You look so good," I said. "I love watching you like this."

"Yeah?" His voice was breathless and caught in his throat as he pressed a second finger in.

"Yeah. You're incredible."

"T-thanks. So are you."

I pumped my cock as I watched him. The lube he'd rubbed onto me made my grip deliciously slick and hot. Pleasure flashed through me like the first crack of lightning.

Jay pressed a third finger in, throwing his head back on the bed and panting. I wondered if he could hit his prostate like this or whether he was agonisingly short. My money was on the second.

His other hand reached out, searching for the toy as he pulled his fingers out. I wanted to bury my face between his cheeks to taste him and drive him wild. I put my hand out, holding his thigh in place before he could move.

"Wait," I said. "I want to eat your arse."

"Even with the lube?" Jay asked. He glanced down at the bottle next to me. "Oh, apparently it's cherry flavoured. I didn't even realise. I just grabbed a bottle out of the box." His cheeks flushed at the implication, but I loved the idea that he had a whole box of tricks we could explore.

I chuckled. "Well, it's not my favourite flavour, but I'll manage. I want to taste your tight little hole and take you apart."

"Oh fuck." Jay nodded wildly. "Please."

I grabbed his hips, pulling him across the bed towards me. Jay wrapped his hands around his knees, holding his legs high and wide, presenting his arse for me. Fuck, he was perfect.

Jay gasped as I licked across his hole. There was something resembling artificial cherry there, but it was overtaken by something deep and musky, something that was utterly Jay. I wanted more. I pressed my fingers in alongside my tongue, aiming for that sweet spot inside him that he hadn't been able to reach.

"Oh shit. Shit! Right there."

Jay gasped and moaned as I took him apart with my mouth. It was a heady feeling to reduce someone to a melted puddle with nothing more than two fingers and your tongue. My own cock throbbed as it rubbed against the mattress, the friction driving me wild, but I didn't want it to end like this. I'd been promised a show.

I leant back and reached for the dildo. It was thick and heavy in my hand, and I had to admit the flared, ridged head and thick body were a little intimidating. I could also see why Jay must love it.

"Do you want me to do it?" I asked, holding up the toy. That would be just as fun as watching Jay. He shook his head.

"No... maybe next time. Today I want to show you." He released his legs, slowly rolling onto his front and kneeling up. His skin was flushed and beaded with sweat, and his hair stood on end like he'd been running his hands through it. I knew he'd enjoyed it when I'd gently pulled his hair the other night, so it wouldn't have surprised me if he'd been pulling at the strands while I ate him.

He took the dildo from me, squirting some lube on it before placing the base on the mattress and holding it with one hand. He shuffled on his knees until he was hovering above it, positioning his body so I could see both his sexy arse, his cock, and his face. My fingers reached for my cock, and I groaned as I grasped it. I was already on edge, my orgasm humming under my skin, waiting just out of reach.

Jay gasped, mouth hanging open as he began to sink down on the thick, ridged head of the toy. He moved slowly, taking it inch by inch. All I could do was stare at the way the toy sank into him, his arse swallowing the thick shaft. His cock leaked precum onto the sheets, and I wanted to wrap my mouth around him, savouring the taste on my tongue.

"L-Leo," Jay said, his voice hoarse and broken.

"You look so good. So fucking good for me, taking all your toy."

"F-f-feels fucking amazing."

"Yeah? You like how it stretches you?"

He nodded, his other hand reaching up to pinch his nipples, rolling the bars between his fingers in turn.

"Are you going to ride it for me? Going to come for me?"

Jay nodded again, a deep moan filling the room as he began to roll his hips. It was desperate and filthy, and I loved watching him move. I began to jack my cock slowly, trying to tease out the inevitable, my eyes never leaving Jay. He began to move faster, his cock bouncing in front of him.

He was so fucking perfect.

Jay's hand reached for his cock, pumping it as he bounced on the dildo, moving faster and more frantically with every second that passed. "Fuck, I'm. I'm getting cl— I'm gonna... Leo!"

Jay came with a shout, ropes of cum shooting across the bedsheets. His chest was heaving, his thighs trembling as he slowly tilted to one side, falling onto the mattress next to me. I leant over and kissed him deeply, groaning against his lips as I jacked my cock.

"C-come on me." Jay's voice was no louder than a whisper, but I heard every word. "Want you to come all over me."

"Yeah? Want me to cover you in my cum?" I could barely say the words. Pleasure burned deep in my abdomen, rolling through my muscles. I rolled onto my side and onto my knees as fast as I could. Jay was stretched out beneath me, looking utterly fucked out. My eyes roamed over every inch of him, taking him in so I could remember this picture forever. My balls tightened and I groaned. I was so close. There was no turning back now. Jay smirked and winked at me, and that was it.

The storm that had been rumbling under my skin unleashed its full force, sending my orgasm barrelling through me. I came with a grunt, shooting my release across Jay, painting his skin. Something stirred in my chest at the sight.

"Wow," Jay breathed. "That was… Wow."

"Yeah." I flopped down beside him, pressing a soft kiss to his perfect mouth. "You're amazing."

"So are you." He softly kissed me again, and I savoured the moment. He'd removed the dildo at some point, throwing it on the bed beside him. "We should clean up, and my shower will only fit one of us."

"You can go first then. In a minute." I wanted to keep kissing him for a minute or two more.

"Okay, but if it won't come off, I'm blaming you." He chuckled, then sighed, almost sadly. I had no idea why. "You're amazing, you know that, right?"

"So are you." He smiled at me, but it didn't quite reach his eyes. For a second, he looked worried as if there was something else going on I didn't know about.

"Are you okay?" I asked, stroking his hair off his face. Concern flared in my chest, mixed with something painful I didn't recognise. Jay's smile widened, and the worry vanished, like wispy fog in sunlight. I almost wondered if it had ever been there, or if I'd been imagining it.

"I'm good. Just sticky and a little exhausted. I think you wore me out, but I am absolutely not complaining. I'm just not sure I want to get up."

"Do you need me to carry you?"

"As fun as that would be, I think I'll manage." He gave me another kiss before swinging his legs off the bed. "I'll be back in a minute. Just make yourself comfy."

I watched him go, two new emotions warring in my heart. The first was concern, and the second was infinitely more complex, but it felt a lot like love.

## CHAPTER TWENTY-TWO

*Cornflower — Single blessedness, Hope*

**Jay**

I GROANED and buried my head in my hands, scrubbing my face for the millionth time and wincing as my hand caught my lip ring at the wrong angle. Motherfucker! That stung.

Today, the universe had decided it had not had enough fun making my life miserable and had decided to add an extra little problem to the mix. And that problem was the website.

Although I had a graphic design background and was extremely comfortable with all things design based, when it came to other parts of computing, technology and I just didn't get on. I'd spent the past five hours attempting to convince the plug-ins I'd installed to please just work, but apparently the powers of the universe had decided to fuck me over. Instead of giving me a nice-looking website with an online ordering platform built in, I'd ended up with a garbled mess that looked like it had been built by a five-year-old.

Except they taught coding in schools now so a five-year-old could probably have done a better job.

Edward had spent the entirety of the past two weeks trying to get me to fork out for a proper web designer or to at least let him ask around to see if he could pull in a favour for me. One of his cosplay friends was good with websites, and Edward was sure they'd be able to help me out and probably for mates' rates too.

Part of me wanted to say yes because I was sure it would be easier, but another, louder part of me felt nothing but an overwhelming sense of guilt at having to get Edward involved. It was bad enough I'd dragged him into this mad bookshop scheme in the first place. Now I apparently needed him to bail me out of everything. I couldn't keep asking him to help me.

His other suggestion of hiring someone was almost impossible. I didn't have the funds.

I'd managed to pay my business rates bill and set up a direct debit scheme to keep paying the rest, but it had meant taking nearly two grand out of my savings, and that was before I considered the rest of my upcoming bills for the month. The shop had only been open for three months, and I was starting to wonder if we'd make it to six.

Ugh, why had I ever thought I could do this?

I fisted my hands in my hair, trying to pull myself back to the present problem. I was going to have to spend my evening trying to figure out what had gone wrong and trying to undo everything I'd spent this afternoon working on.

To add insult to injury, I'd also received three emails from people planning to attend the Impulsion Steampunk Festival asking questions about the workshops, despite the fact that Edward had said he'd handle everything. Two wanted to ask specific questions about a workshop to do with travel in the world of steampunk, and another wanted to know if they needed to bring their own material for the sewing class Edward was teaching. Neither of which I knew the answer to.

I'd told them as much, after spending an hour trying to find the email address of the person they actually needed to talk to.

So much for spending my day off relaxing.

My phone buzzed on the counter beside me. I'd set it to vibrate just in case I got too absorbed in work and missed something important. Leo's name scrolled across the screen and my chest tightened. I'd promised him we could meet up this evening and watch more of *Celestials*, but now I wasn't sure I had time.

Leo *How's the website going?*
Jay *It's going, I guess. Slower than I expected =\ really not sure I'm gonna get it working this week*
Leo *Take a break and come to mine*
Leo *You'll make yourself feel worse if you spend all night staring at it*

I wanted to argue with him because I needed to keep

working and get this fixed. If I didn't do it now, then it was just going to go on top of the ever-growing pile of things that needed doing. That list seemed to be getting longer and longer every day.

I didn't know why I was suddenly busier now, but maybe it was because my fear made every task take twice as long. I was spending more time worrying than I was actually working.

LEO *Do I need to come fetch you?*

I could hear the teasing tone behind his text, and I smiled.

JAY *Probably or I'll stay here all night*
LEO *I'll be there in thirty. Want to stay?*
JAY *Sure =) <3*

I regretted the messages almost as soon as I'd sent them. I shouldn't be goofing off to watch telly with Leo or spending hours wrapped in his arms, no matter how perfect they were, but it was too late now. I'd just have to try and fix this tomorrow while the shop was open, and if not, I had tomorrow evening. I could always skip D&D on Wednesday if I needed to.

Memories of my life in London resurfaced, and I pushed them away. This wasn't that. I wasn't going to make the same mistakes. I could make this work.

I hoped.

· · ·

"Darling, have you forgotten how to answer your phone?" Edward sounded curious, and I rolled my eyes, almost wishing I hadn't answered his call. I relaxed back on my sofa, pushing my laptop off my legs. My shoulders popped as I rolled them, and my stomach grumbled loudly. Had I even remembered to eat dinner? Probably not. I'd been too busy trying to schedule Twitter posts for the next couple of weeks. I'd been trying to be more active on social media, and scheduling posts seemed like a good way to at least get something up. Even if I still couldn't get the fucking online shop working.

"No, I've just been busy."

"There's busy and then there's avoiding me."

"I'm not avoiding you," I said, trying to pretend it wasn't true. I might have been avoiding him just a teeny, weeny, insignificant amount. Or y'know, all his calls and messages for the past week.

"Is this about D&D last week? It's not my fault you rolled a one on that magic potion and got turned into a newt. You didn't have to ride around in Kruk's pocket, you know. You could have chosen his shoulder. Although, you climbing into Leo's lap in real life was adorable, even if poor Sam will never be the same. I think you definitely helped the poor boy confirm his sexuality, though, because he really couldn't take his eyes off you, and his face was a lovely shade of fuchsia."

"It's not about that. I've just been busy trying to get things sorted for the shop." I was deliberately being vague, and we both knew it. I felt terrible because I'd always told him everything, but I couldn't ask Edward to bail me out again. First, he'd gotten me out of living in London, then he'd let me stay with him rent-free while I decided what to do, and then, to top it all off, he'd helped me set up the shop without asking for anything in return. I needed to stand on my own two feet for once, like the adult I was pretending to be.

"I'm not sure I believe you."

"It's the truth. Between the shop, and people asking about the workshops, and seeing Leo, I've just been swamped. You know how shit my time management is."

Edward hummed suspiciously. "How're things going with the *Empire* costume?" I asked, quickly changing the subject to something I knew would distract him. "Did the convention people get back to you? You said they wanted to arrange photo shoots with you and The Masked Gentleman. Are you gonna do it?"

"I know you're changing the subject, and I don't appreciate it."

"You still want to answer the questions though. I can hear it in your voice."

"Ugh, I do." He sighed dramatically, and I knew I'd successfully distracted him for at least the next twenty minutes. Maybe longer if I could find some good follow up questions. "And yes, they did. They want us to do appearances together for all four days, and they're offering photo ops." I heard the shudder in his voice. "If I commit murder, will you please remember to get me a decent lawyer and clear my internet history," Edward said. "I might have been Googling simple but effective ways to kill people, and I feel like that could be used against me as evidence in court."

"And there was me thinking you'd been watching weird porn like a normal person."

"Oh, I don't care about that. Everyone watches porn, and I highly doubt my choices would be considered that shocking."

I snorted. "Probably not. So how long will these photo ops last? Are they the sort people pay for?"

"Don't play dumb. You know they're exactly like that. You've been to enough cons to know how they work."

"Maybe I'll come have a shoot with you then. I might ask if you two can kiss."

"If you do that, I will disown you. And I won't even tell you that Jason Lu is going to be there."

"Holy shit, Jason Lu's gonna be there? Like Jason Lu from *Celestials*? Aka my future husband?"

"I'm sure Leo would have something to say about that, darling."

"Eh, I'm sure he'd understand. It's *Jason Lu*."

Edward laughed. I pictured Edward throwing his head back, eyes sparkling. Damn, I really missed him. Maybe I shouldn't have been avoiding him as much as I had. I'd just been sure he'd know something was wrong as soon as he saw me, and it would all come spilling out. The dark circles under my eyes were a sure-fire sign.

It wasn't like I wasn't going to bed. It was just that I was constantly plagued by horrific nightmares which meant I was only getting about four hours of sleep each night. The only time I slept better was when I was at Leo's. I didn't know if it was because his mattress was softer, or because his sheets smelt so fucking good, or because for some reason I felt instantly calmer with him beside me. I never had nightmares when I was with him, but I couldn't stay there every night. We hadn't been dating that long, and I didn't want to impose. Besides, I was so busy I'd hardly seen him, and it wasn't fair of me to expect him to let me stay with him just because I slept better around him.

Even if that was what I wanted more than anything in the world.

Leo made me feel like I mattered. Like I was important in some way. He made me feel like my self-worth didn't have to be inexorably tied to how much money I made, or how hard I worked, or how successful I was. Somehow I got the feeling Leo would want me no matter what.

I wished my own brain would get the message, but no matter how hard I tried I couldn't seem to get through to myself.

Edward and I chatted for a little bit longer before we finally said goodnight. I promised him I'd go over for dinner at some point soon. I picked up my laptop again and began working. I only had a couple more things to cross off my to-do list tonight, then I could finally fall into bed and hope I got more than four hours of sleep before the nightmares started again.

When I finally crawled into bed, it took me ages to fall asleep and my bed somehow felt full of infinite empty space. I curled myself into a ball and let tears slide down my cheeks, even if I wasn't sure why I was crying.

# CHAPTER TWENTY-THREE

*Primrose — I can't live without you*

**Leo**

SOMETHING WAS WRONG WITH JAY. I could feel it in my bones.

He'd been getting more and more distant over the past three weeks, but it was only in the past couple of days that I'd really noticed it. That was my fault because work had exploded after Mother's Day, and I'd found myself falling back into my old bad habit of staying at the shop far too late. I was absorbed in flowers, and I'd lost track of everything else. I'd seen Jay for Dungeons and Dragons and a couple of nights snuggled up in front of the telly, but that had been it. We'd mostly just been texting, but even that had petered off in the past week.

Jay had said he had lots to do, and I didn't doubt him. He'd been muttering fitfully about the website and social media last time I'd seen him, and he'd been fending off questions left and right about the steampunk festival. People didn't seem to understand that just because The Lost World was hosting the workshops, that didn't mean they were involved. One woman had apparently spent twenty minutes berating Jay about something to do with the number of tables. He said by the end he'd just given up because it wasn't worth arguing. The next time I saw Edward I'd definitely be having words.

The last time he'd stayed over, Jay had spent all night tossing and turning. It had only stopped when I'd put my arms around him and pulled him close, tucking him into me and running my hand soothingly up and down his chest. He'd slept soundly for the rest of the night, but the growing dark circles I'd seen under his eyes were starting to worry me. I got the impression that whatever had happened at mine was becoming a reoccurring thing, and I wondered how much sleep he was actually getting, but Jay brushed the question off every time I asked it.

I remembered sitting on his sofa the first time we'd hung out while he talked about his old job and how he'd worked excruciatingly long days because it was what he'd needed to do. He'd said he didn't want to go back to that, but I knew from experience those habits were hard to break. The guilt from taking even one night off was the hardest. Along with the little voice that said I'd never survive, much less flourish, if I stopped working for even a minute. It had taken a long time to banish those fears.

If I was being honest, they'd never really gone away. I'd just learnt how to deal with them.

Running a new business, especially a small one that

relied on customer support was really bloody hard. And I'd never have gotten through it if I hadn't had a couple of people—like my brother—pushing me on. Aaron had called me every week to ask how I was doing. I'd appreciated that. Even if sometimes he had used half the call to rant about random chef stuff. It had been a nice distraction though, which was why he'd probably done it. Even Aaron wasn't that much of an asshole.

I knew Jay had Edward, and he had me. I just hoped he'd ask for help if he needed it.

My mood didn't improve throughout the day, and I spent the whole time hiding in the back room making orders. I hoped Emily wouldn't notice or would just chalk it up to me being grumpy.

I wasn't giving her nearly enough credit.

"There's something wrong, and you're going to tell me what it is." It was a statement, not a question. I looked up from the arrangement I was working on to find Emily staring at me sternly. Given that I was perched on a stool and she was naturally nearly as tall as I was, she made quite a looming presence. "Come on. I'm good at listening."

I glanced at the front of the shop. "Is Alfie okay on his own?"

Alfie was the guy I'd hired as a third pair of hands. At eighteen, he was fresh out of a horticulture course at Riseholme College, and he'd been helping his mum make wedding flowers since he was six. He was chatty and earnest in a way I'd never figured out how to be, and he'd already spent an hour talking to Albert about Mary. I had a gut feeling he was going to do well here, especially since

Emily had taken him under her wing the moment he'd set foot in the door.

"He's fine." Emily waved her hand. "He's got a brain, and he knows how to use it. Now stop changing the subject."

"I'm worried about Jay," I said matter-of-factly.

"Why? Did he say something?"

"No. Nothing like that." I turned back to my flowers. I was always better at expressing myself when my hands were busy. It allowed me to process my thoughts in a neater way, helping me put them in order without me having to think about it. "He's been working a lot lately. and I don't think he's sleeping. He's been... distant."

Emily hummed thoughtfully. "How's the shop doing?"

"Okay, I think? I know it's been a little quiet, but he didn't seem worried last time I asked." That had been another question Jay had dodged with a smile. Now I was starting to wonder whether it had been a lie. Did he not trust me, or did he not want to worry me?

They were two sides of the same coin, only I didn't know which side was heads and which was tails. I didn't know how it had landed either.

Maybe he thought I'd think less of him if he was in trouble? Maybe he was worried things were falling apart, and he was desperately trying to keep going. I tried to remember everything he'd told me about his ex and his life in London. Kieran sounded like a bloody menace, but I didn't know exactly what he'd said to Jay or how long he'd let Jay believe working long hours was the best thing to do. I couldn't imagine how much it must have hurt Jay to be betrayed like that. If I ever saw Kieran, there was a good chance I'd punch him before he could even say hello.

"Maybe he really is busy. Impulsion is this weekend, and I saw the shop mentioned on the website, and Daniel mentioned Jay was trying to get the online store set up. Maybe he's been getting lots of orders?" There was a hopeful note in Emily's tone, and I desperately wanted to believe her, but something deep inside me was preparing for the worst.

"Maybe. I'll talk to him."

"That's probably the best idea," Emily said, giving me a little smile. "Why don't you go see him tonight? I can take Alfie through closing, and it'll stop you staying late too." She nudged my shoulder. "Come on. It'll be okay. Just talk to him. You're both adults, and you've both got brains and tongues. You should use them for once." I raised an eyebrow, and she smacked my arm. "And not in that way. Or at least not until you've talked to each other. Then you can bang each other's brains out."

"Words first. Got it."

"Besides, you two can't break up. I need that bookstore. I can't go there if you two aren't together. I'm sure there are rules against it, and I really like it there."

"I'm so glad you're thinking of me." I chuckled, but it was superficial at best. The worry sank deeper into my heart. I didn't want to lose Jay. I just needed to make sure he knew I was there for him, and I'd help him in any way I could.

"You're very welcome. Now, I shall go back to supervising my minion."

Emily disappeared back to the front of the store, and I heard her talking Alfie through the ordering system. I picked up a stem of stock, twirling it idly in my fingers, letting a plan coalesce in my mind. I wasn't good at talking to people, but it didn't look like I had a choice.

By the time I left Wild Things, I didn't have much more of a plan in mind. All I'd come up with was "tell Jay how I feel" and "make sure he feels supported", which were more like rough bullet points than an actual plan.

Angie pottered along beside me as we walked slowly towards The Lost World, happily enjoying the last of the afternoon sunshine and wagging her tail at everyone who passed us.

The worry that had formed earlier had seeped into my chest like an insidious poison, planting a seed of doubt where none had existed before.

Maybe I was part of the problem?

Running a new business was hard, and throwing a new relationship into the mix was like adding petrol to a bonfire and then chucking a couple of fireworks in for good measure. Maybe I shouldn't have come on to Jay so strong and given him some time to get settled, especially because I knew exactly what he was going through. I know he was the one who'd kissed me first, but I'd started this by pursuing him. I hoped I hadn't caused more problems than I'd solved.

The shop was quiet, and Jay sat behind the counter, studying something on his laptop screen. He looked up when the shop bell tinkled, but his smile was more pained than happy.

"Oh, hey. I didn't know you were coming by. Did I miss a message or something?" Jay glanced at his phone.

"No. I just wanted to stop in. Is that okay?"

"I mean, I guess… Sure."

"I've got Angie too. Can I bring her in?"

Jay nodded, and I held the door open long enough for my wiggly Staffy to squeeze through. As if sensing something was wrong, she trotted straight around the counter to Jay. His lips twitched, and he bent down to scratch her ears. I heard her tail thumping on the floor.

Jay looked pale, and the dark circles under his eyes had grown since I'd last seen him. He also looked stressed and sleep deprived, like he could do with eating a good meal then sleeping for twelve hours. One glance at him made something in my chest clench painfully. All I wanted to do was wrap him in my arms and protect him, even if it was from himself.

"What are you doing tonight?" I asked, watching his face carefully. He sighed, looking utterly defeated.

"I've got some work to do on the website, some emails to pass on to Edward, plus I need to double check everyone's layouts and requirements for the weekend, and I need to go over the shop's finances for next month. I think I need to make more changes."

"Is everything okay?"

"Not really." He chuckled sadly. He looked at me, eyes wide and full of sadness and fear. "I don't think I can do this anymore."

## CHAPTER TWENTY-FOUR

*Cyclamen — Resignation, Goodbye*

**Leo**

I FROZE. Then, like I was testing whether an icy lake would take my weight, I gingerly moved forward.

"What do you mean?" I kept my voice soft. "What can't you do?"

"Any of this," Jay said. He sounded like he was two seconds away from crying. "I'm broke, the shop is failing, I can't build a fucking website, I have no social media presence, nobody knows we exist, I have people emailing me day and night about these bloody workshops, and I'm working around the clock, but it feels like the more I do the more I fail. I'm utterly useless, and I should never have tried to do this. It's like London all over again."

I took another half step towards him. "It's not though. Let me help you."

"I can't ask you to do that. You have your own business to run."

"Yes, but I can do both. I'm your boyfriend. Please, let me help you." I could see the fear running across his face. It felt like he was slipping through my fingers. He was like water; no matter how much I tried to cup it in my hands, it was going to escape.

"Fuck, that's another thing I'm failing at." He chuckled, but it was a hollow, empty sound. It sent a chill down my spine, and I felt anger rising in my chest. It wasn't directed at Jay though. It was directed at me.

How the hell had I let it get this far? How had I not noticed what he was going through? Anger surged inside me, but it was all directed inwards. I knew how tough this was, and from the beginning of our friendship, I'd wanted to help Jay avoid the traps I'd fallen into. Maybe it was naïve or stupid of me to think I could protect him. Maybe it had never been my place. But now wasn't the time for self-flagellation. Jay was in too deep, lost to the maelstrom of his anxieties, and all I could do was try to not let him get swept away.

"You're not failing," I said. I took another step closer, reaching my hand out towards him. I was terrified it would go straight through him, like he was nothing more than a wisp of air, a ghost. "I know it's tough, but you can do it."

"I don't think I can." He slumped his shoulders. "Kieran was right. I'm useless. Nobody wants me."

"I want you." I took his hands in mine, cupping them together.

"Why?"

"Because you're brilliant," I said. I took a deep breath and cleared my throat. Now was the time to tell him everything I'd ever wanted to say. I had to hope it would be enough. *Oh God, please let it be enough.*

I couldn't bear the thought of losing him because he thought I'd be better off without him. That would be infinitely worse than him not wanting me for any other reason. I would never be better off without him.

"You're smart, and funny, and so bloody dedicated to this. I've never met anyone as driven as you are. You know more about books than anyone I've ever met. I don't want you to give this up. You deserve to live your dream, and I need you to let me help you because I love you, Jacob Morris. More than anything. You are bloody awesome, and I wish you could see what I see."

Jay stared at me, his eyes wide. There were tears clinging to his long, dark lashes. "You love me?"

I hadn't realised I'd said that out loud, but it was the truth. I wasn't going to deny it. "Yes, I do, because you're fucking amazing."

"I'm not." He swallowed, shaking his head. The colour had drained out of him, fear stamped across his face. "Please, I'm not worth it."

"I don't…" I had no idea what was going on. Had I said something wrong? I'd thought I had a handle on the situation, but I suddenly felt more out of control than ever. "You are. You are worth everything."

"No, no. Please. I'm not." He was crying now, fat tears rolling down his cheeks. His breath was coming in ragged pants, and his shoulders were shaking. I reached my arms out, pulling him into me. His fingers clutched at my t-shirt while he cried into my chest.

"It's okay," I murmured, stroking my fingers up and down his spine in the most soothing way I could imagine. "It's going to be okay."

Jay was quiet for a moment, then he let out a long, shuddering breath. "I can't do this."

"Yes, you can."

"No... I can't... not yet." He looked up at me sadly, eyes puffy and rimmed with red. A sudden rush of fear pierced my heart. Please don't let him be doing what I thought he was doing. "You're amazing, Leo. Truly you are. And I think I might love you too... and that's why I have to do this."

"Do what?"

"I-I... I need some space. Just a little." He took another breath. It sounded like he was trying to force the words out. I wondered if there was any way to stop them, to freeze time so he'd never be able to say the words I knew were going to break my heart. "I can't do this right now. Trying to run the shop and trying to have a relationship you're worthy of. You deserve so much more than I can give you. I don't want you to have to wait around for me to get done with work or blow off another date night because I have to fix something. I can't do that to you."

"What if I want you to?" I knew I sounded desperate, but it was all I had left. "I know what you're going through. I know how hard it is. I'm never going to expect you to be at my beck and call because I'm just the same sometimes. We can work it out, I promise. Please. Just... don't do this."

"I'm sorry," Jay said. He tilted his head up, pressing a gentle kiss to my lips. "It's only for now. I mean, that is... just let me have a little space to figure this out. Maybe just until after this weekend is over? I understand if you don't want that... I know I don't deserve you. If you don't want to wait, you don't have to..." His voice trailed off, and there was nothing but defeat in every line of his body. He looked utterly drained. "I know you want to help but... but this is something I need to do for myself for once. I can't let other people fix my mistakes again. I have to take responsibility for myself."

The pain inside me spread, seeping into my bones. I wished I could make him see what I saw, but more than anything, I wished he'd just let me in. Standing on his own two feet was one thing, but I wished he didn't think he had to do this alone.

Nothing had ever felt like this.

Jay was still looking at me, wondering if I'd answer him.

"You don't have to do this alone," I said. My hands came up to stroke his jaw, and I pressed another kiss to his lips.

"Please. Don't..."

"I love you." One more kiss. Just one. Because I had no idea if I'd ever get to kiss him again, and I needed to know this wasn't it. "Just... you know where I am."

Jay nodded his head, but he didn't say anything. He just stepped back, out of my arms. Away from me. I bit my lip, trying to feel something, but my body was numb.

I turned away. "Come on, Angie. Let's go home." She whined, and the sound pulled at my heart. Jay made a little sniffling noise behind me. Angie whined again. "No, baby, we can't stay."

And with that, I turned and walked out of The Lost World, away from the man I loved, away from the man who I'd thought could be my future. I just had to hope I was making the right decision.

## CHAPTER TWENTY-FIVE

*Camellia (Pink) — Longing for you*

**Leo**

EVER SINCE I'D left Jay at The Lost World, I'd been consumed with regret. I wanted to be angry with him for walking away and not talking to me about how he felt, despite the fact he'd made me that promise.

I wanted to feel anything other than despondency.

My chest felt like an empty shell.

Despite everything, I wasn't angry at Jay. I just wished I'd been able to help him. That was what hurt the most—the fact that I hadn't been able to do anything. And that I still couldn't. I knew Jay needed space to figure things out, and my only option was to wait him out.

I could do that. The Yorkshire in me made me stubborn as a rock.

But right now, it just felt like I had a rock in the pit of my stomach.

I wanted to feel something, anything, except the bleak emptiness and longing for the man I loved that sat heavy inside me.

When I woke up the next morning, I wondered if it was even worth getting out of bed. It didn't feel like it. Even Angie seemed to sense I wasn't happy, because she'd spent the night curled up next to me, and as soon as I'd stirred she'd burrowed up next to me, the way she always did when I was ill or upset.

I debated messaging Emily and asking her to run the workshops and getting Alfie to take over the shop. But I knew that would never work. I didn't want Emily finding out what had happened with Jay, not yet anyway. The last thing he needed was the wrath of Emily looming over him. Plus I was still hoping it had been a dream.

My mind kept replaying the conversation I'd had with Jay over and over. Part of me still clung to the hope that this wasn't it, that somehow Jay would come to his senses and realise his mistake. I already knew I'd forgive him if he did because I knew exactly how he felt. I knew he was so caught up in his own fears and anxieties he couldn't think of anything else. As much as I wanted to ignore his request for space, I knew I needed to give him what he wanted. Even if that was going to be incredibly difficult when I literally had to be in the same building as him all weekend.

Well, twice that weekend.

But that was enough.

Another part of my brain was already pushing me to

accept that it was over. It felt like a lead weight in my stomach. I just wished he'd let me in. And I wished I could have seen he was in trouble. I'd failed him in exactly the way I hadn't wanted to.

Eventually, after staring at my ceiling for another thirty minutes, I heaved myself out of bed and into the shower. After a quick wash, I pulled on my clothes for the day—a white shirt, a floral patterned waistcoat that Emily had made me especially for the occasion, and some dark jeans—before pulling my hair into the neatest bun I could manage. One quick glance in the mirror told me I looked a hell of a lot better than I felt.

Twenty minutes later, Angie and I made our way into town. We were a bit later than I'd planned, but I couldn't find the energy to care.

The Bailgate was already thrumming with people setting up stands for the day, and the sounds and smells of sizzling food from a couple of stands doing an early trade in bacon and sausage sandwiches filled the air. I grabbed a couple for Emily, Alfie, and I as well as getting them to chuck in a couple of bits of bacon for my spoilt dog who was practically dancing at my feet in anticipation. At least I could make her happy.

I tried not to look at The Lost World as I went past, focusing my gaze on the cobbled stones in front of me. I'd have to look at it later when I went back to run the workshops, but for now I could pretend to be happy in my ignorance.

Emily and Alfie were already at Wild Things organising some displays. Alfie was wearing a waistcoat that matched mine while Emily was wearing a full-on Victorian day dress complete with embroidered flowers. How the hell she found time to make these things was beyond me, but I couldn't deny it was impressive.

"How'd it go?" Emily asked, a cheerful note in her voice.

"Fine," I grunted as I made my way past her and into the back room. I didn't really want to have this conversation now. In fact, I didn't want to have any conversation at all. "I brought breakfast." I put the paper bag on the side and pulled out my own bacon roll.

"Oh, that's lovely of you, sweetie." Emily paused, and I knew she was looking at me. "Are you sure you're okay? You look awfully pale."

"Fine." I searched around for a reason. "Just nervous. There's going to be a lot of people." As far as excuses went, it was a valid one. I was expected to stand up for an hour each day and teach a workshop in front of twenty to thirty people I didn't know. Why the hell had I agreed to this?

Emily hummed sympathetically. "You're going to do great. Why don't you stay here for a bit and run over your notes and make some orders? That'll take your mind off it."

"Thanks." I took the order list off the wall and read through it while I ate my bacon roll. There was a lot to do, and Emily was right, it would keep me distracted.

For now at least.

I kept my mind focused on work for the rest of the morning, burying myself in flowers. Every time I felt my thoughts wandering, I forced them back to the bouquet in front of me. It helped a little, and by the time two o'clock rolled around, I felt marginally better. Until I looked up and realised I needed to head up to The Lost World and set up.

The workshop was from half-two until half-three and there was a fifteen-minute break between each session to allow the next person to set up. I sighed and rubbed my eyes, cracking my knuckles and wishing I was anywhere except here. I had no idea how I was going to face Jay without breaking down, but it was too late to backout now.

With Alfie's help, I carried some buckets of pre-cut flowers up to the shop, a bag of floral tape, tissue paper, and ribbon slung over my shoulder. I was just going to teach people to make a simple little posy of roses, wax flower, and stock. I had a couple of different colours of roses, which would change the meaning slightly, and together they'd make a pretty combination. Plus, it wouldn't make too much mess either.

The Lost World was teeming with people either perusing the shelves or clearing out of the last workshop when we arrived. I saw Edward, resplendent in blue, cream, and gold with a large top hat adorned with goggles perched on top of his platinum hair, chatting animatedly to a couple of people. He must have seen me because he beamed and called out.

"Downstairs is ready when you are, Leo."

I nodded and made my way towards the stairs, trying not to look for Jay. I had a job to do, and if I saw him now, I knew it would break me.

The workshop space was empty, the tables neatly laid out in little circles… the same way we had it for game night. I paused at the bottom of the stairs and swallowed. My heart was thundering in my chest, my mind flooded with memories of helping Jay clean up after games nights, making him sit down so I could fold down the tables, and exchanging little kisses every time we passed each other.

"Are you okay?" Alfie asked from behind me. "Is there a problem?"

"No." I shook my head and stepped into the room, carrying my bag and bucket over to the table at the front. "Put the bucket down there. Please." I pointed at a space on the table.

"Will you need me to come back later to pick them up?" Alfie asked cheerfully. He always had such a happy grin on his face that I felt bad for being surly all morning and avoiding him and Emily. He wasn't to blame for this fucked-up situation.

"No. I'll manage."

"Alrighty, I'll see you in a bit. Good luck!" He disappeared and left me staring around, wondering what the fuck I was doing.

I didn't have time to dwell on my thoughts, though, because two minutes later people started arriving and taking their seats. The room filled up with happy chatter while bile rose in my throat. I pushed my nerves away, digging a notebook out of my bag that had all my notes for the talk. I'd planned to talk for the first half about floriography and then get everyone making something for the rest of the session. It had seemed like a good plan, but now I wasn't so sure.

Not that I had time to change it. I took a deep breath,

glancing at the sea of faces in front of me. Then I began to speak.

Surprisingly enough, it hadn't been as torturous as I'd imagined.

The twenty-five people who'd signed up were all engaged and seemed genuinely interested in what I had to say. They'd even asked questions about different flowers and why the meanings varied depending on where they were from. By the time the workshop ended, I realised I'd actually had fun.

But whatever mood boost I'd received soured the moment I packed up my stuff and climbed the stairs. Jay stood behind the counter, chatting with a group of customers. He was wearing a white shirt with the sleeves rolled up to the elbows, a blue cravat, and a dark brown waistcoat. There was a dark hat perched jauntily on top of his head, decorated with goggles and bronzed cogs. He looked every inch like a steampunk adventurer off to explore the world, but as I watched him, I saw the dark circles around his eyes and the way his eyelids almost looked puffy. The smile on his face looked like one he'd plastered on, rather than the genuine one I'd seen light up rooms.

He looked like he was pretending not to be utterly fucking miserable.

He looked the same way I felt.

Jay's head turned, his eyes locking onto mine. For a moment I wondered if he was going to say something. Then

I remembered I'd promised to give him space, even if it stung like a thousand wasps. I wrenched my gaze away from him and stomped out of the shop.

Maybe tomorrow would be better.

Except it wasn't. If anything, Sunday was worse.

I'd hardly slept Saturday night, wondering whether I should have said something to Jay or at least acknowledged his presence. By the time I had to get up I'd only had about three hours of sleep.

I pulled on my clothes, hoping I looked more presentable than I felt, then went to work. The shop was still empty when I got there. I grabbed the list of orders and threw myself into work, barely acknowledging Emily or Alfie when they arrived. Emily tried to get me to talk, but I just snapped at her and told her to leave me alone. For once she did. But I was too tired and grumpy to wonder if she'd figured things out.

My mind was whirring. I wished above anything else that I could tell Jay how I felt about him. That I wasn't angry at him, that I missed him, that I hadn't stopped thinking about him even for a minute. That I still loved him.

I caught sight of some mint sprigs and the little bucket of tea roses I had left over, an idea forming in my mind.

But I didn't have time to act on it. Not yet.

As two o'clock rolled around, I dutifully packed up my bag and with Alfie's help, took the buckets up to The Lost World. The bookshop was even busier today, and the last workshop had overrun, so by the time I got everything downstairs it was time to begin. I hadn't even seen Jay. Then again, maybe that was a good thing.

The workshop passed quickly, but I could feel my heart wasn't in it. I tried my best, but I was running low on anything resembling enthusiasm. When I'd finished, it was all I could do to pack up and get out of there.

I needed to think. The idea that had been percolating in my brain was finally coming to fruition, and I needed the quiet of the flower shop to bring it to life.

As I reached the top of the stairs, I glanced around, but Jay was nowhere to be seen. My heart sank. Even though I was supposed to be giving him space, that didn't mean I didn't want to see him. It hurt like hell, but even a glance was better than nothing. I just wanted to make sure he was okay.

On my way out the door, I walked straight into Edward, today dressed in a more elaborate version of the adventuring outfit I'd seen Jay in yesterday. It was beautifully made, but I almost preferred the simplicity of Jay's. He'd looked so handsome.

"Oh, hello! I was just coming to check everything went okay. I've had some wonderful feedback."

"It was great," I said woodenly. "I'm sorry, I have to get back to the shop." I moved to step past Edward, then I paused. I reached into my bag and pulled out the little posy I'd made that afternoon to demonstrate. It had a single red rose set amongst some stock and wax flowers. The rose was a little squashed, which was why I'd used it. Looking at it, I wondered if it was a cliché gesture, but it would have to do for now.

"Can you give this to Jay?" I asked, handing Edward the posy. He looked at me with confusion as if wondering why I didn't give it to him myself. "I have to go."

I left Edward standing on the doorstep and headed for Wild Things.

I had planning to do.

When Emily found me on Tuesday morning, I'd been up since five and was three cups of strong, sweet tea into a bouquet.

When I'd gotten back to the shop on Sunday, I'd realised I didn't have everything I wanted, but by then it was too late to do anything about it. Instead, I'd grabbed pen and paper and started planning, only finishing up when Emily had forced me to go home on pain of death.

I'd spent Monday driving around Lincolnshire trying to find the flowers I needed. Overkill? Probably. But I needed Jay to know how I felt about him, and there was only one way I knew how to do that. Even if he wouldn't quite understand.

I'd spent Monday afternoon putting the bouquet together, taking it apart and rebuilding it at least three times. I had sprigs of spearmint for warm sentiment, bright magenta zinnia for both lasting affection and thoughts of an absent friend as well as stock and an abundance of tea roses. I'd bought nearly every tea rose the wholesalers had, carefully picking out the most beautiful blooms from among them. The rest would do fine for the shop. I'd always said I wasn't a tea rose person, but every flower had a time and a place to be used, and this was their time to shine. They meant "I'll remember always" and I couldn't think of anything more fitting.

By the time I went home on Monday night, I'd been satisfied, but this morning I'd realised I didn't like it at all. So now I was remaking it. Again.

"Feeling any better this morning?" Emily asked, a cheerful note in her voice. I'd lied on Sunday and said I had a headache, using it as a poor excuse for being a miserable bastard.

"Not really."

"What's wrong, Leo? You've been in an awful mood all weekend. Did something happen?" I looked up at her. I don't know what was written on my face, but her expression fell. "Oh shit! I'm so sorry. What happened?"

"It's fine." My voice sounded numb. "Jay just… needs some space."

Emily gave an exasperated sigh. "Fuck! When did he tell you?"

"Friday."

"And you didn't think to tell me?"

"I didn't want to worry you."

"You were just grumpy all weekend instead," she said dryly. Then she sighed again. "I'm going to kick that boy's ass."

"Please don't."

"He hurt you."

"He's hurting too. More than I thought." I sighed,

finishing up the arrangement and trimming the last of the stems, tying them together with some white ribbon. It was the most beautiful bouquet I'd ever created. I didn't think I'd ever make anything that perfect again. "Will you do me a favour?"

"Sure, what is it?"

"Can you take this to The Lost World?" I felt stupid even asking. I was sure she'd tell me to do it myself.

Emily looked at the flowers and then at me, deliberating quietly, then she gave me a small smile. "Sure. Want me to do it now?"

"Just at some point today. Please don't murder Jay while you're there."

"I'm making no promises, but I'll try my best."

"Thanks, Em."

"No worries." She wrapped her arms around me, squeezing me tightly. "It's gonna be okay. I promise."

I had to hope she was right.

It was what I'd been holding on to all weekend.

## CHAPTER TWENTY-SIX

*Geranium — Stupidity, Folly*

**Jay**

IF THERE WAS A BIGGER idiot in the universe, I wanted to meet them and introduce myself.

I'd completely and utterly fucked up. I didn't know what was worse—knowing that I'd fucked everything up with Leo or knowing that it hadn't made a jolt of difference. In fact, it had made everything worse.

I'd cried myself to sleep every night since Friday, curled up in a ball and sobbing into my pillow. The first night had been the worst. Now I just felt numb.

I'd crawled my way through the weekend in a zombie-like stupor. I couldn't tell you whether or not the festival workshops had been a success. I'd barely even registered them happening, and yesterday I'd just bedded down in my blanket fortress and slept, grateful the shop was closed.

I hadn't wanted to get up when my alarm had gone off this morning, and I'd debated simply shutting up shop for the day and hiding under the duvet. But since that was the complete opposite of what I'd hoped to achieve with this ridiculous request for space, I had to drag myself out of bed.

God, I was so stupid. Why the fuck couldn't I just admit I needed help? Why couldn't I let Leo in? He'd offered so many times, but my stubborn brain had been determined that I should do it myself. Those brain weasels had a lot to answer for.

I dragged myself through stock count and was knee-deep in paperwork and wallowing in misery when there was a knock at the door. I wasn't expecting any deliveries or any visitors, but for half a glorious moment I thought it might be Leo.

When I pulled the door open though, I saw Emily holding a bouquet of flowers.

My heart tightened painfully, like it was caught in a vice. Emily looked at me, the expression on her face a clear deliberation between murder and pity. I wondered if I'd get a choice. I probably deserved the former.

"I'd ask if you meant to hurt Leo, but considering you look like you haven't slept in a year, I don't think you're doing much better." She handed me the flowers and gave me a sad smile. "This is for you. From Leo. I think he spent the better part of three days working on it."

"Oh…" I stroked my fingers across the petals of a pretty pink tea rose. The bouquet had an array of them in soft colours, dotted amongst stock and some other things I didn't recognise. The vice around my heart had suddenly been swapped out for an iron maiden. "It's beautiful."

"Yeah, it is."

We stood in silence. Neither of us knew what to say. I wanted to ask a thousand questions about Leo and how he was coping. I'd seen him briefly on Saturday, but the pained look on his face had ruined me, and on Sunday I'd hidden from him in the little stockroom halfway up the stairs.

But that wasn't the point of this. I'd stupidly wanted space to give myself a chance to focus. I couldn't do that if I was constantly thinking about Leo. I needed to sort my life out first, then I could see if he still wanted me. I just had to get through the next couple of days. Things would be easier after that.

Even if I already knew they wouldn't.

"Can you tell him thank you?" I asked.

"Sure." She turned to go, then paused, looking back at me over her shoulder. "He'll wait, but he won't wait forever. I hope this is worth it."

I heard the sadness now, an aching note of it, bubbling under the surface. She had every right to be upset with me. I knew that, even if all I wanted to do was attempt to justify my actions, but I wasn't sure if she was actually upset with me or for me. There was a pained look on her face, but I didn't understand what it meant.

"Jay," she said, her voice catching. "I don't know what's going on, and I know Leo is my friend, but if you need something, just ask. You're my friend too, and I hate seeing you like this. I don't want either of you to hurt."

"Thanks… I'll, um, I'll let you know."

Emily nodded. Then she left without a backwards glance. I looked at the flowers again, wishing they didn't feel like a goodbye.

I couldn't be arsed to close the shop up again, so I just flipped the sign to open and left it. Tuesdays were quiet anyway, and I doubted I'd be disturbed. I walked back towards the counter and found the vase for the flowers, trying not to think about the day Leo had brought me the vase and the first bouquet. It was still the only vase I owned.

For the next couple of hours, I tried to keep myself busy.

I did some more poking at the website, which was starting to look vaguely presentable since I'd abandoned trying to get the plug-ins to work and stuck with the bare minimum.

I ordered some stock, momentarily revelling in the idea of new books.

I served a couple of customers and helped a mum find some good books to read to her six-year-old. I had quite a nice selection of diverse kids' books, and we spent an hour talking through them and deciding on the best ones for her son. In the end, she'd bought three children's books and something for herself. It had been a nice distraction, but the best feeling was knowing I'd helped someone find books they'd love. That was why I'd opened this shop in the first place. It had been nice to remember that.

Of course, my peace and quiet didn't last long.

Hurricane Edward arrived just after two, a swirl of wrath wrapped in black and gold. He didn't even use my full name when he saw me, a sure sign he'd gone beyond upset to furious. I'd only ever seen Edward this mad once before, and that was when someone at a comic con had tried to start a debate with him about the place of women in fandom. The troll had said women had no place except to look pretty. Edward had been one minute away from a ruthless, verbal dissection explaining exactly how stupidly small-brained that idea was by the time I'd intervened. Not that I hadn't been tempted to let him continue.

"Darling, what is going on? I have been informed by a little bird that you asked Leo for some space, and I have come to see what has driven you to such madness." I sighed. Emily had clearly ratted me out. I'd gotten through the whole weekend without him finding out, mostly because I'd hardly seen him, only to be undone in four hours. I knew I shouldn't have introduced Edward to Emily at game night. Edward ignored my sigh and continued.

"Have you, in fact, lost your marbles? Do you need me to find you some new ones? Or would you like me to list all of the reasons this is a horrible decision?" He fixed me with a glare, looking like some beautiful avenging angel. "Perhaps though, we can start with you explaining yourself?"

"Aren't you supposed to be on my side? You're my best friend." Edward rolled his eyes at me.

"Of course I'm on your side, which is why I'm doing this. I'm attempting to prevent you from doing something monumentally stupid."

"Please, babe. I can't deal with this. I just... I just needed some space."

Edward's expression softened. "Deal with what? Is this to do with why you've been avoiding me lately?"

"No." Edward raised an eyebrow and my resolve crumpled. I was tired of fighting. I just needed to tell someone. "Maybe? I just… I can't do this anymore." I flopped down onto the floor behind the counter, bringing my knees to my chest. I hoped the shop wouldn't suddenly fill up. Now that I'd sat down, I didn't know if I could get back up.

Edward's boots clacked on the carpet, suddenly appearing in front of me. I hadn't realised the laces were gold. He sat down, cross-legged.

"Can't do what?" he asked, softly. "Darling, please tell me what's wrong?"

"This." I gestured around me airily as if that would explain it. "The shop is failing, babe. I'm not making enough money, and nothing I'm doing has changed that."

"But I thought you were building a website? And a social media profile? And there were so many people in here during the festival."

I chuckled hollowly. "Yeah, but that was one weekend, and most of them weren't local. And I'm trying to get the website stuff sorted, but I'm failing at that too."

"Why didn't you say something? I could help you. I already said I know someone I can put you in touch with. He's Welsh, very lovely, does a fabulous Aqua Man cosplay. The Jason Momoa version, not the comics." Edward's expression was earnest, and whatever wrath he'd come in with had dispersed. He was more summer breeze than hurricane now.

"I can't… You've done enough."

"What do you mean 'done enough'?"

"It's just…" I took a deep breath. How could I make him

understand? "You came and got me from London, you let me live with you for nine months without taking rent, you invested in my business—which is now failing—you spent hours helping me set it up, and you still come to help out even though you have better things to do. I-I..." I took another deep breath, trying to steady my racing heart. "I can't keep relying on you to swoop in and rescue me like my knight in shining armour. I can't let anyone do that. I need to stand on my own two feet for once. And that means I have to do this by myself."

"Well, that's the biggest load of bollocks I've ever heard."

"What?" I stared at him. Edward was looking at me like I'd suddenly grown three heads and started spouting gibberish.

"Do you know why I did those things? It's because I love you, you utter dumbass. You are my best friend in the world, and I wanted to help you. I didn't do those things because I had to. I did them because I wanted to. And Leo's the same. I bet you he knows exactly what you're going through because running a new business is fucking terrifying."

"But—"

"Don't you 'but' me. These things are hard. Really fucking hard. And that's why you need friends and people to help you. Do you think I do everything myself?"

I paused. I'd never thought about that before. I'd always assumed he did, but now I wasn't so sure, simply because of the way he'd said it. "No?"

"You don't sound sure."

"That's because I'm not."

Edward chuckled, but it was a fond noise. "You're adorable, my love. No, I don't. I have a PA who helps answer my emails and does some of my social media and helps organise appearances for me. His name's Lewis. I'm sure you've met him. He's got pink hair and a voice like a foghorn when he's angry... anyway, that's not my point. I couldn't do half the things I do without him because he gives me time. And also, I'm absolutely useless with half the things he does for me, so it's easier to get him to do it rather than worrying about it myself." Edward was very good at making his point in a roundabout way, but I had to admit it made sense. Especially now I thought about everything he did on a day-to-day basis. "It's not a bad thing to ask for help."

"But... I keep needing help." Edward's logic was like a magical weapon of light, beating the brain weasels back into their box and destroying the doubts they'd sown, but they weren't going to go down without a fight.

"And that's okay. Nobody's expecting you to do this yourself." He reached out, placing his hand on my knee. "Standing on your own two feet and being responsible for yourself doesn't mean you have to put your mental and physical health at risk. And it doesn't mean you have to put your life on the back burner either. You found a man who adores you and who tells you that every single day. Let him love you and trust him to help you."

"I'm not even sure Leo will still love me after the stunt I pulled," I said, shaking my head.

"Of course he does."

"How do you know?"

"Because of this," Edward said, pulling out a slightly squashed posy from his pocket. "I'm sorry. I meant to give it to you the other day, but I forgot. I don't think it matters though, because those flowers say more than this ever could." I stared at the battered red rose and then back at him, raising my eyebrow. I had no idea what he was talking about.

"What do you mean?" I glanced up at the bouquet that was sitting on the counter.

Edward sighed exasperatedly. "You know for somebody who likes books, you're very ignorant."

"Rude. We're not all living out some gothic Victorian fantasy life like you."

"I feel like that was supposed to be a dig, but I'm taking it as a compliment." He smiled sweetly. "Flowers have meanings. There's a whole language built around them. What do you think Leo did his workshops on?"

"Okay… and?" I got the feeling I was missing something very obvious, but my common sense was still slow to function thanks to my long running exhaustion.

"And every single flower or bouquet that beautiful man has ever given you has had a meaning! Honestly, darling, I love you, but you are very dense."

"Wait… all of them?" My mind began to whirl. I looked up at the bouquet on the counter… at the colourful selection of tea roses, the stocks, and the others I couldn't place… and then I thought about the thornless yellow roses, and the daffodils, and the tulips, and all the other flowers that Leo had given me over the past few months.

Had Leo been telling me how he felt about me all along?

"Every single one," Edward said. He pulled out his phone, tapping frantically. "Here, look at this." He shoved the screen under my nose. It was a website listing flower names and their meanings. My fingers were trembling as I took the phone from him. "The meanings are a little varied depending on the website, and I think there's a bit of difference between the UK and America, but this is a pretty good one."

"You knew?" I wanted to be mad at him, but I was too busy being overwhelmed by the list in front of me.

"I had my suspicions. I thought you had figured it out."

"No! I've never heard of this before."

Edward sighed and patted my knee like I was a small dog. "It's a good thing you have me."

I wanted to argue with him, but then my eyes found daffodils on the screen and my thoughts ground to a halt.

*Daffodil — Regard, Unrequited Love, Respect*

Oh...

I scrolled down faster, looking for more meanings.

*Rose (Red) — I love you, Love, Desire*
*Rose (Yellow) — Friendship, Joy, Gladness*
*Rose (Tea) — I'll Remember Always*
*Rose (Thornless) — Love at first sight*
*Roses (Assorted Colours) — You're everything to me*

And finally...

*Tulips—Love, Passion*
*Tulips (Pink)—Perfect Love*

The breath disappeared from my lungs as the words on the screen punched into my chest. This couldn't be real. This couldn't be happening. I looked up again at the bouquet on the counter, my eyes stinging with tears as they fixed on the colourful tea roses.

And then ringing from the bell over the door pierced the air.

## CHAPTER TWENTY-SEVEN

*Hawthorn — Hope*

**Jay**

THE SOUND SENT a shockwave through me, dragging me back to the present.

The present where I sat on the floor behind the shop counter, trying not to cry. Very professional. I shoved Edward's phone back into his hand, motioning to him to keep quiet.

"We're not finished with this," I hissed as I ran my hand through my hair and climbed to my feet.

There was a woman examining the new release shelves. Her dark red hair was pulled up into a long ponytail and she was wearing retro, cat-eye glasses. They were a pale, mint green. Something about her was oddly familiar, but I couldn't place it.

"Hey," I said, trying to at least act like the professional I was supposed to be. "Welcome to The Lost World."

"Oh hi," she said, turning and giving me a smile. Her face was even more familiar now that I could see all of it, but I still had no idea where I'd seen her before. "I didn't see you there."

"Sorry, I was looking for something under the counter." I chuckled. "I should really be more organised."

"I totally get that."

"Is there anything in particular you're looking for?"

"Not really. Just browsing." She ran her finger across the cover of a new release, smiling at it fondly.

"Well, up here we have the new releases, adult fiction—mostly science fiction and fantasy with some horror and crime—and then downstairs we have YA, children's fiction, romance, a little bit of literary fiction and there's also some writing spaces and armchairs if you need somewhere to chill." After one of our game nights, I'd ended up leaving a couple of extra tables out because I couldn't get them in the cupboard, and someone had said they made a nice writing space. I'd added a few extra bits, like a hot drinks station to one of the low units at the side, and I was really pleased with it. Now I just needed writers to use it.

"Really? You have writing spaces?"

"Well, more a couple of tables and chairs, nothing fancy really, but there's a kettle and some tea, coffee, and hot chocolate sachets. And some power outlets too. I have the Wi-Fi password somewhere too if you want it." I looked at the notebook covered in scribbles and the scraps of paper sticking out of it. "Somewhere" being the operative term.

"Actually, if you don't mind, I'll go without it. I've been looking for somewhere quiet to get some work done. Is that okay?"

"Sure, go ahead. Just watch out, the stairs are quite steep. Let me know if you need anything."

"Thanks." She gave me a big smile, and with a last look at the book, she headed towards the stairs.

Edward popped up beside me as soon as she descended. "Who was that?"

"I don't know, but she looks oddly familiar." I pulled at my lip, trying to convince my brain to dig deep into its memory archives to find what I was looking for. I stepped around the counter, heading for the new release bookcase and picking up the book she'd been looking at—*When Emily Addison Speaks*.

It was a hardback with a shimmering black wrap embossed with silver lettering. The book was a new one that I'd had the hardest time getting my paws on because it had sold out everywhere as soon as it was released. I'd managed to get two cases of American imports from Gardeners, but I thought that would be all I'd get for a while.

I turned the book over, noticing all the praise dotted around the blurb. It was a romantic fantasy about a girl who could manipulate people's emotions in a world where magic was forbidden. She had to spend all her time pretending to be something she wasn't, hiding away from people in an attempt to keep herself safe. Until she met another girl who could do the same thing. If that wasn't an allegory for queerness, I didn't know what was.

I'd been a big fan of the author, Annabel Monteforte, for a long time. She had started small, struggled for a while, and built up a huge online fanbase. She hadn't been an overnight success, but she'd never given up. I'd always admired her tenacity, but what I loved most was the way her words poured off the page and into my heart. Each one of her books made me feel something I'd never experienced before. It was heady and beautiful. I'd been saving *When Emily Addison Speaks* to read later, mostly because I wasn't sure I'd be able to deal with the book hangover I knew I'd get from it.

I flipped the back cover open and froze. Smiling up at me from the author photo was the same woman who was now writing in the basement of my shop: Annabel Monteforte.

The air in my lungs escaped in a little squeak as I carefully put the book back on my shelf. Then I flailed my arms, gesturing frantically to Edward, who was looking at his phone and peering at my flowers. Oh shit, the flowers. The messages. Leo. Argh, why did everything have to happen at once?

"Edward." I hissed, practically running to the counter. "Edward!"

"What? Why are we whispering?"

"Do you know who that woman is?" I leant in closer, hoping she couldn't hear us. The last thing I wanted was to scare off my favourite author by being a complete dipshit. "It's Annabel Monteforte."

"What?" Edward started at me. "You can't be serious?"

"Deadly. It's her. Holy shit. I'm going to die. Freakin' Annabel Monteforte is in my shop!"

"Okay. Okay. We need to be cool."

"Yeah. Cool. Okay, I can do cool."

Edward chuckled. "Maybe stop freaking out over her for a second and go back to freaking out about the flowers and the fact that Leo is clearly in love with you and, although he's giving you physical space, would clearly like to remind you how he feels for a minute."

"Yeah… I can do that." I took a deep breath, releasing it slowly. "What are these?" I asked, pointing to the bright pink flowers I didn't recognise. They had a slightly rounded shape with long petals.

"Zinnia. They mean 'thoughts of an absent friend'. But, magenta ones also mean 'lasting affection'."

"Oh… So we have 'lasting affection', 'you're everything to me', and 'I'll remember always'." My heart swelled with every word as the realisation sank deeper into my chest. I'd been an idiot.

"Don't forget the 'warm sentiment' from the mint leaves," Edward said, pointing at some little sprigs of green I hadn't noticed. "And the 'affection' and 'lasting beauty' of the stock. And the 'love' of that little red rose there. I told you he still loved you."

"I still… I fucked everything up though."

"Have you? Have you really?"

"I don't know." This bouquet of flowers told me one thing—that Leo still had feelings for me, that he still cared, that he missed me—but I was still worried, even if my old worries had been replaced by new ones. I'd been terrified I couldn't give Leo the attention he deserved and that our relationship would come second while I got my feet underneath me. Now I wasn't sure I could be the boyfriend he deserved. Leo deserved someone better than me. Someone who wasn't going to run away when things got difficult. Someone who'd actually talk to him like we'd promised we would.

God, I was such a fucking idiot. If I wanted to make things right, if I ever wanted to have a chance of getting Leo back, there were some things I needed to do first. I turned to look at Edward.

"I don't suppose you happen to know anyone who's good with websites?"

He smiled and nodded. "Of course. What do you need?"

Two hours later, I had an email from Edward's Welsh friend, Reuben, confirming that he'd work on the website, his initial thoughts on what we could do quickly, and the promise of a Skype call as soon as possible to chat things out.

Reuben had even offered to do it for mates' rates because he and Edward were close, and nothing I could say would change his mind. He'd said the world needed more queer safe spaces, especially ones that weren't clubs, and he was happy to help. I'd have to ask Edward what sort of books he liked and put together a little thank you package for him.

I also had a string of WhatsApp messages from Lewis, offering to give me a crash course in social media in return for keeping Edward from stalking The Masked Gentleman's Instagram. I wasn't sure how achievable that was, but I promised to try. I'd probably just change Edward's password. That would keep him distracted for a few days.

Edward had also procured a large packet of chocolate chip shortbread, which was helping to settle my nerves. I was waiting for the overwhelming surge of guilt because I was sure I was being a needy pain in the ass, even if everyone had been incredibly lovely so far.

My to-do list was already looking a hell of a lot more manageable. Every time I caught sight of the flowers on the counter and the little posy propped up against the vase, I was spurred on to be better. If I could get this under control, I could apologise to Leo, and I would feel like I was the kind of person he deserved.

Edward had disappeared up to my flat to make us some tea, and I was nibbling a biscuit while making a list of what I needed the website to do for Reuben when I heard footsteps coming up from downstairs. Annabel appeared with a relaxed smile on her face, carrying her laptop bag and a couple of children's books.

"Hey, Annabel. Did you manage to get your writing done?" I asked, pushing my laptop out of the way so she could put the books down. She didn't say anything about me figuring out who she was, but she didn't seem too bothered by it.

"A little bit, but I have to admit I spent a lot of time looking at your children's book selection. It's amazing! I'm going to get these for my niece."

"Thanks." I felt my face heating which probably made

me look like a complete idiot. I grabbed a paper bag and began scanning the books through using the phone app I had. It was so much easier than using a huge till. "I really wanted to have a diverse selection of books. There's more through there." I pointed at the other room. "It's mostly science-fiction and fantasy and a lot of queer books."

"I love that. It's nice to see a space like this nearby. It's so warm and welcoming. Did I see a sign for a games night on the pinboard near the stairs?" Annabel picked up the bag of books and tucked them under her arm while she searched for her wallet. I mentioned the total before continuing.

"Yeah, we run a game night every other Wednesday. I'd love to get a book club started, and I've had some offers to run an inclusive pop-up pampering session. I just haven't had a chance to get them started."

"Well, it would be awesome if you do! I'll tell my younger sibling to get down here for games night. They've been looking for somewhere to game, but they're only seventeen, and they're a bit nervous."

"Send them along. Everyone's very welcoming, and we'd love to have them."

"Amazing. Thanks." She gave me a beaming smile and turned to leave.

"Before you go," I said, taking a deep breath, still not quite sure whether I should ask the question on my tongue. "Would, um, would it be too much trouble… um, could I get a selfie with you please?"

"Sure." Annabel pulled out her phone, and I ducked around the counter to come and stand next to her. If there was ever a time to act like a normal human, it was now… I just had to manage it.

"I, um, I love your books by the way. But I'm saving the new one because I know I won't get anything done while I'm reading it."

She laughed. "I'm the same when I read books I love. I was surprised you still had some." She shook her head. "Sorry, that sounds so arrogant. I mean, I cried when my editor called me to say they'd sold out and were going for a second print run within the first week. I honestly thought she was joking. I told her to stop pulling my leg."

"I get that. I'd probably be the same." I smiled as the camera clicked on her phone and then held up mine to take one too. This whole thing felt utterly surreal. "I've actually got a couple of boxes of *When Emily Addison Speaks*. We're not the busiest shop, and I don't know if people realise we've got copies."

"Oh, would you like me to sign some?" Annabel said it so genuinely it was clear she wasn't joking. My brain had short-circuited though. All I could do was nod and stammer out a couple of words.

"Um, yeah… that would be… um."

"What he means to say," said Edward charmingly, appearing with a tray loaded with a new tea set—floral patterned this time, "is that he'd love that, and he'd be incredibly grateful, but only if you want to. We don't want to delay you."

"Yeah, that."

"It's no bother," Annabel said, giving me a smile. "Do

you want to do it downstairs? That way I won't get in anyone's way."

"S-sure... Yeah, let's do that."

"You go," Edward said, giving me a nudge and a little smile. "I'll watch the counter. Would you like some tea?"

"That sounds great," Annabel said. "Lead the way."

I nodded, taking the tea tray from Edward, still sure the entire situation was a waking dream. I was sure I'd come awake any moment to find myself on the stool behind the counter and the shop empty.

But by the time I was sitting at a table with Annabel freaking Monteforte, drinking tea, eating shortbread, and chatting about books while she casually signed a pile of hardbacks, I realised no dream I'd ever had—besides maybe the sex dream I'd had about Leo—had ever been so lovely. Annabel was very funny and engaging, and she seemed genuinely interested in the shop. We ended up exchanging a huge list of book recs. My to-be-read list was getting longer by the second, but it would be worth it.

Annabel left an hour later, thanking me again, which was bonkers because I was the one who was incredibly grateful to her. I shook my head as I climbed the stairs to grab my laptop. I had about ten minutes before my Skype call with Reuben, and I also needed to text Emily. A plan had been forming in my mind all afternoon, but I needed her help.

Edward was happy to watch the counter for a little longer in return for the final piece of shortbread, so I took my laptop, its charging cable, and my notepad upstairs to my flat.

Reuben was a lovely guy with a thick accent who looked like he'd just come back from walking in the wilds of the Welsh hills. He reminded me a little of Leo. It only took an hour to talk through everything, and I was astounded when he said he'd have it up and running by the end of next week. I'd sent him all my carefully designed graphics, and Reuben had stuck a maintenance screen on the website, directing people to email me while everything was under construction.

With every passing minute, the worry in my chest eased. Maybe I could do this. Maybe everything would work out the way I'd originally hoped it would. And maybe asking for help wasn't the worst thing in the world.

I just wished I'd realised that four days ago.

Reuben and I were just finishing up our conversation and chatting about the latest season of *Celestials* when Edward burst into my living room. His face was white as a sheet, like he'd seen some sort of ghost. I was absolutely willing to bet he'd been stalking his nemesis on Instagram again, and I sighed internally, preparing myself for yet another long rant.

But he just held out his phone and said, "Darling, I think you need to see this."

## CHAPTER TWENTY-EIGHT

*Apple Blossom — Good fortune, Better things to come*

**Jay**

I TOOK the phone from Edward, my brow wrinkling in confusion. Edward was a dramatic soul, but I'd genuinely never seen him like this. It was like someone had died.

I looked down at the app he had open. It was Twitter, and it was logged into The Lost World's account. I'd given Edward access when I'd set it up, just as a backup in case anything ever happened to me. I knew he didn't use it much though, but that wasn't the important thing. The important thing was the little notification button, which seemed to be in the process of exploding...

"What happened?" I asked, clicking on it and staring at the rapidly increasing number of new follow notifications and comments. People were saying things like "awesome!" and "I'll check it out!", but I couldn't figure out what they were referring to. I hadn't posted anything today. Or had I? I couldn't remember what I'd scheduled to post at the beginning of the week. Nothing I had thought of was exciting enough to warrant this kind of response though. "What's going on?"

"Annabel Monteforte posted a selfie of the two of you on her Twitter and told her hundred and twenty-five thousand followers about the shop." Edward's voice was breathy with shock, and he looked like he needed to lie down.

"Holy shit..." I stared at the notifications. I could barely keep up with them. I scrolled through the feed, trying to find the original post. "Reuben, can I call you back later?"

"Yeah." I heard him say. "Sounds like you're gonna be needing that website sooner than you thought. I'll go and make a start." He disconnected the call, but I wasn't looking at my laptop screen. I was still staring at Edward's phone. I'd found Annabel's post.

*Had a fabulous afternoon at @TheLostWorldbooks today in Lincoln (UK)! It's a tiny indie bookshop that's super LGBTQ+ friendly & the owner, Jay, is so helpful—seriously my TBR is so long now! Please check them out & support them. We need more places like this <3*

She'd posted the photo of the two of us standing in front of the counter. You could see the huge rainbow flag hanging behind us. It was the perfect backdrop. She'd posted a second tweet on the thread that made my heart drop through my stomach and into the floor.

*P.S. They still have copies of* When Emily Addison Speaks, *and I may have signed some ;)*

This couldn't be true, could it? Things like this only happened in movies. Nobody actually met their favourite author, took a selfie with them, and then had said favourite author tweet about how lovely they were. It just didn't happen.

Except apparently it did because there was no denying the growing number of notifications or the way the shop's follower count had just jumped from a couple of hundred to nearly a thousand in twenty minutes or the growing number of direct messages and tweets tagging the shop from people asking if there was a way to order books.

Holy shit. People wanted to order books.

Lots of people. Wanted lots of books.

"Jay, are you okay? You've gone very pale, darling. You look like you're about to be sick." Edward's voice sounded far away, like he was standing at the other end of a tunnel.

"I... I'm fine... I think." A shiver ran across my skin, which was odd because I felt too warm. How could I be hot and cold all at once? And why did my chest suddenly feel ridiculously tight, like I was being hugged by a giant boa constrictor. God, was this what it felt like to wear a corset? No wonder Elizabeth Swann had fallen off a cliff in the first *Pirates of the Caribbean* film.

I jumped as Edward's hand brushed against mine. He gently pried the phone from my grasp and made a little humming noise. Then his fingers interlaced with mine, his thumb gently rubbing my skin. "Darling, are you with me?

Can you breathe for me please? In and out. Nice and slow."

I nodded, my body suddenly coming back online. I gasped then let the air out in a shuddering exhale. I took another deep breath, letting it out slower this time. Then another. And another, until the tightness in my chest loosened, and I felt like I could breathe again.

"Thanks," I mumbled. I ran my hands through my hair and pushed my glasses up my nose as my brain started to come back online, like a computer after rebooting. "I, um, I think I might need your help. I think I'm suddenly going to have a lot of orders to fill. Do you think I should have people email me? That might be easiest, right? Then they can email me their details and orders, and I can ask them to PayPal the money over that way I have a paper trail."

I pulled my phone out of my pocket, noticing a ton of notifications from GMail. It seemed people had discovered the website and the little notification Reuben had posted. His timing couldn't have been more perfect if he'd tried. He was definitely getting a thank you package and a lifetime supply of free books.

"That sounds like a good plan," Edward said. He was looking at his phone again, a tiny frown in between his eyebrows, his mouth drawn together in what was commonly known as Edward's "thinking pout". "I think we might need some help though. Give me a second." He tapped the screen a couple of times, lifting the phone to his ear. "Lewis, my love, I need your help. What? No! I haven't done anything! Why do you always assume I'm the one who's caused trouble?"

I chuckled, shaking my head as Edward sweet-talked Lewis into giving us a hand, asking him to take over Twitter and help streamline the email while Edward and I took over the orders. I was going to need packing material, labels, and boxes, and I wasn't sure if the post office was still open. I'd have to send Edward to check. I'd need to double check my stock list too. And whether I had enough printer ink to do receipts for people. I wasn't even sure my printer still worked.

But that wasn't what I was thinking about as I dismissed all the notifications. For once, my mind was strangely clear and calm. I knew I could deal with the shop and the orders and everything that was about to happen because I knew I had help. Instead, I was thinking about Leo and everything he'd said, both out loud and with his flowers. I was thinking about what I could do to make it up to him, to prove that I was sorry, and to show him I wanted a relationship with him more than anything in the world.

I pulled up my WhatsApp and typed out two messages. One to Emily and one to Leo.

Now I just had to hope I could pull off what I was thinking.

## CHAPTER TWENTY-NINE

*Hyacinth (Purple) — Sorrow, Please forgive me*

**Leo**

IT HAD BEEN NEARLY four days since I'd last spoken to Jay. Three since I'd last seen him. And every day felt like a lifetime.

Objectively, I knew that four days meant nothing in the grand scheme of things. But my heart still ached for him. I kept checking my phone, hoping for something, and every time I saw nothing, my heart cracked a little further.

Emily had taken the flowers to the shop like I'd asked. She'd said Jay looked terrible and hadn't said much, but that had been it. Since then she'd refused to talk about him. I got the feeling Jay had been blacklisted, in which case he was going to have to do something grand to get back in Emily's good books.

I wondered whether Jay did grand gestures. Probably

not. Even if he did, I wasn't sure I'd like all the attention. The worst thing I could imagine was a bunch of people looking at me. Those big public proposals always made me cringe. I couldn't understand why someone would want that much attention.

I shook my head, turning back to the paperwork in front of me. The numbers swam in and out of focus, and I couldn't seem to keep my attention on them. I couldn't stop thinking about the gorgeous, tattooed man with the bright eyes and beautiful mouth who was just up the road. It would only take me two minutes to get to him. To tell him that I still needed him, that I still loved him. But he was out of reach, and it wasn't up to me. It was up to Jay.

I didn't want to push him before he was ready. That would just make everything worse.

Maybe if I still hadn't heard from him in a couple of days, I'd send him a text. Just to make sure he was still alive. I didn't think that would be too much. Emily would know, but I knew if I mentioned it, she'd confiscate my phone.

I sighed and let out a little growl of frustration. This was fucking ridiculous. Angie snuffled in her bed.

"Exactly," I muttered darkly. I put the paperwork to one side. It wasn't happening today. I glanced up at the clock. It was getting late. I should go home and pretend I wasn't alone. Maybe I would even jerk off to relieve the tension crawling under my skin. I wasn't sure it would help in the long run, but it might make me feel better for five minutes.

I dropped my pen on the table and swiped my phone off the desk, absentmindedly checking for notifications while trying to decide whether I felt like cooking or not. The temptation to order another round of takeaway was strong. My sour mood hadn't made me want to spend time in the kitchen. All I really wanted to do was go home and pass out until tomorrow or until Jay made up his mind. That was probably very sad, but it was all I had the energy for. I didn't even want to watch any more of *Last Call*. The show had lost its appeal now.

As I glanced at my phone, I noticed two notifications. One was a cryptic message from Emily, offering to open the shop in the morning. I had no idea why she'd offer. It wasn't like I had any reason to stay at home.

Or maybe I did. I opened the second message, holding my breath.

JAY *Can you come to The Lost World?*
JAY *This evening*
JAY *If you're free that is. You don't have to. I mean I'd understand if you didn't want to*

A smile pulled at the edges of my mouth; the first one in days. Even in text form Jay was rambly and adorable. I wasn't sure if this was a good or bad sign, but the fact he'd given me an out instead of just insisting gave me hope. It was all I had, and I was going to cling to it. Just for a few minutes more.

LEO *Sure. Give me 10*

I grabbed my jacket, giving the shop a once over to

make sure it was ready for tomorrow before flicking off the lights and walking out the door, Angie beside me. As I locked up, I realised that whatever happened, I wasn't going to want to get up tomorrow. I quickly messaged Emily to take her up on her offer.

My feet carried me up the hill, hope rising in my chest. I tried to temper it with the thought that this might be it, that Jay was going to end things. But it was no use. I'd always been an optimistic person, and now it was all I had.

The shop was closed, but there was a light on. I knocked and waited. It seemed to take an age for Jay to get to the door. Then I heard muffled footsteps and the sound of a bolt being drawn back. The door opened and Jay's face appeared.

He was still pale and tired looking, but he looked better than the last time I'd seen him. As if it was a different kind of tiredness. His bottom lip was red and swollen like he'd been worrying it with his teeth, and his dark curls stuck out at odd angles. I wanted to sweep him up into my arms, hold him close, and take his worries away. It was clear my feelings hadn't changed. I was still in love with him. Maybe more than ever.

I'd always given my heart away freely, which was strange because I wasn't great with people. But if someone had made the effort to get close, I'd always found myself giving them a piece of me. Perhaps I loved too hard and too fast because it had always blown up in my face. Maybe it was why I'd shut myself off over the past few years, too unwilling to let people get close because I knew what would happen when they inevitably decided they didn't like the differences between my exterior and interior.

"Hey," Jay said. "You came."

"You asked me to."

He nodded. "Still, I appreciate it. You, um, you didn't have to, but I'm glad you did." He pulled the door open wide, beckoning Angie and I inside. The shop looked the same as before. Except my flowers were displayed on the counter, and there was a huge stack of boxes overflowing with padded envelopes and smaller boxes piled on the floor in front of it.

"Did I miss something?" I asked, staring at them. "Did you get the online orders working?"

"Something like that." Jay gave a little chuckle. "I might have gone sorta viral on Twitter. Which I will add, was completely not my fault and highly unintentional."

I raised my eyebrow.

"It's a long story," Jay said. "I'll tell you later."

"Later?" A flare gun fired in my chest like a beacon of hope guiding me towards the light.

"Yeah. There's, er, there's something I need to do first. Can you… Are you okay to wait here?" I nodded and Jay visibly exhaled. "Cool. Great. Just… just give me two minutes."

He headed towards the stairs, practically running up them. I waited as promised, my whole body thrumming with tension. I had no idea what was going on or what Jay was doing. I tried to distract myself by looking at the nearest set of shelves, but even the books didn't distract me. I rubbed my hands together, trying to focus on something other than my racing pulse. This was worse than every single horror movie Aaron had ever forced me to watch.

The minutes seemed to stretch on infinitely. Each second lasting a thousand lifetimes. I was sure more than two minutes had passed. It felt like two years.

Then I heard Jay's footsteps on the stairs. Slower this time, more measured. My heartbeat quickened. I felt like I was a condemned man awaiting an executioner. Or maybe I was awaiting rescue. I wouldn't know until Jay was standing in front of me again.

"Can you close your eyes?" he called. "I promise there's a reason. You just… I need you to trust me."

"Okay." It was all I could do. I could have argued or demanded he tell me what he was doing, but that wasn't me. I wanted to trust him, so I closed my eyes. And I waited.

I heard Jay come down the last few stairs and take another deep breath, muttering something to himself that I couldn't catch. There was the sound of paws pattering across the carpet and a soft greeting.

"Hey, baby girl. I missed you," Jay said, his voice barely audible. I had to strain to hear him, but I loved the fact he was talking to Angie. She was my whole world, and I needed someone who'd accept that. Jay seemed to love her almost as much as I did. "What do you think? Yeah?… I hope so too." He exhaled. I tensed. This was it. "Okay… You can open your eyes."

I did and my mouth fell open.

Flowers. Jay was holding a bouquet of flowers.

But not just any flowers… lily of the valley, tiny blue

cornflowers, and what looked like white violets. And tulips. Pink tulips.

I stared, my eyes roaming over every flower. Did Jay know what he was saying? Fuck, please let him know. Please let him be telling me what I thought he was.

"T-these are for you." His voice was shaking as he held them out for me. "I, um, I hope you like them. And I hope they tell you a little bit of how I feel. Because I'm so fucking sorry for how I acted. I shouldn't have pushed you away when I panicked. I should have let you in and told you how I felt. I was just so fucking scared this was going to be like London all over again. That I'd fucked up. I was so convinced I needed to do everything by myself."

"You never had to do that," I said, finally finding my voice. I reached for the flowers, taking them from him. No one had ever brought me flowers before. They were the most beautiful thing I'd ever seen. "You never had to do it alone."

"I know. At least, I know that now."

I looked at the flowers again, my finger reaching up to gently stroke the petals of one of the tulips. Jay had said this would tell me how he felt, but I wasn't sure if it was just a gesture or if he'd worked out my secret.

"They... they mean 'perfect love' don't they?" he asked. His voice was soft, and when I looked at him, there was a shy smile on his face. "I, um, I finally realised all the flowers you'd given me had meaning, apart from being really pretty."

I felt my face heating. I'd never had anyone figure out my secret before. I used floriography in my arrangements, but I'd never told anyone except Emily. "Did Emily tell you?"

"No." Jay shook his head. "It was Edward. I think I was frustrating him, and he beat me round the head with it. Metaphorically, not literally. Although I think if he'd had a book on hand at the time, he would've hit me with it. He's sympathetic but only up to a point, and I was subjected to a lecture about the horrible mistake I was making. Which I agree with. He'd probably have said so sooner, but he only found out today."

I let out a little chuckle. That was something I could definitely believe. "Where did you get these?"

"Um, Emily got them for me. She helped me put them together. I'm no expert though, so I'm sorry if it looks like it was assembled by a hyperactive toddler." He looked almost sheepish, but I couldn't understand why. Sure, the arrangement was a little rough, but I hadn't noticed that until he'd pointed it out. And I didn't care because the arrangement was made with love, and that was all that mattered.

"I love you, Leo. And I'm so sorry for everything. You're the best man I've ever met, and I want to spend every day proving that to you. I want to be the man you deserve."

"You're already that," I said. I tucked the flowers into the crook of my arm and reached out my other hand for him. His fingers interlaced with mine, and I pulled him close. My eyes roamed over him, drinking all the details of his face in again. My whole body was thrumming, like someone was running an electrical current through me, and I couldn't stop smiling. "I love you too."

"Can you forgive me for being a stupid, stubborn

asshole and a massive twat?" Jay stepped closer, his body pressing against mine. He licked his lips.

"I forgive you." I tilted my head, releasing his hand to cup his jaw, bringing his lips to mine. His mouth was soft and sweet—the same as always—but the barest touch of him sent heat flooding across my skin. It had only been a few days, but it felt like forever. I swiped my tongue across his lip, teasing his piercing, and Jay moaned, melting against me.

"Would you like to go upstairs?" he asked. His eyes were already glassy with lust, his cheeks dusted with a beautiful blush. "I want to make this up to you."

"Whatever you want."

Jay smiled playfully, took the flowers from me, and darted over to the counter, producing a second vase full of water. I chuckled. I assumed Emily had brought that too. I watched as Jay bent slightly, my eyes following the swell of his perfect arse. When he stood, he saw me watching. He winked and wiggled his arse teasingly, giving me a coy smile.

"Are you coming?" He turned to walk towards the stairs.

I grinned, then strode across the room and scooped him up in my arms, gently putting him over my shoulder. Jay shrieked and giggled as I carried him up the stairs, Angie following at my heels.

## CHAPTER THIRTY

*Honeysuckle (Coral) — I love you*

**Leo**

I SHUT Angie in Jay's open-plan kitchen-living room because the last thing we needed was to be interrupted by an inquisitive Staffordshire Bull Terrier.

Jay was still chuckling from his position on my shoulder. He'd also discovered that if he leant down far enough, he could grab my arse. Something that amused him greatly.

"Do you want me to put you down?" I asked, attempting to fake a stern voice as Jay grabbed my arse while I made sure the door was shut firmly behind us.

"Fuck no."

"Then stop grabbing my butt."

"But it's such a nice butt, and I missed it." He sighed. "I missed all of you."

"I missed you too." I gently tilted forward so he slid off

my shoulder and I caught him in my arms on the way down. Jay grinned and wrapped his legs around my waist, refusing to be put down. He leant forward to take my mouth in a deep kiss, flooding my body with heat.

"I love that you can pick me up. It's really fucking sexy."

"Oh?" I quirked my eyebrow, turning the pair of us so I could lean him against a wall. His arse rested perfectly against my cock. He smirked and ground down against me as he kissed me again, his tongue pushing into my mouth. It was a small movement, considering I was still holding him, but it was enough to make his desires perfectly clear.

"Fuck me like this?" he asked, pulling his lip between his teeth and looking up at me with wide eyes. "Please. I want you to pin me against this wall and fuck me hard until I'm full of your cum."

I let out a low rumbling growl, and Jay moaned. I squeezed his arse, pulling him against me so he could feel the hard press of my cock through our clothes. "You don't want me to take you to your room, spread you out on the bed, and eat out your tight little hole?"

"Urgh, later," Jay groaned, leaning his head back against the wall. "But first I need you to fuck me. I need you inside me so fucking bad."

"Yeah?" I pressed kisses down his neck, sucking and licking at the exposed skin. Jay made the most beautiful little moans as I did. He gasped as I gently nipped the skin at the base of his neck. I worked my way back up to his lips, nipping at them as I kissed him again, barely pulling back to growl out, "You need my thick cock?

"Fuck yes. Give it to me." He was perfect. There was only one problem. I only had two hands, and both of them were holding Jay. I wasn't sure I'd be able to unbutton my jeans without putting him down. And as far as I was aware, neither of us had lube. Or a condom. Bollocks.

"Do you have any lube near here?" I asked, desperation clear in my voice. "I think I'm gonna have to put you down, at least to get your jeans off."

Jay chuckled and pulled at his lip again. "So, um, you won't need lube... I may have prepped already. Just in case." I raised my eyebrow and Jay grinned. "Don't give me that look. This was going one of two ways and you know it. Either you were going to forgive me and we could fuck and make up, or it would've gone horribly wrong in which case I'd probably have come up here to cry, order pizza, and stuff my hole with my dildo."

I groaned. "You're such a tease."

"You haven't seen anything yet."

"Show me," I demanded, gently lowering him to the ground. I stepped back. The hallway was softly lit, but there was enough light to see by. Jay popped open his jeans, sliding them over his thighs to reveal nothing but his hard cock. "Commando?"

"It was a toss-up between this and a jock strap."

"I bet you'd look very pretty in a jock."

"Next time." He winked. Then he turned, putting his arms and chest on the wall and pushing his arse out. Between his cheeks I saw a flat, black disk. I groaned, my hand reaching for my cock, rubbing it through my jeans. "Do you like it?"

"Fuck yes." I ran my finger over the plug, gripping the smooth edges and gently teasing it in and out of Jay's hole. Jay gasped, then the sound melted into a desperate moan.

"Shit! Please, just fuck me."

"Do you have a condom?" I asked, leaning over his shoulder and kissing down his neck while my fingers kept teasing the plug.

"I'm safe…" he said, looking up at me. He looked desperate. "I mean, I got tested after I left London. So, if you want…"

"Are you sure?" I squeezed his cheeks. The thought of being inside him with nothing between us was sexy as fuck.

"Yeah, plus I put a fuck ton of lube on that plug. My sheets were like a fucking slip-and-slide."

I snorted then I kissed him, gently tugging on his lip, loving the way he melted against me. "I got a test after my last relationship. And I've been very single since then."

"Dry spell?" Jay wiggled his eyebrows, but his teasing grin shifted into an expression of desire as I gently teased the plug from his arse.

"You could say that." I reached for my jeans, popping the button and pushing them down far enough for me to pull my aching erection out of my boxers. I didn't want to waste any more time stripping off the rest of my clothes. I desperately needed to fuck him. "Not any more though."

I slid a finger into his arse, and then a second, letting out a little growl at how wet and stretched he was for me. I needed to be inside him, and I couldn't wait any longer. I spun him in my arms, grasping his hips and lifting him. I pinned Jay against the wall as he wrapped his legs around me, and the head of my cock pressed against his pucker.

"Oh God, yes." Jay's head thumped back against the wall. His arms locked around my neck as his eyes met mine, wide with lust behind his glasses. His lips were red and swollen, and I felt his erection pressing into my stomach. Jay's desperation was clear, but he couldn't do anything until I let him. "Put it in. I fucking need it."

I pulled him down onto my cock, pressing slowly inside him. I gasped as heat enveloped my dick. He was so hot and wet and tight around my cock, and I knew I wasn't going to last long. I was too wound up by the whole situation. I stilled him as I bottomed out, giving him a moment to adjust. Jay's chest was heaving, and sweat was beading on his forehead.

"Fuck. You feel so good," he groaned. His mouth met mine, his kisses hot and desperate as his tongue pushed into my mouth. "Fuck me… Give it to me."

"Yeah? You need it baby?"

"Yeah… need your fucking dick."

I growled, nipping his lip, my fingers squeezing his arse. I began to move my hips, thrusting slowly into him. I wanted to draw the pleasure out, but it wasn't going to be possible. I didn't have that sort of self-restraint. At least, I didn't right now.

"Harder," Jay cried. His fingers tangled in my hair, tugging it and sending a shiver of pleasure straight down my spine. "Harder!"

Another low growl rumbled through my chest. If Jay wanted it hard, I'd give him exactly what he wanted. I snapped my hips up, pounding into him. Pleasure shot through me, setting my nerves alight. I felt the familiar burn of my orgasm approaching, but I wanted Jay to come first. I wanted to feel his channel tightening around me as I fucked him. His cock was still pressed into my abdomen. The friction must have been perfect judging by the noises sliding from his lips in broken words and half moans of desperation. Fuck, he was so perfect like this. So needy and delicious. All mine.

"Touch yourself," I said, my breath ghosting over his ear. "Wanna feel you come."

Jay whimpered and nodded. One hand snaked between us, gripping his cock and pumping it hard and fast as I pounded into him. My thighs were burning, but I didn't care. I needed to come.

"Oh, shit. I'm going—shit, Leo!" Jay cried out as he came, his cock painting our t-shirts with thick ropes of cum. His channel pulsed around me, squeezing my cock and pulling my orgasm out of me with the force of a rocket.

"Fuck!" My body locked up as I came, pumping my release inside him. My chest was heaving and my muscles screaming.

"I love you," Jay whispered, kissing me softly.

"I love you too."

"That was fucking amazing."

"Yeah... it was." I shifted my weight and grimaced. Clearly my knees were not impressed with this. And neither were my shoulders. I was going to need to do more exercise if this was going to become a regular thing. Which I really wanted because pressing this beautiful man up against the wall and fucking him until he screamed my name was really fucking sexy.

"You can put me down if you want."

"I think I'm going to have to," I said. My jeans were still somewhere around my knees. I wasn't going to be able to move without falling over and looking like a complete tit. "Not unless you want to end up on the floor. And not in a sexy way."

Jay chuckled, then pulled a face as my softening cock slipped out of him. I lowered him gently to the floor, giving him another kiss. I debated pulling my jeans up, but it was easier just to kick them off. Jay had stripped his t-shirt off and was padding down the hallway in just his socks, which had little cartoon burgers and chips all over them.

I smiled, my heart overflowing with love. I still couldn't believe everything had worked out the way it had, although I was still missing details. Like how he'd managed to go viral on Twitter.

Jay stopped at the doorway to his bedroom and looked back at me. "You coming? I thought we could lie down for a minute before we shower. You're welcome to stay if you want, although I'll understand if you don't."

"I'll stay. I don't exactly have a clean t-shirt to go home in." I looked down at myself and the wet patches of cum that were splattered across my shirt. I peeled it off and balled it up in my hands as I walked down the hallway towards him.

Jay snorted. "Don't worry. I'll stick it in the wash and then on the radiator. It'll be dry by the morning."

"If you're sure."

"Of course. I'll do it in a minute. I'm just gonna go to the bathroom first and, um, clean up." He waved at the bed. "I'll be back in two seconds."

Jay disappeared towards the tiny bathroom, and I made my way towards his bedroom. I dropped my ball of clothes on the floor then perched on the edge of his bed to undo my hair, running my fingers through it as I shook it loose. There was something very satisfying about letting my hair down after a long day, and I sighed happily as I stroked my fingers through the long strands.

I heard the bathroom door open, and Jay appeared. I spread myself out on the bed, opening my arms for him. He smiled and slowly sauntered across the room to me. It gave me time to drink in his body, refamiliarising myself with the lines and curves of his frame and the ink that crawled across his skin. He climbed onto the bed, snuggling up against me and sighing happily as he rested his head on my chest. I wrapped my arm around him, pulling him close, my fingers skimming over his skin.

Something inside me clicked into place, a knowledge that this was it now. We'd made it through the first wobble between us, and if we could do that, then we could survive anything. Our relationship would be stronger now, and I knew I'd never let Jay go because he meant more to me than I'd ever thought possible.

"What're you thinking about?" Jay asked. His fingers were tracing the lines of the peonies on my chest.

"You. And me. About how I'm never letting you go."

"Yeah?" He looked up at me uncertainly as if he was expecting me to suddenly dump him now that we'd fucked.

"Yeah. I love you."

"I love you too. And I'm still really fucking sorry."

"You don't have to keep apologising."

"I kinda do though. I was such a fucking dickhead to you. I pushed you away because I was so scared that you'd hate me for failing and for not being able to do everything by myself. Even though I know you understand how tough this new business shit is. I mean you offered me so much help, and I was too stupid and stubborn to realise you actually meant it." His cheeks tinted.

"You thought I didn't mean it?"

"Kinda?" He shrugged sheepishly. "I mean, I thought I had to do everything myself or I was failing. Edward, um, Edward might have had some choice words to say on that as well."

I chuckled and pressed a kiss to the top of his head. "It's okay. I get it."

"I'm still sorry though. I'd say anxiety is a bitch, but I shouldn't blame that. So yeah, I'm gonna apologise again."

"It's okay. I understand why you did what you did, and there's nothing for me to forgive."

"Are you sure?"

"Yes." I chuckled. "I'm sure." Jay nodded, soothed for now. I wondered if his anxiety would keep telling him I hadn't forgiven him. One way or another, I'd make him believe me. We all made mistakes and fucked things up, but it was how a person dealt with the bad that truly showed their character. I understood why he'd been scared because I'd been there as well.

I ran my fingers across his skin, casually looking over

his tattoos and tracing the lines of the cross of the Hanged Man that wrapped around his shoulders.

"Can I ask you something?" I asked.

"Sure. Always."

"What does this mean?"

"The Hanged Man?"

"Yeah. I know it's from tarot but I don't know what it means, and I'm assuming, given the size of it, it means something to you."

Jay nodded and snuggled deeper into my side. "It has a variety of meanings depending on when or how it appears, but it's usually to do with being stuck in a rut, suspension, and metamorphosis. It's about sacrificing people and things we're trying to hold on to. I got it after I moved here. Edward took me to a tattoo parlour to distract me, and I ended up getting this. Well, starting it anyway. It took a while." He took a deep breath, his fingers running up and down my chest. "For me, it's about letting go and moving down a new path. Letting go of the things I was holding on to—like Kieran and London—the things that weren't working and moving onto the next part of my life. It was the first step in… healing, I guess. Or maybe acceptance would be a better word."

"I think it's perfect," I said. "I don't think any of my tattoos have that much meaning. Most of mine are because I like flowers."

Jay chuckled. "That's a perfectly valid reason."

I skimmed my fingers down his side, casting my eyes over the rest of his ink and admiring the different images.

Then I stopped and stared, unable to stop a chuckle from bubbling out of my lips. "What's this?"

"Oh my God, you found my eternal shame, didn't you?" Jay groaned and buried his head in my chest. "Would it help if I offered an explanation?"

"I'd want to know anyway," I said with a laugh. I looked at the tattoo again. It was a pair of vampire fangs, dripping blood, and what looked like a wolf paw.

"Ugh, I knew it was a bad idea when Edward suggested it."

"Why doesn't it surprise me that he's involved?"

"Alright, so, you know how my full name is Jacob? And he's Edward. When we started chatting, we realised we were a walking *Twilight* joke. Especially because he's pretty, pale and blond. I mean Edward looks like a fucking vampire already." He sighed. "We were talking one night, and I'm not even sure how we got to this—I think we were drunk—but we said if we ever met, we should get matching tattoos. And because of the whole *Twilight* thing, we joked we should lean into it. I didn't think it was ever going to happen, but it did, and now I have a bloody vampire and werewolf tattoo." He laughed softly, and his shoulders shook. When he looked up at me, there was a fond smile on his face.

"I'm guessing Edward has one too?"

"Yup. His is a tramp stamp."

I chuckled, shaking my head. Strange as it sounded, I could absolutely picture Edward with that tattoo. "I think it's cute."

"The tattoo or the fact that Edward has a tramp stamp?"

"The tattoo." I reached down and pulled him up for a kiss. "I love how close you two are."

"Thanks. I, um, I kinda like the tattoo too. I know it's tacky, but it's cute. It reminds me of him."

"I mean, I have a tattoo of a piece of toast on my foot, so you can't beat that."

"Wait, what? Seriously? You've gotta show me now." He nudged me playfully and then kissed me again. "Is this going to just dissolve into showing each other our weird tattoos?"

"I mean, do you have one that's weirder than a piece of toast? Or your vampire fangs?"

"Toast first, then I'll consider showing you."

"I might just see it later."

"You'll never find it without me," he said, laughing as he straddled my lap. His arse settled perfectly on my cock and a little groan slipped from my lips. Jay's smile widened deviously. He shifted his hips, rubbing his arse against me.

I growled and pulled him in for another kiss.

## CHAPTER THIRTY-ONE

*Lily of the Valley—Return of happiness, Humility*

**Jay**

"I'M NOT sure I can do this," I said, looking around at the packed shop and nervously fiddling with the sleeves of the dark blue jumper Edward had forced me into. "I think I'm going to be sick."

"You're going to be just fine, darling. I promise." Edward smiled and brushed a stray curl out of my face. "You are very charismatic and charming, and this isn't an exam. There aren't any wrong answers."

"No. This is much, much worse." I looked at the local news presenter who was chatting with Leo and her cameraman. Why the fuck had I agreed to this again?

After Annabel's tweet, the outpouring of love and support for the shop had been incredible. In all my wildest dreams, I'd never imagined becoming as popular as we had in the past two weeks. The amount of orders we'd received had already paid all the shop's bills for the next four months, and there were still more pouring in. Especially because a couple of other authors had picked up Annabel's tweet and retweeted it with comments about supporting indie bookstores.

Lewis and Reuben had been a godsend in all the chaos. Lewis had taken over half the running of my Twitter account as well as wrangling my emails into something resembling order and had colour-coded them in order of importance for me to deal with. It had helped a ridiculous amount and had stopped me from getting overwhelmed by the sheer volume of email I was receiving. Lewis had also taken it upon himself to delete any hate mail I got for daring to be a queer safe space since, as he said, I "didn't need to deal with that bollocks".

Reuben had built a functional web store in two days that managed to cope with the volume of orders and was easy as fuck for me to understand. He'd even written me a how-to guide so I could update it myself and add new books to it whenever they came in.

Throughout all the pandemonium, Leo had been a steady rock by my side. Every evening he'd come to The Lost World and helped me box up the last of the orders to be posted the next day before we made dinner and relaxed.

I'd had the nagging feeling that I should be spending my evenings working because I was so sure there were things I was meant to be doing, but Leo had gently insisted a break would be good for me, and I'd had to admit he was right. I felt a lot better spending my evenings on the sofa or in bed with him and getting some solid sleep. It made everything so much easier to deal with.

My days were even busier now. It hadn't just been the online community that had rallied around the shop. It had been the local community too. My physical customer numbers had nearly tripled, which wasn't saying much when some days I'd only seen a handful of people, but it was definitely a huge upswing, and everyone had been genuinely friendly and supportive.

Last week, I'd gotten a note from the regional BBC news team, *Look North*, who wanted to do a feature on The Lost World as part of their evening slot. They'd drop in to film it one morning, and it would be shown a couple of days later. I'd umm-ed and ahh-ed for so long that Edward had decided to reply to the email for me. I'd wanted to be cross with him for taking the decision out of my hands, but I was kind of glad he had. Otherwise the email would have probably still been sitting there at Christmas.

I'd been worried the shop would be deserted while they were filming—because it was eleven o'clock on a Wednesday morning—which wouldn't be the greatest look. Luckily, Lewis had put out a couple of tweets asking for people to stop by, and it seemed to have worked. The cameraman had already been capturing footage of the shop and a beautifully dressed Edward behind the counter.

He'd gone for "understated" in a gothic style, white ruffled shirt and black jeans, with his gold-laced black boots. Even trying to be subtle, he still managed to look more stunning than any man I'd ever seen. He looked like the Netflix Alucard brought to life, minus the sword and vampire fangs.

Edward had even managed to drag Leo in, despite the fact that Leo didn't work at the shop. I think Leo had also been roped into being interviewed as a fellow local businessman and customer. I wasn't quite sure if he appreciated that or not.

"Are you ready, Jay?" the reporter asked, giving me a beaming smile. Her name was Kirsty and she'd been really lovely since the moment she arrived, which put me at ease. She'd already talked me through the sort of questions she was going to ask and what they wanted me to talk about. Kirsty had explained they'd edit out her questions to make it feel more natural and intersperse the interview with footage from the shop so the whole thing wouldn't just be me rambling to the camera. It was only a five-minute slot, which didn't give me too much opportunity to fuck up. Even so, a crushing weight had settled onto my chest, and I was already baking in the jumper and shirt Edward had insisted I wear. It wasn't even my jumper!

"Sure," I said. I sounded more confident than I felt, which was a good sign at least.

"Great. If you just stand here." Kirsty directed me to stand on a pre-approved spot, which apparently had good lighting. "Then we can get started."

I nodded, taking my place. I took a deep breath and tried to smile. Fingers crossed I didn't look like I was about to throw up.

"Are you nervous?" Kirsty asked.

"Yeah, a little." I chuckled nervously, twisting my hands

together out of sight of the camera. "I've never done anything like this before."

"Don't worry, you're going to do great." She gave me another smile, checked a few things with the cameraman, and then started. "Okay, Jay, can you introduce yourself and the shop and tell us a little bit about the sort of things you do here."

Behind Kirsty, I saw Leo. He gave me a little nod and a smile that lifted me, making me feel like I could do anything. For once, I actually believed I could.

"I'm Jay, and I'm the owner of The Lost World book and game shop here in Lincoln. We've been open since January, and even though we sell books from lots of genres, we have a strong LGBTQ+ theme. We're here to not only sell diverse books but to provide a safe space to all members of the LGBTQ+ community."

The more I spoke, the easier it became. This shop was important to more people than just me, and I wanted to share it with the world. I wanted people to know we existed, and I wanted them to know they'd be safe here.

Kirsty nodded and smiled as I talked about our game nights and my plans for a book club and pop-up pampering with Emily and her sister. Now that I was feeling more in control and financially stable, there was no reason for me not to start those things.

It was strange how quickly the whole thing went when I got talking. I'd thought it would be like pulling teeth, but suddenly Kirsty was saying that they'd got everything they'd need. I wasn't quite sure where the time had gone.

"See? I knew you'd be great," Kirsty said, giving me

another of her beaming smiles. "You're a natural." She gave me the details for when they thought the segment would air—probably in a day or two—and her email address in case I had any questions. They shot a few more bits of footage of the shop, and then that was it.

As soon as they left, I collapsed onto the stool behind the counter while Edward procured a cup of tea and a couple of ginger biscuits for me. I dunked the biscuits in my tea and nibbled them while half leaning against Leo, who was very generously acting as a wall. He stroked my shoulder gently.

"Do you think it went okay?" I looked up at him, clutching the last bit of my biscuit. I wondered if Edward had the rest of the packet stashed away somewhere, but I couldn't ask him because he was actually making himself useful for a change and helping a customer.

"You did great," Leo said, leaning down to press a kiss to the top of my head. "I'm still not sure why they needed me. They could have just interviewed Edward or Sandra from the chocolate shop when she popped in to say hello."

"It's because you're gorgeous and charming, and they couldn't resist." Leo hummed and raised an eyebrow. I chuckled. "Do you need to get back to Wild Things?"

"I should. Alfie was opening up today since Emily had an appointment with the social worker, and I don't want him to think I've abandoned him."

"He's got Angie. He'll be fine."

"True, but she's not the best florist in the world. Yesterday she tried to eat a carnation I dropped. She wasn't impressed when I made her spit it out."

I snorted. "Well, make sure you're back here at six thirty for game night. I have no idea what Edward has planned, but he said something about being kidnapped by elves, so who the fuck knows what's going to happen. It can't be any worse than when we had to face those fucking ceiling squid."

"You lived," Leo said, giving me a wry smile.

"They broke my lute. I was very upset."

"I'll buy you another one."

"Oooh, are you my half-orc sugar daddy?"

"Only if you promise never to say that again."

"Deal." I grinned and tilted my head up, begging for a kiss. Leo indulged me before leaving me behind the counter. I watched him go, my heart overflowing with warmth. I felt like I could melt off the stool into a puddle on the floor like some sort of ice cream. Eighteen months ago, I'd never dreamt of being this happy. I'd been utterly miserable in London, barely eking out a passable existence. I'd thought my life was good then, but it turns out that working sixty to seventy hours a week while your boyfriend complains about every move you make is not the key to happiness. If only I could have told past Jay that.

Edward strolled over to me, leant on the counter, and brushed his hair out of his face. "So, I just have one question. How do you feel about drinking games?"

# CHAPTER THIRTY-TWO

*Ambrosia — Your love is reciprocated*

**Leo**

"I'll choose the red one," I said, pointing to the conical flask of red liquid in the centre of the table. I had no idea where the hell Edward had gotten six different sized glass flasks or what he'd used to make the "magic potions" inside of them, and I wasn't going to ask. Sometimes it was better not to know.

Edward grinned over his Dungeon Master screen. The look on his face would have put most movie villains to shame. "Can you all roll a constitution check for me please?"

"This is going to go really badly, I can tell," Jay whispered from beside me, picking up his twenty-sided die and rolling it in his palm. "Where the fuck did he get this sadistic idea?"

"I'm not asking, but clearly your best friend is an evil mastermind."

"He's two steps and a nuclear blast away from being a supervillain." Jay shook his head, watching everyone else at the table roll. He looked up at Edward. "Are we allowed to know what happens if we fail?"

"No," Edward said sweetly, "but I promise it's nothing bad."

"Said the supervillain," Jay muttered. I chuckled and rolled my die. It landed on a thirteen, which, with my modifier added, made me pretty certain I'd be safe from whatever Edward had planned. For now at least.

"Oh bugger." Jay sighed dramatically, and I looked down at his die. A natural one. "I'm in trouble."

"So," said Edward, "Your host, Lord Taenaran, pours out the potion and you all drink. Taenaran drinks first, just to prove to you it's not poisoned." He gave Jay a sweet smile. "And then he says, 'As you see from looking at me, it's but a simple charm. You will come to no harm. All you must do, if you needed a clue, is to speak in rhyme, for the rest of the time'."

"Motherfucker," Jay hissed. "I'm terrible at rhymes."

"Well that's hard, considering you're our bard," I said, giving him a wry grin. I wasn't much better at rhymes, but luckily Kruk wasn't the most charismatic of characters so I could get away with being a bit quieter. I was guessing the potions all had different effects, so hopefully someone would choose another one soon.

I had to admit, when Edward had set up the scenario where we had to play a drinking game with an elven king to rescue our beloved non-player character—who took the form of a golden retriever but we all suspected was a human prince trapped in dog form—I'd been a little skeptical, but it had been a fun evening so far. The scenario suited Edward's flair for the dramatic.

"You're not helping."

"Are you whispering, Jacob?" Edward asked. "If so, I hope it's in rhyme. And since you rolled a nat one, I think Castien will be feeling the effects for a while, even when you drink another potion." Edward grinned, while Jay groaned, before looking at the rest of us. "Since the rest of you did well, you'll only have mild effects, and it'll wear off as soon as you drink the next potion. So who wants to choose next?"

"Oooh me!" Daniel said, pointing to a glittering green concoction. "I choose that one."

It all went downhill from there.

Edward's potions made us all sing, dance, think we were drunk, transported us to a puzzle room that we had to find our way out of, which took us nearly forty minutes despite the fact it only had four doors, and finally made the object of our heart's desire appear in front of us.

"Kruk, in front of you, you see a beautiful axe inlaid with silver. With it, you know you could kill many of your enemies, bring prosperity to your people, and be the mighty hero you've always dreamed of being." I gave a small smile because that was Kruk's dream. I liked playing characters with uncomplicated backstories. I'd never been one for lots of angst and drama.

"Castien, in front of you, your true desire emerges. The

one thing you want in the universe more than anything else."

"Oh shit," Jay whispered. I was confused. What could Jay's character want that made him look like he'd prefer to hide under the table? "I've been set up."

"You see the face of Kruk, looking as handsome as ever. He's looking at you like you're the only person in the world who matters, and he's also holding a beautiful lute so you can play for him because apparently he doesn't mind the fact that you're tone deaf and can't hold a tune."

"I resent that." Jay was smiling, a slightly pink tint to his cheeks. He rolled his eyes at Edward. "I can't believe you set me up like this."

"It's because I love you."

"Who can see these images? Is it just me, or can the others see them too?"

"Everyone," Edward said sweetly.

"Ah fuck it!" Jay waved his hands in the air. He turned to me, half laughing as he spoke. "Kruk, I think you're the handsomest, sweetest being I've ever met, and I love you."

And then he hopped out of his seat and into my lap, pulling me in for a kiss as the rest of the table cheered.

I stared at the stream of comments under the video Jay had sent me, my eyebrow half-raised in bemusement. It was the clip from *Look North* about The Lost World, which had aired a couple of days ago as well as being shared online by several BBC outlets.

It had also gone around Facebook and Twitter, for

reasons I couldn't quite fathom. There were some lovely comments about Jay and the shop, as there should be, but there were also a lot of comments about me... thirsty comments.

"Did you read the comments?" Jay asked, looking up at me from where he was lounging against the pillows on his side of the bed. Angie and I had stayed at his flat last night, and Angie seemed to quite enjoy getting a sofa all to herself since I wouldn't let her sleep on Jay's bed.

Jay was grinning, and I knew he'd read every single one of the comments. Which was obviously why he'd sent them to me.

"A few," I said dryly. "I think my favourite is the woman who said she wants to lick me like a Mr. Whippy cone. That's a disturbing visual."

"Don't you like being licked?"

"Not by random women on the internet."

Jay snorted. "I like how a video about my bookshop ends up becoming about you."

"My apologies. I told you they should have interviewed Sandra."

"Edward will be so disappointed he's hardly in it," Jay said, leaning over my arm to peer at my screen. "He'd happily soak up all the attention from horny women on the internet."

"Only because he knows it would drive poor Lewis nuts.

"Edward describes their relationship as 'lovingly-tormenting'. Edward drives Lewis crazy, and Lewis gets his revenge by making him do fan photo-ops with his nemesis." Jay shook his head and chuckled. "Or something like that anyway. I still can't believe I hadn't known Edward had a PA. It all makes so much sense now. He was always grumbling about things like photo ops or emails or not being allowed to do things, but I thought it was just Edward being his overdramatic self."

"It does make sense when you think about it."

"Mmm," Jay hummed, scooting across the bed and burying his head against my chest, snuggling deeper into my side. He exhaled deeply and pressed a kiss to my abdomen. "Do we have to get up and go to work? Can we just stay here all day?"

"Sorry, but no. It's Saturday, and we have customers to deal with."

"Ugh, you're so mean."

"Just be glad I didn't make you get up at four thirty to go to my wholesaler."

Jay shot me a look of abject horror. "No thanks. Even when we're living together, I shall never, ever do that. You can leave me and Angie in bed."

My heart lurched at Jay's suggestion. I couldn't deny that I'd thought about us living together, picking him up every night after the shop closed and walking home, hand in hand with Angie moseying along beside us. Making dinner and curling up on the sofa with the latest episode of *Celestials*, staying up late and wearing each other out. Having friends around to watch films and play games, maybe even running a Dungeons and Dragons campaign for all of them. I'd always wanted to give Dungeon Mastering a try.

I didn't know how long the term on his flat was, but I knew most standard contracts were a minimum of six months... although since the flat was part of the shop, maybe it was different. Maybe we could live at mine and keep his place for when we were too tired to go all the way to mine or if it was pouring it down since none of us liked walking in the rain.

"You're stealing my dog too?" I chuckled. "I get to drive to Spalding in the freezing van while you two stay snuggled up at home?"

"Yeah, pretty much." Jay's smile faltered for a second. I knew he was wondering if he'd said something wrong. As if bringing up us living together was the wrong thing to say.

"I'm sure Angie'd love that. And I would too." I leant down and kissed him. "The living together part. Not the being turfed out of bed at four thirty by myself."

"Sucks to be you. But I'd make it up to you." His eyes flashed with desire as his fingers skimmed up my thigh. "And we could start now."

"Yeah?"

"I mean, if we've got time?" he asked teasingly. "I wouldn't want to make you late for work." He wrapped his hand around my cock, and I groaned as I began to fill his hand. I glanced at my phone. Emily would be at Wild Things, so if I was a tiny bit late, it wouldn't matter. Jay slid down the bed and wrapped his lips around the head of my cock, running his tongue over the velvety skin.

Fuck it, I was going to be late.

"We've got time."

# CHAPTER THIRTY-THREE

*Monkshood — Beware*

**Jay**

I FELT like I was floating on air for the rest of the morning, and it wasn't because it felt like Leo had sucked my brain out through my dick.

Everything felt like it was falling into place, and I believed more than ever that things between us would last forever. There was this solid weight of certainty in my chest when I thought of Leo. It was a comfortable feeling that enveloped me in warmth, its glow spreading across my skin and lighting me up from the inside out.

Leo hadn't even flinched when I'd brought up the idea of us moving in together. In fact, the soft smile on his face made me think he'd been imagining what our life together would be like. I knew I was. It was something I couldn't stop thinking about. I knew we should probably take things slowly, but since my wobble, I felt more assured and confident.

I wanted a life with Leo. I wanted to wake up beside him every morning, even when he had to get up stupidly early to go to the wholesaler. I wanted to walk to our respective shops together, our fingers linked, and then walk back again in the evenings. I wanted to make dinner together and watch whatever stupid TV shows we were obsessed with before falling into bed with him. I wanted us to build a life together: him, Angie, and me. And maybe we could even get another dog… I mean, The Lost World deserved a shop dog just as much as Wild Things did.

I was still thinking about how to suggest getting another dog to Leo at lunchtime. The shop had been steadily busy throughout the morning, the late-May sunshine drawing people into town. It had been great to have people coming in to browse, buy, and even sit downstairs for a bit to write. One of the local writing groups had asked if they could meet at the shop once a month for a couple of hours on a Saturday, and today was their first meeting.

The doorbell tinkled, and I looked up from the order sheet in front of me where I was making a rough note of everything I needed next time I put an order in.

"Welcome to The Lost World," I said, or tried to say, because as soon as I had the first syllable out of my mouth, the rest dried up like a puddle in the desert. Standing in front of me was a man I never wanted to see again for the rest of my life: Kieran.

"Hi, Jay," he said, giving me a little wave as he walked up to the counter. "It's good to see you."

"I can't say the same about you." My voice was ice cold, and I knew I sounded rude, but I didn't care. "What are you doing here?"

"I came to see you." He looked surprised like he'd expected me to welcome him back with open arms. I suppressed a laugh. I had no idea where the fuck he would have gotten that idea. "I thought you'd be pleased to see me."

"What gave you that impression?" I asked. My hands were shaking with anger. I couldn't believe he had the nerve to come here, especially after everything he'd put me through. Then again, that was so typically Kieran. He never imagined someone wouldn't be pleased to see him.

"Well, I thought now that you've had some time to calm down after everything we could talk. I mean, you did leave rather abruptly last year. I only knew where you were after I saw that video of you on Facebook." He looked calm, and I was starting to wonder why I'd given this man seven years of my life. I mean, I'd been wondering it for a while, but now he was standing in front of me, and I couldn't remember why I'd ever loved him.

I smiled to myself and shook my head. "You know, that happens when you lie to your boyfriend of seven years, emotionally manipulate him, and then fuck his best friend behind his back. Be honest with me, Kieran, how many men did you fuck when I was at work? Working the job that *you* encouraged me to take. I just can't figure out whether it's because you genuinely thought I should take the job, or whether it was the money, or whether it was because me working crazy hours would give you more time to fuck around."

I chuckled and shrugged my shoulders. "You know what? I don't actually care. You were a shitty boyfriend, and I'm glad I left. And y'know, when someone leaves you and doesn't contact you, maybe you should take that as a sign they don't want to see you anymore."

Kieran was staring at me, doing his best impression of a goldfish. I almost wanted to take a photo to show Edward, although that was probably a bad idea because if Edward found out Kieran was here, it was likely he'd commit an extremely brutal murder. And I was not in the mood to clean up that kind of mess.

"But I thought... I mean... I made a mistake, Jay, and I apologised for it. You should at least give me a chance to explain."

I held up my hand, giving him my best withering look. "No, you said you were 'sorry I was upset' and 'sorry I found out this way'. That's not an apology. You were just sorry you got caught, and I don't want to hear any of your pathetic explanations."

"Don't be an asshole, Jay. You're making mountains out of fucking mole hills. What did you expect me to do? You neglected me!" His voice was full of venom, and I shook my head sadly. Clearly, Kieran hadn't learnt anything from this experience. I almost wanted to feel sorry for him. After all, I had a great life now, and all he had was the pathetic remnants of a relationship he was still trying to cling to.

I wondered what had prompted him to make the journey to Lincoln. I assumed whatever man he'd shacked up with after I'd left had dumped him, and now he was starting to realise just what he'd thrown away. Maybe he thought I'd go crawling back to him the moment he showed up because it was inconceivable to him that I was better off without him.

Well, it sucked to be him because I'd moved on, and I had zero regrets. I almost wanted to laugh. Instead, I schooled my face into a serious expression and told him everything I'd been wanting to say for the past fourteen months.

"You should have talked to me. You know that. But we never were very good at communication, so I'm going to make this next bit very clear. I never want to see you or hear from you again. Move on with your life, and maybe next time you have a boyfriend don't treat them like they're disposable. Because I can guarantee you this'll just happen again. Now, get the fuck out of my shop."

Kieran stared at me, then he turned on his heel and stalked away, slamming the door of the shop behind him. A couple of browsing patrons in the next room looked up at the sound, and one of them stuck his head around the gap.

"You okay, Jay?" he asked.

"Yeah, I'm fine. Just an aggrieved ex-boyfriend." I waved my hand and sat down on my stool. Now that the moment had passed, I felt how hard my heart was thundering in my chest. Adrenaline flooded me, and I thought I could hear my pulse. "Didn't expect him to show up. Ever."

The man, whose name I thought was Gem, gave me a nod of solidarity. "I get that." He put the books he was holding on the counter. "It's the worst when they surprise you. Do you need anything?"

"You don't happen to have any gin, do you?"

"No." He laughed, then reached into the leather satchel he was carrying and pulled out something wrapped in colourfully striped foil. "But I do have a caramel wafer. Chocolate is usually a pretty good fix I find."

"You're a lifesaver." I looked down at his pile of books. "Oh, I loved that one," I said, pointing at one of the colourful covers. "Have you read their other series?"

"No worries. No, not yet. Do you have it?"

"I might have the first one." I thought carefully for a second, hopped off my stool, and headed for one of the units in the second room. One of the units had some drawers at the bottom that I kept stock in. I opened one, then a second, searching for what I wanted. It was a nice distraction from everything that had just happened.

"Here you go," I said, carefully pulling the book from the stack. Gem took it, turning it over in his hands to read the blurb. I closed the drawers and headed back towards the counter, not wanting him to think I was pressuring him into buying it. Just because I loved the book didn't mean it was for everyone.

"It sounds great," Gem said. He put the book on the counter with the rest of his purchases, and I began to put them through. "Did I hear you're starting a book club?"

"Yeah, it'll be once a month on Thursday evenings. I was thinking maybe one book a month? I'm open to suggestions for books too." Mostly so I wouldn't have to choose them. I was so indecisive. I knew if it was down to me, I'd never choose anything. There were just too many books to choose from.

"There's an initial meeting on Thursday at seven, so we can talk about what books we want to read and see who's interested."

"That sounds perfect. I'll be there," Gem said, putting his new books into his bag.

"I'll see you then, and thanks for the caramel wafer." I perched on my stool again as Gem walked away, studying the wrapper before opening it and biting into the sweet, chewy treat. I turned the whole day over in my head, from my morning with Leo, to my surprise confrontation with Kieran, to Gem's kindness.

It was strange to think how much I'd changed in the last year, and the last couple of months especially.

Once upon a time, I would have given anything for Kieran to show up and say he'd been looking for me and that he'd made a mistake, but now I realised just how unhealthy our relationship had been. I was blossoming in Lincoln, living the life I'd always dreamt of with a man I loved more than anything in the world. A man who was almost too perfect for words and who I still couldn't quite believe was mine. But he was, and I was eternally grateful for that. I couldn't wait for us to build a life together because I knew it was going to be incredible.

# CHAPTER THIRTY-FOUR

*Calla Lily—Magnificent beauty*

**Leo**

"I saw Kieran today."

I froze, my serving spoon halfway out of the pan, the spoonful of homemade fried rice hovering above the stove. Jay had said it casually, and when I looked over at him, he stopped pouring drinks to give me a smile.

"He came into the shop and said he'd been looking for me and wanted to talk about everything that had happened between us. I told him to get fucked." Jay sounded pleased with himself, but I saw hints of worry behind his glasses.

"I'm proud of you," I said. I put the spoonful of rice back into the pan and turned to face Jay. I put my hand on his waist, slowly turning him to face me, my other hand reaching up to cup his jaw. "You're amazing."

"Thanks." Jay stretched up and kissed me. "I was shaking the whole time though, but not because I was scared. I was just so angry at him, y'know? I can't believe he thought he had the right to demand I talk to him." He sighed and then chuckled. "I can't believe he came all the way from London too. What an idiot."

"Agreed. First-class idiot."

"Is it terrible to say..." Jay trailed off, pulling at his lip. "Is it terrible for me to say I'm almost glad he came? Not because I wanted to see him but because it gave me a chance to put things to bed and tell him everything I'd wanted to say for the past year."

"It's not terrible," I said. I kissed his temple. "Sometimes it's good to be able to put the past to rest. I think a lot of people wish they could tell their exes those things."

"I guess I just got lucky." He chuckled and grinned. "By the way, don't tell Edward what happened. He's sworn a bloody vendetta against Kieran, and I don't want to have to scrub blood out of the shop carpet."

"Yeah, it's murder to get rid of."

"That was terrible, and you know it." He nudged me playfully. "Besides, I've moved on. I used to hate Kieran. Now he's just... nothing. It would be stupid to give him any brain space."

I turned back to the pan, picked up the serving spoon, and started to dish out dinner. "I'm still proud of you though."

"I'm proud of me too. Now, let's go watch terrible eighties murder shows. Apparently the next episode is the beginning of a new arc involving the mob!"

"Spoiler!" I laughed, watching Jay dance his way through to the living room.

Technically, we were at my house, except in my mind, I'd already started thinking of it as ours. I'd already worked out where I could clear space for Jay to move his things in and where we could put another wardrobe if we needed one. I could probably ask Daniel and Emily to give us a hand moving things in, and we could load up the shop van with boxes. I was sure Edward would help too. It wouldn't take too long with five of us.

And after that... who knew? I was excited for the future though. For the first time in a long time, I didn't feel alone or unseen. I felt loved and wanted. I felt whole. Who'd have thought that one bunch of flowers would change my life?

Jay called, telling me to hurry up and mentioning something about dying of starvation while he waited. I chuckled to myself and shook my head, carrying the bowls through. Jay was already curled up in his spot, and Angie was on the floor at his feet. She'd already pegged Jay for a soft touch who'd give her treats.

He always tried to deny it, but when I caught him giving her a bit of chicken, he just grinned and shrugged. "She's our baby. We have to spoil her."

I sighed. I was never going to win that argument. Mostly because I couldn't deny it. Angie had always had me wrapped around her little finger, and now she had Jay as well. I had no idea what would happen if we ever got another dog. My bank balance would probably be the thing that suffered the most.

We watched a couple of episodes, and Jay migrated

from his corner to my side, spreading himself out so his head was in my lap. I rested my hand on his side, feeling the warmth of perfect contentment burning in my chest. This was the closest thing I could imagine to perfection.

Afterwards, we left Angie in the kitchen though Jay promised to come and get her later. He'd taken to letting her sleep at the foot of our bed and was apparently immune to her snoring. I'd thought a super king-size bed would be big enough for the three of us, but I was still the one who ended up with the least space. Not that I minded because Jay spent most nights wrapped in my arms, his head resting on my chest and a leg thrown over mine.

Jay took my hand and pulled me up the stairs, tugging me into our bedroom. His lips met mine in soft kisses full of heat and desire as his fingers reached for my t-shirt. I stripped naked, loving the way his eyes lit up in delight and roamed over my body. He gently pushed his fingers against my chest, and I went backwards onto the bed, propping myself up on a mountain of pillows so I could watch Jay while I stroked my cock, precum slicking my fingers. Jay stripped slowly, teasingly revealing perfect, inked skin inch by inch. I loved every part of his body, from the top of his head to the tips of his toes. One day, when we had nothing else to do, I was going to lay him out and kiss every single inch of him.

His cock was already hard between his legs, and he crawled onto the bed, a bottle of lube in hand. He pushed my legs apart and settled between them on his knees, looking down at me. His eyes burned bright with hunger, a mischievous smile on his lips. I already knew I'd let him take whatever he wanted from me. We'd started switching more, and I loved feeling him buried deep inside me. Jay had been worried at first, but he needn't have been. I loved the way he fucked me.

I couldn't take my eyes off him as he reached a hand between my legs to press his cool, slick fingers to my hole. He was so beautiful. I jacked my cock as he fingered me, groaning in pleasure at the dual sensations.

Every second seemed to last a lifetime and yet was simultaneously over too quickly. When Jay finally pressed his dick inside me, I let out a deep moan, gripping the sheets and throwing my head back. His lips caressed mine as he made love to me slowly, taking his pleasure from me with every grind of his hips. Whispered words and groans filled our room, and sweat glistened on our skin.

Jay came with a broken cry, filling me with his release. It didn't take me long to follow him over the edge with a guttural moan, velvety pleasure enveloping every inch of me.

Afterwards, he lay against my chest as we kissed, each kiss punctuated with little words of love and affection. Our relationship had blossomed and bloomed into something so beautiful I could hardly believe it. I couldn't describe it either.

How could I possibly find the words to say what Jay meant to me or how I felt about him? There weren't enough words in the universe to convey my feelings. All I could do was show him, each and every day, how much he meant to me. This man was the one I'd been waiting for all my life, and now he was here, safe in my arms. I intended to keep him there. Whatever came for us, good or bad, we would survive it together, hand in hand. There was no love like this, and I was going to cherish it.

Forever.

## EPILOGUE
### 17 MONTHS LATER

*Tulip (Pink) — Perfect love*

## Jay

"Thank you. Merry Christmas!" I called as the last of my Christmas Eve shoppers grabbed their purchases and stepped out of The Lost World into the freezing December air.

I closed the door behind them, flipped the sign to closed, and slid the top bolt across for good measure, letting out a huge sigh of relief as I did. Retail at Christmas was insane, and I was glad it was over for another year. Sure, I enjoyed helping people pick out Christmas presents and wrapping books in colourful paper, but holy shit, the stress was not worth it.

I groaned as I stretched my arms above my head, feeling a deep ache in my bones. I was so glad I'd decided to shut the shop from now until the New Year. I had eleven blissful days ahead of me, where I could do nothing except lie on my sofa with the dogs and my boyfriend, eat my weight in chocolate and those honey peanuts Leo kept buying, and mainline episodes of TV until I passed out. It would be glorious.

We'd debated going to various family members' homes for Christmas but ultimately decided we wouldn't be able to make it work with the businesses. We'd tried it last year and it had been a disaster, and we'd ended up stuck on the M5 at eleven at night trying to get down to my dad's. This year, we were staying home, and my dad was coming to stay. According to the last text I'd had, he'd made it safely to Lincoln and promptly decided to go exploring.

He was going to be staying in the flat above The Lost World, so there was a fifty-fifty chance he wouldn't actually turn up for Christmas and would instead stay here and read his way through my stock. I'd probably have to come and pry him out of the shop with a crowbar.

I'd introduced Dad to Leo last summer, and they'd hit it off instantly. They were both quiet, reserved types who didn't need a lot of words to say what they meant, but once they'd started talking about books and then plants, they'd lost me as they carried on an intricate conversation about something to do with roses. I'd zoned out by that point. It meant the world to me that they got on because I couldn't imagine my life without either of them in it.

"Okay, time to clean up," I muttered to myself. I heaved myself up from where I'd been leaning against the door and looked around the shop. Fairy lights twinkled in the window and along the tops of some of the bookcases twirled around brightly coloured tinsel. We had a little fibre-optic tree as well whose branch tips slowly cycled through the colours of the rainbow. It was decorated with the brightest baubles I'd been able to find, and as a result, it looked like a rainbow had vomited all over it.

It was ridiculously gay, and I loved it.

Until earlier today, it had also had a few labels on it from people wishing for books.

I'd started the tradition last year after a couple of people on Twitter had asked if they could buy books for people who might need them or couldn't afford them as presents. So now, people could leave an anonymous, numbered label on the tree asking for a book or two while I made a note of their details on a spreadsheet, then people could come in and fulfil them, either anonymously or by name. I'd posted some of the requests on Twitter too, and they'd all been filled within a couple of hours. I was humbled by the kindness of people who just wanted to make sure everyone got something for Christmas.

I started flicking the fairy lights off and straightening the shelves, singing old Christmas songs quietly to myself as I did. Soon, I'd be able to go home and crash out.

There was a snuffling snore from behind the counter and then rustling before a small, boxy head poked itself from around the counter and sneezed.

"Bless you. I wondered when you'd finally drag yourself out of bed." I chuckled. "You're not a very helpful assistant, you know."

Rupert looked at me again and sneezed before pottering over to me to plop down on my feet, his customary tactic to get attention. After all, it was hard to move when you had fifteen kilograms of Staffy sitting on your foot. He looked up at me and smiled, his knitted Christmas jumper making him look just the right amount of adorably ridiculous.

Rupert was another rescue we'd taken in last year. He was absolutely soft as butter and a complete pushover, which was a little at odds with his scarred appearance. He'd been found dumped in the countryside, missing half an ear and with open wounds on his face from what the rescue centre said was probably dog fighting. My heart had broken as soon as I'd seen him. I'd taken one look at him in the kennel and known we had to take him home. Leo and I had been a little worried about how he and Angie would get on, but Angie had just sniffed him once and started licking his stumpy ear. She mothered him constantly, and it was kind of adorable to watch.

"You know, if you sit on my foot, I'm not going to get anything done," I said, reaching down to stroke his soft, blue fur. "Not that you really care." Rupert's tail thumped on the floor, indicating he didn't. "Hmm, didn't think so."

I kept straightening the books I could reach, but it was a pointless exercise.

There was a knock at the door, and I winced as Rupert jumped up, woofing softly as he wiggled his way over to the door. I frowned. Leo wasn't supposed to be here for another thirty minutes and Dad for another hour. It wasn't like either of them to be early, but if they were, I could rope them into helping since Rupert could only sit on one person's foot at a time.

I slid the bolt back and pulled the door open, a grin

spreading across my face. Leo and Angie stood in the street under the golden glow of the streetlights, both wrapped in coats. Leo was holding a bouquet of flowers.

"Hey," he said. "I know we're a bit early. Is that okay?"

"Of course, but the entry fee is steep. I'll warn you now. One kiss." Leo chuckled and kissed me as he ducked through the door.

"Prices have gone up."

"Next year it might be two. New year price hikes and all that."

"Hm, might have to consider if it's worth it." He grinned and bent down to scratch Rupert's head.

"So rude. And after I bought you more honey peanuts."

"Because you ate them all."

"Because I ate them all," I said with a grin. "In my defence, they're just too delicious." I looked at the flowers Leo was holding. They were a beautiful arrangement of pine and what might be stephanotis and several things I didn't quite recognise. My flower knowledge had gotten a little better over the past eighteen months, but it wasn't perfect.

"Who are the flowers for?" I'd assumed they were for me, but they could be a late arrangement we needed to drop off on our way home. It wouldn't be out of the question for Leo to offer to do something like that. He was sweet like that.

"They're, um, they're for you." He passed them to me gently, and I gazed at the soft petals and beautiful, blooming foliage. I loved all of Leo's arrangements, but there was something extra beautiful about his winter ones. I think it was because he could make something stunning out of very little. Somehow Leo made you think you had the most beautiful blooms in the world in your hands.

"They're beautiful. Thank you." I tilted my head up and pressed a kiss to his lips. They were soft and cold and tasted of the honey lip balm he'd started using. "What's the occasion?"

"I just wanted you to have them."

The sweetness of the gesture curled around my heart. What had I done to deserve such a sweet, wonderful man? I couldn't imagine my life without him, and I was starting to consider whether we should make things permanent. In the back of one of my drawers was a little black box, tucked away, waiting for the right moment. I'd seen the band in the window of an antique jewellery store that we passed on our way home, and one lunchtime I'd snuck out to take a closer look at it. It had been perfect, so I'd taken it home.

All I had to do was work out when to ask the question.

I looked down at the flowers again, then blinked, squinting between the greens, whites, and reds. There was something shiny wrapped around one of the flower stems.

"What's…" my voice trailed off as my fingers brushed against something hard and metallic. All the breath rushed out of my lungs, leaving me feeling light-headed. "Holy shit."

There was a ring carefully tied to a single red rose that sat in the centre of the bouquet. I stared at it, my eyes filling with tears. My hands were shaking as I touched it again, feeling the cool metal under my skin. When I looked up,

Leo was down on one knee in front of me, Angie and Rupert sitting on either side of him.

"What's happening?" I asked stupidly, even though I knew what was going on. I just needed to hear Leo say it, needed him to say the words to prove to me the moment wasn't a dream. "Is... is this real?"

"Yeah, it is."

"Really?" I sniffed and realised there were tears running down my cheeks. I probably looked *highly* attractive as I sobbed my eyes out and tried to stop my nose from running. But that didn't really matter right now.

"Really." Leo reached for my hand, interlacing our fingers together. "Jay, from the first moment I met you, I knew you were special. I've spent so many moments imagining our future together. I thought it was time I did it for real." He took a deep breath, his thumb stroking the side of my hand. "Jacob Morris, will you marry me?"

"Only," I said, dropping to one knee in front of him, "if you'll marry me too. You'll just have to wait until we get home for your ring though."

Leo's face was the picture of stunned surprise, and I giggled. "O-of course."

"Then yes, I will marry you." I threw myself into his arms, not caring that I was still holding a giant bunch of flowers or that we were surrounded by two highly affectionate Staffies who loved to jump on us. All I cared about was being in the arms of the man I loved. Our lips met in the perfect kiss. It was a kiss that said so much. And I knew Leo felt it all.

We broke apart, and I grinned. "I guess you ought to put that ring on my finger now."

"I guess I should." I'd thought it would take him ages to untie it, but with two pulls on the ribbon tying it to the rose, the ring was in Leo's palm. He took my hand and slid the ring gently onto my finger. It was a perfect fit.

"I love you so much," I said, pressing another kiss to his perfect mouth.

"I love you too." He rose to his feet, holding out his hand to pull me up. "Shall we go home? Your dad is going to meet us there. And maybe a few others as well."

"A few others?"

"Well." Leo blushed, looking slightly sheepish. "I thought you might like to celebrate with everyone."

"That sounds perfect," I said. "Let's go home."

I fetched Rupert's and my coats, wrapping us both up against the cold. I left a couple of lights on, so we could bring my dad down later. Then I took Leo's hand and stepped out into the street. At some point, it had started snowing, and now a light dusting covered the cobbles and the surrounding shops transforming it into the perfect winter wonderland.

Leo's fingers squeezed mine as we walked up the hill under the shadow of the cathedral, lit up in beautiful golden lights. It could have been the setting for a fairy tale, but this was real. My fantasy had become reality, and I couldn't wait to live it every day for the rest of my life.

When we got home, everyone was waiting for us in the glow of the Christmas lights under a hand-painted "Congratulations" banner that I'd definitely not seen before. My dad squeezed me in the tightest hug with tears in his eyes before Emily and Daniel did the same. Their foster son, Elliot, gave me a high five before asking me if there would be chocolate cake at the wedding, because he only really liked chocolate cake. I promised him there would be. He'd been with Emily and Daniel for nine months now and was honestly the sweetest kid I'd ever met. Plus he'd taken to D&D like a duck to water, so he got bonus points for that.

Edward nearly crushed me before pressing a soft kiss to my forehead, not bothering to hide his tears. I felt like I'd been blessed by some sort of elven king. He probably wouldn't have let me go if Izzy hadn't pried him away with a low chuckle, before giving me a bear hug of his own. There was a pairing I'd never seen coming, but it was funny how the universe surprised you. Who'd have thought Edward's greatest enemy would become his true love? Definitely not me. In fact, when he'd first told me, I'd laughed. For ten minutes. There'd been tears and everything because I'd been convinced he was joking.

Apparently not.

But fate was funny like that. It was almost like a game of D&D—roll your dice and see what happens. And if you're lucky, you get your happy ever after.

That die I'd rolled when I'd first decided to take a chance on Leo had finally revealed its result.

A perfect natural twenty.

*The End*

# ACKNOWLEDGMENTS

This novel has been an exercise in self-indulgence and allowed me to inject my fully nerdy self into my writing. But it wouldn't have come to life so spectacularly without the support of many people.

To Rosie, for always being there for me and cheering me on. Thank you for introducing me to fandom, cosplay, board games and nerd life; I am forever grateful. This one is for you, and for all that time we spent writing anime fanfiction together as teenagers. At least the language of flower knowledge came in useful one day!

To my husband, for encouraging me to keep writing and for always being a nerd with me. I couldn't ask for a more awesome partner in life.

To Toby, for bouncing ideas around with me initially, for encouraging me to bring Leo and Jay to life and for introducing me to Dungeons and Dragons.

To Carly, Alie and Gwen for cheering me on throughout my writing.

To Susie, for encouraging me when I wobbled, and for loving Leo and Jay as much as I do.

To Natasha, for bringing Leo to life and blowing my mind with this amazing cover. Seriously, I'm getting this printed for my wall.

To my D&D people for going on adventures with me and introducing me to a whole new world. And to my Starfinder crew – thanks for all the laughs and disasters. I'm absolutely not sorry that we ended up as some odd combination of *Suicide Squad* and *Guardians of the Galaxy*. I love you all.

And finally, to all my readers, whether you're new to me or you've been here since the start, thanks for joining me on my journey and for supporting me. I can't wait to bring you more books… especially because Edward's story is going to be fun!

**ALSO BY CHARLIE NOVAK**

Off the Pitch

Breakaway

Extra Time

Final Score

Standalone

Screens Apart

Short Stories

One More Night

*For a regularly updated list, please visit:*

*charlienovak.com/books*

# CHARLIE NOVAK

Charlie lives in England with her husband and a dachshund named Biscuit. She spends most of her days wrangling other people's words in her day job and then trying to force her own onto the page in the evening.

She loves cute stories with a healthy dollop of fluff, plenty of delicious sex, and happily ever afters – because the world needs more of them.

Charlie has very little spare time, but what she does have she fills with cooking, pole-dancing, reading and ice-hockey. She also thinks that everyone should have at least one favourite dinosaur…

Website charlienovak.com
Facebook Group Charlie's Angels
*For day-to-day-musings, giveaways and teasers.*

Plus sign up for her newsletter at charlienovak.com for bonus scenes, new releases and extras.

facebook.com/charlienovakauthor
twitter.com/charlienwrites
instagram.com/charlienwrites
bookbub.com/profile/charlie-novak
amazon.com/author/charlienovak

Printed in Poland
by Amazon Fulfillment
Poland Sp. z o.o., Wrocław